"I am not an invalid!" Cal roared

Before Patrice could move a muscle to stop him, Cal leapt onto the hood of the vehicle right behind him and proclaimed his wrath to the world. "The only thing wrong with Cal Sullivan is that his ex-wife is driving him crazy!"

Patrice hoisted herself onto the hood of the car and confronted him. From below, Casey's voice wailed up at them.

"Daddy! Mom! I don't believe this! Get off that car right now!"

"I'm not coming down without him."

"And I'm not going anywhere until you admit I don't need a stretcher."

But Casey's embarrassment had captured Patrice's attention. "How about that?" she said. "Did you ever think we'd get too outrageous for *her?*" Suddenly they were laughing so hard they had to throw their arms around each other to keep from sliding off.

Another voice boomed up at them. "Hey, buddy, that's my car! Get your butts off it!"

Dear Reader,

If January puts ideas of "getting away from it all" into your mind, our Superromance authors can help.

Lynn Erickson's adventurous and very twentieth-century heroine, Tess Bonney, finds herself face-to-face with *The Last Buccaneer* when she is transported through time to the Spanish Main.

Out on the west coast, Nora Carmichael's ordered life is suddenly thrown into chaos when her apartment is invaded by *The Dog from Rodeo Drive.* Author Risa Kirk gives Lane Kincaid, her wonderful hero, the formidable task of convincing Nora that both he and the puppy are perfect for her.

In Boston, Stephanie Webb and her boss, Ben Strother, reluctantly join forces to bring their parents together, but their parents, it seems, have plans of their own. They arrange a vacation in Hilton Head so that their stubborn children will give in to the inevitable—*their* mutual attraction. *The Parent Plan* is a must for Judith Arnold fans!

Media personality Patrice Sullivan returns to North Carolina for her zany daughter's wedding and finds her "ex" as sexy and infuriating as ever. Peg Sutherland's *Simply Irresistible* is just that—a touching and lighthearted romp that stitches together a relationship clearly never meant to end.

In the coming months, in addition to more great books by some of your favorite authors, we've got some new talents to showcase. There's lots of excitement planned for 1994, so go ahead and get away from it all—and then come back and join us for all the fun!

Marsha Zinberg
Senior Editor

PEG SUTHERLAND

SIMPLY

Irresistible

Harlequin Books

TORONTO • NEW YORK • LONDON
AMSTERDAM • PARIS • SYDNEY • HAMBURG
STOCKHOLM • ATHENS • TOKYO • MILAN
MADRID • WARSAW • BUDAPEST • AUCKLAND

ISBN 0-373-70580-8

SIMPLY IRRESISTIBLE

ABOUT THE AUTHOR

Peg Sutherland's books have garnered praise from fans and critics alike. In her latest Superromance novel, *Simply Irresistible,* Peg's wry sense of humor takes flight. The result is a sexy, rollicking comedy that will delight her old fans and win her new ones the world over as she treats us to a new look at the Old South. Peg says, "I wanted to write something that would lift me up and make me feel better—like the old drawing room comedies I love."

Peg lives with her husband, Mike, a magazine editor, in Charlottetown, North Carolina.

Books by Peg Sutherland

HARLEQUIN SUPERROMANCE

398—BEHIND EVERY CLOUD
428—ALONG FOR THE RIDE
473—ABRACADABRA
525—RENEGADE
553—LATE BLOOMER

HARLEQUIN TEMPTATION

414—TALLAHASSEE LASSIE

Don't miss any of our special offers. Write to us at the following address for information on our newest releases.

Harlequin Reader Service
P.O. Box 1397, Buffalo, NY 14240
Canadian address: P.O. Box 603,
Fort Erie, Ont. L2A 5X3

CHAPTER ONE

FOURTEEN DAYS at the fat farm. Two hours and twenty minutes under foil and chemicals at the salon. And twenty-three minutes in front of a magnified makeup mirror.

But one minute into the lobby of the Omni Charlotte and Patrice Hilton Sullivan knew she still wasn't ready for a reunion with her ex-husband.

Especially when her ex-husband was on the arm of a woman with all the talent required to appear on the cover of *Cosmo*—in other words, an abundance of firm cleavage. No woman Patrice's age would be ready for that, particularly when the occasion was to discuss her grown daughter's impending wedding.

When, she wondered irritably as she gave her lipstick a final check in the shiny chrome framing the hotel elevator, had she grown so ridiculously preoccupied with her looks? Was it part of the natural order as the big four-o loomed ahead, teeth bared, waiting to pounce? Had it been those eight years spent watching twenty-something lookers move up rapidly in the world of TV news while the forty-five-year-olds were yanked off the air and shoved behind the scenes? Was it the dazzling twenty-six-year-old the network had asked her to train just nine weeks ago?

Or was it simply Cal?

Nope, she told herself. Never that. Never Cal.

Maybe job insecurity in a business where looks were as big an asset as brains and voice.

But Cal? Never.

Whatever the reason, it was discouraging to realize that fat farms and champagne-blond hair, even the judicious application of Sultry Sable to disguise the first hints of the dreaded eyelid droop, couldn't belie the fact that you were old enough to have a daughter walking down the aisle.

But a carefully executed nonchalance can fool the world into believing you don't give a damn about your ex-snake, Patrice coached herself.

You might even fool yourself if you act the part well enough.

Patrice remembered to pull her shoulders back, suck her tummy in and lift her chin. Then she turned on the cool, confident smile that had been part of her major artillery in her eight-year struggle up the network hierarchy, the smile that ultimately converted millions of network news viewers into International Cable News regulars. In long, self-assured strides, she marched across the jade-colored carpet to stand over the couple swallowed up by the puffy cushions of a floral love seat.

"Hello, Cal. Were you under or over?"

Surprise, quickly replaced by something Patrice would have labeled delight if she hadn't known better, flickered across the face she knew in intimate detail. Then it settled into safe pleasantness as Cal cut a quick glance at the young woman beside him.

"Over or under what, Trish?"

Ah, the voice. Still mellow and deep, a little soft around the edges from the North Carolina drawl he hadn't had to tame, as she had. After eight years apart—eight years of long-distance bickering and ex-

tended, painful silences—the voice still stirred...
something.

"Why, par of course. You have been on the golf
course, haven't you, Cal?"

He smiled.

It wasn't fair. Without even standing, he overshadowed her presence with that damned smile of his. That
wider-than-wide grin with the never-say-die dimples and
the brush of a dark mustache.

Dimples! She held on to her own smile to hide the
black sulks darkening the edges of her subconscious.
*Dimples, at his age? Laugh lines, that's more like it, just
like the ones around his eyes.*

His snapping, bet-you-can't-top-this brown eyes.

"Actually, I haven't had much time for golf lately."

That figured. She'd spent two months of careful
preparation for this moment—it had taken a full ninety
minutes just to decide on the raw silk suit and red shawl-
collar blouse she wore. And Walker Calhoun Sullivan
looked as casually rumpled as if he'd stepped off a golf
course half an hour ago.

And he hadn't even been playing golf, which raised a
lot of other possibilities she didn't want to consider.
Like why he had wanted to meet here in this hotel lobby
with a dishy blonde on his arm in the first place.

He stood. Young and Nubile stood. Patrice clenched
her jaw tightly as it sank in that the woman was taller in
canvas flats than she was in sling-back pumps.

"Trish, this is Tory McIntyre. Tory, this is Casey's
mother."

Offering her hand, Tory smiled. A drop-dead smile
that was, unfortunately, as genuinely warm as it was
gorgeous. Patrice would have preferred a vacuous, pat-
ently phony smile. She made an executive decision that

it would be perfectly acceptable—not at all a breach of ex-spousal etiquette—if she hated the woman.

Almost as much as she hated being called Trish.

She shook the hand offered. It was cool and slim and ringless. Patrice willed her mind away from calculating how much she'd spent in recent months in an effort to feel elegant and attractive for this meeting. Whatever the grand total, it was money down the toilet. No matter what the mirror told her, one look at Cal's dimples and Tory's cleavage and she felt dumpy, lumpy and frumpy.

And she didn't even rate a name in the introductions. She was simply someone's mother, a someone not much younger than this...this...Patrice deepened her smile and reminded herself that name-calling was beneath her.

"Trish, you look sensational!" Cal's hair—that thick, curly, dark, soft hair—was windblown and disheveled, not agonizingly styled for studied casualness, as hers was. A teal-and-pink golf shirt, open at the neck to reveal thick, dark chest hair—and not one little curl of it gray, she noted with a certain amount of pique—was vibrant against the healthy color in his cheeks and his sun-browned arms. The knit shirt molded well to his chest, which was broader now than before, and his belly, which was flatter. "Doesn't she look sensational, Tory?"

Flatter? Where is it written that a forty-one-year-old ex-husband gets a flat belly? Patrice treated the Fates to a few lines of the kind of salty dialogue that was common behind the scenes in a network newsroom. Slightly mollified, she then lowered her eyelids in the sultry once-over that Cal had always claimed gave him a hardon in less than two minutes flat. She only prayed the look would remind him that, at his age, he needed way more than two minutes to prepare for takeoff.

"Why, thank you, Cal. So do you. Middle age agrees with you."

He chuckled, so accustomed to her barbs that he obviously wasn't bothered. He leaned toward her and she kissed the air near his cheek. Too near his cheek, she realized an instant too late. He smelled of bayberry soap. She remembered the scent far too intimately. It called up memories of nudging him awake with sloppy wet kisses in private, bayberry-scented places that...

She pulled back and smiled again, grateful for the training that let her smile benignly without revealing even the tiniest hint of what seethed inside.

"So, how's Chicago?"

Patrice didn't want to talk about Chicago. She didn't want to think about how relieved she'd been to walk off the set the night before, with months of freedom stretched out in front of her. She didn't want to think of her young trainee, who might fill in from time to time while she was gone. She didn't want to think of her best friend Lettie's predicament or Cmienski's ultimatum. "Chicago? Windy."

"Casey said you'll be here for two months to help with the wedding."

"That's right." *In a manner of speaking.*

His honey-brown eyes twinkled; he suppressed his dimples. That's how she knew he planned to take a little dig at one of her weak spots. Deceit was not in Cal's soul. Neither was rancor; his little digs were all without even a hint of malice.

"Are you sure they can manage without you, Trish? I'd hate to see the largest news-gathering agency in the world go belly-up just so you can help Casey decide between ivory lace and ecru satin.''

''I seriously doubt if Casey is considering either ivory lace or ecru satin.''

Cal laughed and so did Tory, which further piqued Patrice. Unreasonably, she didn't want the young woman to know her daughter well enough to get the joke.

They stood in the uncomfortable little triangle for minutes too long before Cal gestured them into their seats—Patrice into the puffy floral chair, Cal and Tory back onto the matching love seat.

Patrice kept her eyes carefully averted from the natural blonde with the minimum of makeup. Tory was dressed for sport, too. Her arms looked long and lean and well muscled. She probably had a great golf swing.

If they ever made it to the course, that is.

''It won't do any good, you know.'' Cal's deep voice was all friendly warmth, his teeth white and straight under the neatly trimmed mustache. That had been part of the trouble—who wanted to be married to a man who was so close to perfect?

Actually, as she recalled, that had been Cal's complaint against her, not vice versa.

''What won't do me any good?''

''Trying to talk Casey out of it. That is what you've got in mind, isn't it?''

Patrice clamped down on her impatience. ''Still like getting the jump on me, I see.''

Cal didn't chuckle this time. ''This isn't about one-upmanship, Trish.''

For a change? she wanted to ask. But that was uncalled-for, she supposed, even with an ex-husband. Especially since, in retrospect, it was a bit hard to tell who had played that game the hardest. She was spared finding a substitute response by the appearance of a man in white shirt and sport coat. Husky and ruddy, he edged between the couch and chair and clapped a proprietary hand on Cal's shoulder.

"Here you are. We'll be ready to start in fifteen, Cal."

So that was it. They must be meeting here so Cal could work her in between speeches, one of those performances where his mere presence seemed to motivate people to greater heights. The charisma that had made Cal one of the most in-demand motivational speakers in the country was still going strong.

And it was also, apparently, going to cut in on one of the most important discussions she'd had with him since the night she told him she wanted to take the network job in Atlanta—and he told her there was no way he would go with her.

She supposed that shouldn't surprise her. Getting his share of the limelight had always been one of Cal's priorities, hadn't it?

"I'll be right there, Sol." Cal turned back to Patrice. "Sorry, Trish. I'm wrapping up before some fiber-optics group heads out for its company golf tournament."

She conjured her most withering look, which didn't even draw a sheepish glance from her ex. The man had no conscience.

"But I'm here right now, Trish, and I'm willing to listen. Although I doubt if we'll accomplish much more today than we've ever accomplished when we try to talk about Casey."

"Cal, why don't we pretend—just for the sake of conversation—that there's some chance we might agree on this? How would that be, for a change?"

He opened his mouth as if to disagree, then back into the love seat and propped an ankle on his knee. "Okay, Trish. What do you think we ought to do?"

"I didn't come here to shove a solution down your throat, Cal." It was happening already. They hadn't even started the real conversation and she already felt the steam rising in her. Some things never change.

"You didn't?"

"Cal!" Tory poked him in the ribs. "Cut her some slack. This is serious."

Terrific. An ally. An ally with perfect skin and C-cups that didn't even need underwire. Yet. Just what she needed, an ex-husband with a beautiful, understanding, wise and compassionate girlfriend. There went every chance of truly hating Young and Nubile.

Some days, nothing went right.

"I know this is serious," Cal protested. But Patrice could tell from the barest indentation of his right dimple when he tried to twitch away a grin, that he knew she was peeved. She knew he sincerely cared what happened to Casey, but he also thought his ex-wife was overreacting. Again.

That, too, galled her.

She grabbed the arms of the chair and started to push herself up. "I thought, with a nineteen-year-old daughter about to make the same mistake we made, you might be ready to act like an adult and..."

Leaning forward in a smooth, swift motion, Cal darted a hand out to cover hers. "Hold on. You don't think Casey's..." He paused, his eyes moving almost imperceptibly in Tory's direction. "I mean, she hasn't told me she's . . . what makes you think . . ."

Patrice felt her cheeks warming in spite of herself. Damn the man and his shotgun mouth. It was nobody's business—especially not Tory McIntyre's—that Patrice had been pregnant when they said their vows.

She broke stiffly into his stumbling words. "I was referring to the fact that Casey is only nineteen and wants to get married, Cal. Don't you think that's something we should be concerned about? Since we understand the consequences of that mistake only too well?"

Cal dropped back against the cushions. "You had me worried. Casey's always been a little . . . out of control. But I never thought . . . you're sure she's not . . ."

"A little out of control?" Patrice realized her voice was also getting a little out of control. She paused to compose herself, to make use of her professional voice, the one trained to convey information dispassionately and calmly. "If Casey has been a little out of control, whose fault is that, pray tell?"

Cal leveled a piercing look on her, the one that said he was mentally disassembling her to examine the parts and figure out how she ticked.

As if he didn't already know.

"Moving back here to live with me was Casey's decision, not mine." His voice was so calm, so unruffled. Patrice didn't like him using his professional voice against her, not wanting to admit that she had just done the same. "She was fifteen and plenty old enough to decide for herself. And the fact that she's lived with me has nothing to do with what's going on now."

"Nothing to do with it!" That, of course, was the least bothersome of the comments he'd just made. But now was hardly the time to blame him for stealing her daughter away. Besides, they'd fought that battle four years ago, and plenty of times in between. Telephone company stock had surely soared thanks to their marathon long-distance battles over Casey. "How can you say that? You've let her get away with murder for years, Cal Sullivan, and now she's trying to throw away her future on some wild-eyed fairy tale and that's got nothing to do with you?"

"Casey is headstrong. If anything, I'd have to say that's more your fault than mine."

Patrice narrowed her eyes. The rational, adults-only discussion she had planned with Cal was turning into another of their blame-tossing skirmishes. She drew a deep breath and told herself this should be no harder than broadcasting a live report from a blacked-out Middle Eastern city with firebombs going off in the background.

Why, then, could she handle war-torn cities with cool aplomb, while Cal always left her feeling as if she should retreat to a bomb shelter?

"Okay, Cal, she's headstrong and we both know why." *Good, that sounds calm.* "Which is why you should have known better than to try and guide her through her teens. But you chose to try it anyway, and now she's not only headstrong, she's also got her head full of impracticality and..."

Wait a minute. She stopped herself. Now who was getting off the subject?

"That's all right, Trish. I always enjoyed your lectures. They remind me of the guidance counselor's office. Remember the guidance counselor's office, Trish, when they sat you down and gave you that long, stern look and you knew you'd pushed them too far again?"

Tory jabbed him again and muttered a warning. Cal grinned. He was needling her. It was working. Didn't it always?

"No, Cal, I can't say that I remember getting hauled down to the guidance counselor's office."

"No, I suppose you don't. You always did the right thing, didn't you?"

His words chafed, hitting as they did on one of the many reasons they hadn't been able to make their marriage work. Patrice was too rigid, to his way of thinking. Too adult for him was Patrice's interpretation. Not at first, certainly. Both of them, she was sure, remembered the teenage Trish Hilton—as headstrong as their daughter, Casey Hilton Sullivan, had ever been. Unleashed from a harsh and demanding childhood, Trish had ripped through her first year of college away from home like a cat through a yarn basket, joyously creating uproar wherever she lit. Trish Hilton had wanted the world to know she didn't accept its shackles anymore.

Until it shackled her with something she couldn't shake off.

Trish Sullivan had changed fast, back to the serious-minded, responsible person she had been in childhood. Thank goodness, Patrice had told herself a million times, and too bad Cal hadn't grown up with her.

But she didn't want Casey to have to learn things the hard way. She didn't want Casey throwing away college and opportunities and choices just because she thought she'd fallen in love.

Patrice softened. This might be Cal, but this was also the father of her daughter. "Cal, I'm sorry. I love Casey. I want what's best for her. Can we talk about that for a minute? What's best for our daughter?"

There was no humor, no teasing in his voice, only a sincere concern that matched her own. "Are you sure you know what's best for her, Trish?"

Anger smoldered again. She tried to dowse it. "I know that getting married at her age can't possibly be the best for her. Surely you can see that."

"I know you think I'm not taking this seriously enough. But I've thought long and hard about it, Trish. Maybe getting married would be the best thing for her. Maybe a stabilizing influence would be good for her." He hesitated. "You seemed to think it calmed you down. Didn't it?"

"This has nothing to do with me." She bit the words out between rigidly clenched teeth, wondering why the list of things her dentist had warned her to avoid after her last crown hadn't included visits with ex-husbands right above peanuts and hard candy. An oversight, she was certain. "This is about Casey. And I think we owe it to her, as her parents, to try and talk some sense into her."

"Good luck."

"What?"

"I said good luck." He stood, taking Tory's hand and pulling her up with him.

"Is that all? You're just going to dump this in my lap with a blithe 'good luck' and wash your hands of it?" Patrice stared up at the resigned half smile on his face long enough to realize that he was, once again, planning to steal the show with a grand exit. She struggled up out of the foolish, fluffy chair and faced him. "This is just like you, Cal Sullivan. Abdicating all responsibility, bouncing along as if life owes you nothing but a good time, while—"

"No, Trish. This is just like you. Demanding to control all the cards, even if it's not your game to play."

"This is not a game! It's my daughter's life. Her future."

Cal put a hand on her shoulder and squeezed. "Trish, you're wasting your time. You know what Casey is like and I think you know as well as I do that she doesn't respond to reason and she damn sure doesn't respond to strong-arm tactics. If you want to try to bully her into doing what you want her to do with her life, good luck. And I'll see you at the church in two months."

She sputtered. As he walked away, Tory on his arm, she sputtered. Despite Patrice's years of experience in speaking fluidly and glibly in times of stress, Cal Sullivan could still leave her sputtering in his wake.

She wondered, as she used every bit of willpower in her five-foot-four frame to keep from stamping her foot in frustration, if North Carolina had the death penalty for murdering ex-husbands. Because she would surely kill him. Before this two months was over, she would surely lose it and take one of her sling-back pumps to that hard head of his.

Well, at least she would look terrific for film at eleven.

CHAPTER TWO

PATRICE ALMOST RAMMED the pricey back bumper of her rented Mercedes into a cement piling in the hotel parking deck as she gave in to her urge to let off steam. Shoving the car into drive—where was a good four-on-the-floor when you needed it?—she burned rubber pulling out of the lot. The sound soothed her injured pride.

"That's better."

She smiled at her adolescent antics, then gunned the battleship gray sedan through three yellow lights, heading away from the unfamiliar towers of concrete, glass and steel that uptown Charlotte had become in the past decade.

"I hope he gets arthritis in his knees," she muttered as she turned down a stretch of Queens Road just minutes from the central business district. The bare branches of centuries-old oaks met in the middle of the street, where they were budding a pale green.

The first signs of spring soothed Patrice. She drew a satisfied breath as she envisioned Cal hobbling from a golf cart to his tee shot.

Then, Young and Nubile, draped on his arm as they walked away from her, flashed through her mind. "Yeah, arthritis in the knees. And other places, too."

Sunshine danced off the trees and she pushed a button to slide the driver's-side window down. The breeze, warm and fragrant of spring, ruffled her overpriced hair and made her wish for a convertible. The kind of convertible she'd talked Cal into right before their wedding—one with a loud engine and flashy lines and enough power to sail into the wind. Her satisfied smile deepened. She sank back into the seat, remembering.

The kind of convertible she'd also talked Cal into selling right after Casey was born. Her smile faded.

The winding street with its wide median triggered a nostalgia Patrice hadn't anticipated. Charlotte had been her city once—the city where her unplanned pregnancy had taught her the consequences of immaturity and where an unplanned career had earned her the rewards of being good at what she did. The city she had once felt they owned, she and Cal. The city that had held her comfortably in its embrace. As she looked around at the familiar sights, that safe and snug feeling returned.

She seemed to see herself everywhere she looked—in the couple jogging along the wide sidewalk in front of expensive homes that managed to look both cozy and substantial; in a young mother lifting a baby stroller over a crack in the sidewalk where the roots of a giant oak had buckled the concrete in the old, elegant Myers Park neighborhood; especially in the woman in baggy jeans and a patchwork smock hacking back last season's growth of monkey grass. Any of them could have been Patrice a decade and more ago.

Charlotte was nothing like bustling, cutthroat Chicago. Right now that was just how Patrice wanted it.

She resisted the impulse to let the soothing mood of the city settle over her, but it was so tempting. She had felt the knot in her gut—the knot that was weekend anchor deadlines and pressure to get the latest big story on the international scene—loosening the minute she stepped on the plane in Chicago. And now, as she sank into Charlotte's pleasant languor, the knot almost unraveled completely.

Despite her resistance, the city seduced her with memories.

1973

THE FIRST TIME she saw Cal, he'd caught her red-handed in an act of larceny.

She called herself Trish, and she was not yet nineteen. Brown hair streaked with gold swung free, almost to her waist. After eighteen years of being the responsible, level-headed big sister, the one everyone had depended on, the one who made decisions she was too young to make, Trish Hilton had exploded into Charlotte for the freedom of college.

Halloween was notorious for campus pranks and Trish Hilton could barely wait for the dead silence of predawn to instigate the plan she and her new best friend had hatched. About three in the morning, after most dorm lights were out and even campus security officers let down their guard, she and Ludie Hartnett had dashed across concrete and wet grass toward the Student Union. Giddy laughter swelling in her throat, Trish had allowed herself to forget the responsibility of taking care of three younger brothers every day after school for seven years.

She was free. She was wild. She didn't have to be perfect anymore.

The giant jack-o'-lantern—the Pi Kappa Alpha jack-o'-lantern that had won the contest that afternoon and was scheduled to be the centerpiece for a campus Halloween party that night—was heavier than either she or

Ludie had anticipated. Muffling their giggles, they lugged it between them, darting into the shadows whenever possible. They would stash it in their room and watch the uproar when Halloween dawned on campus, enjoying the satisfaction of knowing they'd caused the ruckus. Then, when the witching hour was over, they would return it to the Union.

Just to show they could.

They dragged the pumpkin into the woods fringing the campus. Trish sank against a tree while Ludie dashed to the dorm to make sure the coast was still clear. Laughing silently, sucking air into her heaving lungs, Trish scanned the dark woods for any sign of movement.

Her eyes lit on Cal Sullivan. Tall, wiry, dark haired. The taut lines of his maleness struck the laughter from her throat. Where had he come from?

His dark eyes held her entranced as he moved toward her. She recognized him from around campus. An upperclassman. A well-known charmer and a celebrity from his work on the campus radio station. Nothing to worry about, she was certain, even here in the dark. Still, her heart pounded. Her mouth went dry. She had been caught. Common sense told her to run, but she was too mesmerized to move.

When he stood in front of her, his dark eyes shadowed, he smiled. "I ought to turn you in."

She smiled back because something in his smile said he never did what he ought to do. "But you won't."

"I might."

She recognized the seductive quality in his voice, not from her limited experience with the country boys back home in York, South Carolina, but from watching too many movies. She wondered what would happen if she tried flirting back.

Stealing pumpkins was one thing; she wasn't sure she was daring enough to flirt with a college man.

Head lowered, she gazed up at him from beneath her half-closed lashes, her heart pounding with her brazenness. "What could I do to convince you to take pity?"

"Keep looking at me like that," he said, backing away with a warm, wicked promise in his eyes.

From that night on, Walker Calhoun Sullivan became part of Trish's protest against the ever-perfect daughter and big sister everyone had always expected her to be. Cal, whose fire spoke to the carefully banked fire in her. Cal, a bearded senior who hosted the classical music program on the campus station and dreamed of a TV career. Cal, who loved the devil in her and made her forget her good-girl compulsions.

In his car, along the wooded paths of the campus, in the library stairwell, he kissed her senseless. His full lips teased at her fine, small mouth, leaving her crackling with a need she barely understood.

He touched her, his hands capturing her breasts or cupping her buttocks, pulling her closer without ever disturbing the propriety of her worn jeans and snug T-shirts.

He aroused her but didn't push her, until she grew frustrated with the line of decorum he had drawn. So frustrated that she burst into his off-campus apartment one Sunday morning and shoved him back against the pillows when he rose up in surprise.

"What the..."

"What's wrong with me?" she demanded, pinning his shoulders to the bed and straddling the white sheet across his midriff. She hovered over him, her gold-streaked hair mingling with the thick dark curls on his chest. The sight made her heart pound.

"Wrong with you? Nothing."

She poked a finger in his chest. It barely gave, it was that hard. "Then why don't you want me?"

"I do, but..."

"Then why haven't you done anything about it?"

His dark brows arched innocently. His dimples quirked. She realized then that he'd known all along exactly what he was doing. He was letting her stew, waiting for her to boil over. Knowing she would.

Belligerent with anger, she flattened her palms against his chest and shoved. "Damn you, Cal Sullivan."

She almost jumped off the bed right then and whirled away. But her bare palms had never touched his bare chest before and the sensations arrested her. The thick curls wound softly around her fingers. The tiny beads of his nipples surprised her with their hardness.

"I didn't want to pressure you," Cal protested, his voice dipping and almost disappearing as she continued grazing his nipples with her palms. She liked the fuzziness that clouded his eyes, the hoarseness in his voice. "I knew you'd let me know when the time was right. I know you've never..."

"And I never will, at this rate," she murmured, suddenly aware of movement beneath the sheets. She pressed her crotch against the rustling motion; it was warm and swelled against her.

He groaned and smiled. "Trish, don't do that."

She leaned over and kissed him softly, running the palm of one hand lower on his chest to his flat, hair-covered belly, then turning her cheek to rub across his bearded cheek. "One of us has to. Cal, I'm the only virgin in the freshman class. You don't want that on your conscience, do you?"

His dimples vanished. "Trish?"

Her straying fingers stilled as she realized he wore nothing beneath the sheet.

"Trish, that's not the only reason is it?"

She summoned her courage and continued her hand's downward journey. She gasped, realizing only when it was too late that her eyes had widened as she struck hard flesh. "Oh, my."

Cal, too, gasped. But still he took her by the shoulders and forced her to clear her vision and look him in the eye. "Trish, I mean it. That's not the only reason?"

Barely able to breathe as she explored the silk and steel of his desire, she forced the words out. "No, Cal. That's not the only reason."

"TWIT." IRRITATED WITH her sentimentality, Patrice shoved aside the memories.

She pulled into the shaded parking lot between the sedate brick condominium building where she was staying and a Tudor-style home set back from the street. She tried to focus on the shiny leaves of the towering magnolia tree, the chirp and chatter of birds. But the memories were stronger.

Her rash behavior had hardly resulted in a story-book ending. Within six months, Trish had discovered that her impulsiveness was going to land her with more responsibility than she'd ever had as a big sister—she was carrying Cal's baby.

At first it had seemed like another part of the big adventure of being a grown-up who owed explanations to no one. Another way of thumbing her nose at the peo-

ple who'd spent so much time making sure she knew
exactly what she *should* be doing. Flaunting her wild-
ness had been fun. At first.

Cal was almost ready to graduate, with the promise
that the part-time work he'd picked up at a local FM
station would become full-time as soon as he had his
diploma in hand. And Trish had no real career long-
ings—if she could putter with her plants and herbs and
be assured she was living a life her mother never would
have chosen for her, she was content.

So for Cal and Trish, parenting had sounded like another lark. It was buying a red vinyl baby stroller from
the Salvation Army, emblazoning it with bumper stick-
ers touting peace and ecology and rock 'n' roll forever.
It was boasting offhandedly about their decision to experience natural childbirth. It was crawling out the sec-
ond-story window of their stuffy little apartment to sit
on the roof and count the stars and wait for the baby to
move. It was learning how to make love around a swollen belly. It was being the first in her crowd to brag
about being pregnant as they stood in Latta Park, amid
a clear brook and blooming azaleas, and said their
vows.

And then it was Casey Hilton Sullivan, squalling and
red faced and bald, squirming in Trish's arms and refusing to give in to a serene moment of bonding.

At that moment, Trish had known the big lark was
over.

This was where responsibility set in once again—more
responsibility than she'd ever dreamed of when she'd
chafed at watching out for rowdy younger brothers and
helping with the dinner dishes and the laundry and fix-
ing the morning oatmeal after her mother dashed off to
work.

Patrice tried reminding herself, as she unlocked the furnished executive condo, that Charlotte and its memories were now a part of her long-finished past. As was Cal Sullivan.

Then why, she wondered, does everything feel so disconcertingly the same? As if eight years—years of working long, grueling hours and making not a few cutthroat decisions to scratch her way ahead in a tough business—hadn't passed since she and Cal parted paths. As if there were still valid reasons to be irritated by the differences between them. As if the competition between them hadn't been cooled by her move into news and his embarking on a whole new career as a speaker and trainer.

As if they had never stopped being Trish and Cal Sullivan, the darlings of "Daybreak Charlotte."

Patrice pitched her silk suit jacket onto the arm of the unfamiliar couch, not even pausing to be amazed at her carelessness. She kicked off her heels, mindless that they landed under the polished dining table, and ignored the blinking light of the thoughtfully provided telephone answering machine as she continued stripping off her new clothes on her way into the bedroom of the leased condo.

Thank goodness for the machine. Whoever it was, she didn't want to talk to them. In coming here she'd been glad to get away from everyone and everything in Chicago.

And in her rush to do that, she had run headlong into all her unresolved feelings about Cal.

Trish and Cal. Cal and Trish. She stared at her reflection in the mirror over the sink as she ran water to remove her makeup. With the back of her hand she patted the flesh under her jawline.

Lord, she was sick of this sudden preoccupation with her looks. All she knew was that Cinda Reisling, her new trainee at ICN, was light-years away from worrying about a sagging jawline. And Lettie's job grew more precarious with each new sag and crinkle. Maybe Lettie was right; maybe Patrice should look into restoring that come-hither look to her it-can't-be-morning-yet eyes. Maybe that was the only way a woman could maintain her precarious toehold.

"And how much longer would that keep the network satisfied? Another decade? Then another tuck? And another?"

She lathered her face with soap, then splashed it with clear, warm water. She caught sight of herself again in the mirror, free of artificial color. But the color in her cheeks bloomed almost as high as it had all those years ago on campus, in that little dive of an apartment, in Latta Park.

That's what wrangling with Cal again does for you, she told her reflection.

The Sunny Sullivans, one local magazine story had labeled them. It had started almost as an accident. And before it was over, it could definitely have been labeled a full-scale head-on collision.

1980

IT WASN'T UNUSUAL for Trish to drop Casey off at kindergarten, then stop by WDTV on her way to her job at The Greenery Nursery and Garden Supply Shop. She liked to sit along the edge of the morning show set in one of those rigid, orange molded plastic chairs and watch Cal on the air.

He was so warm and lovable in his cardigan sweaters, with his big smile and deep dimples and teasing eyes, his teddy-bear beard now shaved back to a more conservative but still bushy mustache. Whether he was joshing his way through the weather roundup or setting the Thanksgiving Day Carousel Parade Princess at ease during her first TV appearance, Cal Sullivan was a doll.

No wonder everyone in Charlotte and the surrounding Piedmont area of the Carolinas wanted to start their day with Cal Sullivan. So did Trish. Especially the way she had this very morning, when he'd nuzzled his damp curls into her neck right after he'd jumped out of his four o'clock shower.

"Mmm. You look yummy." He'd slid his hand under the sheet and run his fingers over her curves.

Her sleepy, grunted protest had turned into a little groan of awakening pleasure as his hand settled over her breast. She wriggled in his arms, finding his lips full and warm beneath his soft mustache.

"Better not start this," she murmured as his tongue traced the corners of her open mouth.

"Too late."

She arched into him, savoring his recklessness, wondering vaguely what had happened to her own. "Cal, you have to be at the station..."

"Let me worry about that, woman."

He crawled in beside her, warm and wet from his shower.

"Cal, you're getting everything wet!"

"Everything?" He lowered his hand, seeking the damp warmth that had nothing to do with Cal's shower. "Oh yes, everything."

Yes, Trish enjoyed starting her mornings with Cal. But this morning, her usual stop at the station turned into something not quite extraordinary.

A guest had canceled at the last minute, a woman from the Mecklenburg County Extension Office who was supposed to talk about saving poinsettias from one Christmas to the next. The show's producer, when he spotted Trish, had a brainstorm.

"Say, Cal, doesn't Trish work at a nursery?"

That was the beginning. The one-time, last-minute, no-time-to-panic guest shot had turned into a weekly segment. Their chemistry crackled over the cameras. And they looked so good together—Cal so tall and broad shouldered and dark, Trish so fair and sun streaked and apple-cheeked fresh. Viewers couldn't get enough of the Sunny Sullivans.

Within the year, Trish was co-host, the glamorous notion of television quickly compensating for her work at the nursery and the elemental satisfaction she'd always felt from growing things. The move, Cal assured Patrice, didn't bother him in the least. In fact, he was thrilled. Delighted.

They were a hit. A big hit.

PATRICE SIGHED. Just thinking about it made her weary. Between unwelcome memories of her life with Cal and the equally unwelcome battle to protect Casey from one of life's worst mistakes, Charlotte could become as unpleasant a place as Chicago had been for the past year.

Longingly eyeing the silk lounging pajamas she hadn't had time to stuff into a drawer before her meeting with Cal, she opted instead for the spandex workout togs hanging from the back of the walk-in closet.

Once dressed, she pulled her shoulder-length hair into a clip, plugged her workout video into the VCR and headed for the near-empty refrigerator. On her way, the answering machine blinked impatiently at her. She couldn't ignore it any longer.

Frowning at the flashing light, she paused to punch the button and listened as she continued into the kitchen for a glass of mineral water.

The voice was young and loose and brought a smile to her lips.

"Hey, excellent Ma, it's your wretched excuse for a kid. How's it hanging? So, like, call me when you hit the crib. I can't wait to tell you all my plans. Did I tell you about my new job? It is totally nonheinous. Truly large." Casey giggled shrilly, a very unbridelike sound but one that was very familiar. "Listen, let's have lunch tomorrow and we'll catch up. Oh, and I want you and Dad to have dinner with Will and me tomorrow night. Okay? Wow, this is, like, so cool that you're going to be here to help. Catch ya later."

Hearing her daughter's childish voice made Patrice ache in every bone. She had tried so hard with Casey to be the perfect mother, to give her the kind of carefree youth she herself had never been able to enjoy. Patrice had been determined not to screw up her daughter's life, especially after she and Cal split eight years ago.

And everything had been fine, including her loosely structured custody agreement with Cal, until Casey reached that state of belligerence and rebellion known as adolescence.

From the time she turned thirteen, Casey turned daily life into a war zone. Increasingly, as mother and daughter fought about makeup and boys and curfew and clothes and grades, Casey had turned to Cal for support and shelter. Cal had urged Patrice to lighten up. Patrice had tried vainly to make him understand her fears about drugs and AIDS and all the other dangers that threatened the innocence of teens today.

Patrice knew she was right. Knew she owed it to Casey to do all she could to rein her daughter in.

But in the end, being right hadn't mattered. All that had mattered was that fifteen-year-old Casey had decided, finally, to live with her dad.

"He won't be on my case about every little thing I do!" Casey had taunted her.

Patrice had been certain that much was true.

She'd missed so much these past four years—and now here she was again, playing the heavy. It wasn't a role she relished. But it was her role, she supposed, the role she'd filled so well all her life.

She pulled the bottle of mineral water out of the refrigerator as the machine whirred forward. Once again, Casey's exuberant voice filled the air.

"Oh! Almost forgot. You won't wear, like, a suit or anything when we go out to dinner, will ya? I mean, you probably didn't even bring any suits, since you won't be working. No need for stylin' and profilin', right? Yeah. Well, okay. Later, dude."

Patrice uncapped the bottled water with a frustrated twist, started to reach for a glass, then paused and took a long gulp straight from the bottle.

It could have been worse, she supposed. It could have been Clarence Cmienski, her boss at ICN, demanding to know why she hadn't shown up for the command performance meeting he had scheduled right before her departure. Or her editor wondering if the book—which was, along with Casey's wedding, her excuse for this sabbatical—was moving along on schedule.

Or it could have been Truman if he had somehow tracked her down. Gorgeous, young, vibrant Truman Matthews, on whose account every red-blooded woman at ICN envied her. Truman, whose bad-boy streak had reminded her so much of Cal when they first met, until she finally realized exactly what it was that had drawn her into a silly liaison with a twenty-nine-year-old hard body with a wicked gleam in his dark eyes.

Yes, it could have been Truman, whispering something naughty onto the tape while he wondered, like everyone else in Chicago, if levelheaded Patrice had suddenly gone off the deep end.

Sometimes she wished she could.

Someday she might just do so.

CHAPTER THREE

CAL GLARED AT THE little digital numbers and blinked to clear the perspiration stinging his eyes. Twelve point two-nine minutes on the stair-step machine that was just one of the many fitness machines he had equipped his basement with some months ago.

More than twelve minutes and he'd barely taken eight hundred steps. His concentration was shot.

He gritted his teeth and stepped up the pace, irritatingly aware that some vigilant inner ear listened for signs, for irregularity, for warnings he wouldn't have worried about seven months ago.

"This isn't a race, you know."

Tory's sardonic voice came to him over the steady mechanical squeak of the machine, the same voice that had goaded, urged, encouraged, mocked and soothed him for the past four months.

Hard to believe that she had ever been just another employee, like the two other young women who ran the office of his public speaking and training consultation firm. One to keep the office running smoothly, one to market him effectively. And one to keep him alive.

Because, like it or not, that had been the reason Doc Tipton had insisted that Cal hire a personal fitness trainer. Three months after the early-morning rush to the hospital, Doc had realized that Cal wasn't following the orders designed to prevent another exciting am-

bulance ride. Enter Tory. Cal had resented Tory that
first month, until her sharp mind and even sharper
tongue had forged a powerful friendship despite the
difference in their years.

Cal merely grunted at her and kept up the pace,
watching the numbers click off on the digital meter. It
was a race—against time and old age and even, if only
a little bit, against fear. But Tory, despite all she'd been
through, was too young to understand that.

He wondered if Trish would understand. The way she
looked, he doubted it.

"I thought you were going to tell her. Why didn't
you?"

Tory's words momentarily captured his attention.
Good question. He'd really intended to. In fact, Trish
had been the first one he'd thought of calling seven
months ago. She had crowded into the thoughts whirl-
ing through his mind as he lay on the stretcher, wondering if there was any point in trying to convince
heaven's messenger that a mistake had been made.
Surely they'd meant to finger someone older, more
worn-out, somebody with gray hair, for heaven's sake.
Thinking of Trish while they were poking him with
needles and hooking him up to gadgets had scared the
hell out of him.

Almost as much as the prospect of dying.

Cal sensed that the machine had slowed again and he
glanced over at Tory, resting on the incline bench in her
lightweight warm-up suit. He saw no hint of what she
had been through in the two years before he met her; no
physical weakness, no sallow skin, not even any self-pity
in those alert brown eyes. Despite the scars on her back
and leg, Tory was whole and healed in a way Cal often
envied. Long, lean and built like a brick outhouse—his

pop's words, not his, although it would be hard to argue with the assessment—she stared at him with her confident smile and those eyes that claimed to know what was in his head better than he did.

After four months, he supposed she did. Insight wasn't his strong suit. Ask Trish.

Dammit, forget Trish.

"You *were* going to tell her—at least that's what you said last night."

"It's none of her business." Cal flung his head back to toss the perspiration-soaked hair off his forehead. He'd convinced himself of that seven months ago. No reason to second-guess himself now.

Tory leaned back on the bench and absently started lifting weights. He wondered, less from curiosity than just plain concern, what went through her head when she got that faraway look in her eyes. If regrets or bitterness ever threatened to poison her, he never saw any sign of it.

"I see."

When she spoke, there was no strain in her buttersmooth voice, despite the weights totaling a hundred-plus pounds that Cal had left on the machine when he finished his upper-body work. She spoke as easily as if she were hefting a half-full bag of groceries. What was the world coming to when a twenty-five-year-old woman could lift weights easier than a man? Especially a woman who had fought back from a crippling accident and drug addiction.

He liked her voice, though. He hadn't at first. Something about it had jangled his nerves. Then he'd realized it was too smooth to suit him. He kept listening for a hint of something rough around the edges, throaty and seductive. Like Moira's voice.

No, he'd already admitted it, so why backslide? Like *Trish's* voice. Good thing he'd realized exactly what it was he liked best about Moira before he'd slipped the ring on her finger.

"Then what was I doing there, Cal? Was I something to... show off? To make her jealous?"

Cal laughed a little sheepishly. He'd never had to be very good at figuring himself out. He'd always been so transparent everyone else could do it for him. That's what Trish always said, so it must be true. "Is that bad?"

Tory hesitated only a moment before laughing with him. She might have been his age, given the aplomb with which she had corrected her frailties. Another perfect woman; he was surrounded by them. Except Casey, bless her.

"Why? Do you... are you still interested in her?"

"No way. Never." Cal stopped, peeved at his urge to keep protesting. "Well, she's attractive, of course."

Damned attractive, in fact. Maybe better-looking than he remembered, even going all the way back to those days when her hair danced almost to her plump backside, when she hadn't bothered with makeup and the only color in her hair came from the sun. More attractive, certainly, than she ever looked gazing unflinchingly at the camera from behind that news desk in Chicago. Technically, he supposed, she looked great on the air, but she was too controlled, as if she had no heartbeat, no blood in her veins. That's why she looked so good, unembellished except for the high color of excitement, when she broadcast live from places like the Persian Gulf and Red Square.

Cal realized that Tory had let the weights settle back to the bottom of the pulleys so she could stare at him;

he also realized that his pace, once again, had slackened to almost nil.

He brought out the dimples just to prove he had nothing to hide. "Well, sure, she's attractive. But I don't like her type. I mean, the type she's become. You know what I mean. The superwoman type. That's not what . . . anyway, that's all over."

He knew blathering when he heard it. He clamped his mouth shut and returned his attention to the stair-step machine.

"Then why?"

Narrowing his eyes and his lips, Cal abruptly stopped his efforts and jumped off the machine. Tory shot up to a seated position and dropped her light tone.

"You know better than that. Ease off slowly. Cool down a little first."

Cal picked up a towel and mopped the excess perspiration off his head, arms and shoulders.

"Get off my case, Tory."

"That's my job, Cal."

"Patching the broken?"

He saw the moment of solemnity in her eyes. "I know the territory."

Tory's gentle but firm spirit as she had coached him in the physical regime that slowly brought him back to full strength had been tempered, he knew, by her own experiences. And the places where she had helped patch his psyche, as well as his weakened inner organs, barely showed, he supposed.

Her psyche, he knew, still needed patching. But he didn't know how to repay her with his help. Only one thing would make Tory's healing complete. And that wasn't in his power to accomplish. Only the courts could grant Tory's healing.

At least he could offer her a home. That had been more important to her than the bigger bucks she could make working elsewhere: a safe place to work and regain her confidence and demonstrate to the courts that she had rid herself of the prescription drugs that had ruled her life in the months of agony after her auto accident.

It was some compensation for all she had done for him; some, but not nearly enough. "Sorry if I made you uncomfortable."

She shrugged. "So if she's not your type anymore, why'd you want to make her jealous?"

He propped a leg on the stepper machine and stared down at her. She looked almost as young as his daughter, but he knew she was twice as mature as his flighty offspring. He also knew he wouldn't choose the path she had taken to maturity for anyone, much less his daughter.

But he wasn't being asked to do much choosing on Casey's behalf anymore. All he could do for Casey was try not to worry. He did anyway, mostly because he blamed himself that there was something to worry about in the first place. Lord knows he'd done his best. From the moment Casey showed up at his front door four years earlier, he had quit being irresponsible, irrepressible Cal. No more staying out all night and running wild in an effort to forget Trish. No more spending money as if it were water. No more fast cars and faster women.

Cal had worked hard at responsibility. College funds. This house. He'd even tried to remarry, thinking a stepmother would be good—until he'd realized why he had chosen cool, blond, husky-voiced Moira to fill the role.

Regardless, his best shot at being a responsible father hadn't been good enough. As Trish never failed to remind him. The result was that he couldn't imagine ever admitting his insecurities to his ever-perfect ex-wife.

He shrugged off the thought and grinned at Tory. "Isn't that what meetings with exes are all about—making them jealous? Reminding them what they're missing?"

"Yeah, well, I didn't like the way she looked at me, thinking I'm your little playmate." She threw his T-shirt in his face and gave him a hard, accusing stare. "I only went because I thought you were going to tell her and wanted some moral support."

Cal draped the shirt over his bare shoulder. "I know. I'm sorry. I intended to. I really did. I just…I couldn't. I didn't want her to…talking about it always makes me feel…"

He hesitated, struggling to find the words to describe exactly how he felt about being betrayed by his own body. Before he could speak, the door to the workout room burst open, slamming against the wall with a force whose source Cal knew without even looking up.

Casey had arrived.

She swept into the room like a gale-force wind, flipping her shoes off in a gesture that had been familiar to Cal long before Casey was old enough to wear shoes, much less remove them. It was one of Trish's signature gestures. Taller than her mom, and needle thin where her mom had always been sweetly round, Casey shared Trish's capacity for attracting attention wherever she appeared. With a disconcerting sense of déjà vu he'd realized sometime during the past year that the hooded gaze she'd inherited from her mother would no doubt be seductively appealing leveled at the right young man. And her graceful carriage more than made up for her lack of shapeliness.

Lace-trimmed leggings hugged her straight legs and bony hips, and the lemon yellow patch pockets on her see-through, red gauze top were strategically located to hide the fact there was very little to hide. A black silver-studded dog collar encircled her long, thin neck. Chunky silver rings with stones in every color hung from eight fingers and her straw hair was razor-cut into a semblance of the regulation flat-top Cal had worn in elementary school.

Yes, she might have blossomed into something of an unconventional vamp, but she was still the same old Casey.

Except for the tattoo of a peacock on her right ankle. That was new.

As he absorbed his daughter's appearance, Cal flinched at the thought of the impending meeting between Trish and Casey. He hoped Trish wasn't squeamish.

"I like the bird." He gestured at her ankle.

She laughed, a hearty, head-thrown-back laugh from low in her chest, a laugh that deepened the dimples bracketing her always impish smile. His dimples. His smile. And his laugh, a laugh that always tapped into his soul. He laughed with her.

"Come down to the shop—we'll get one for you." She wrapped her arms around him for a hug, then pulled back and made a face as she held her arms away from her body. "Yuck! Perspiration. How totally heinous."

"Doctor's orders."

Casey grimaced at Tory. "Straining the body. Activating the sweat glands. What a disgusting line of work. Your mother must be so ashamed of you."

Only Cal noticed the remorse that flickered across Tory's face at his daughter's innocent teasing.

Casey dropped to the floor, twisted her legs into a pretzel shape and leaned back against the padded incline board. "Speaking of maternal types, did you see Mom today?"

"We did."

Casey looked from one to the other and raised a pale blond eyebrow. "Both of you? Oh, I'll bet that was cool."

"Your dad was too *c-h-i-c-k-e-n* to explain who I am. He thought it was a much better idea to simply let her think I'm his main squeeze."

Casey squinted her eyes and raised her hands in supplication. "Spare me. Spare me from the one-upmanship of ex-parents. Daddy, how could you?"

"So I'm a jerk. I couldn't think of a clever way to work it into the conversation." He feigned a weak old man's voice. "'Oh, by the way, Tory isn't my lover, she's my nursemaid.'"

Tory thumped his shoulder with her fist and Casey kicked at him with one of her long, thin bare feet.

"Your *trainer,* Daddy. Your trainer." She puffed out her cheeks and mimed lifting weights over her head. "Quit acting like such a wimp. What's the big deal? You'd think you'd engaged in some kind of disgustingly abnormal behavior—which I heartily advocate, by the way—instead of having a little heart attack."

The words gave Cal a jolt, as they always did. A shot of adrenaline that sizzled through his veins and startled the organ in question.

A heart attack. On the one hand, it was hard to believe it had ever happened. On the other hand, Cal knew his life had changed irrevocably that morning seven months ago when his heart sputtered and squeezed shut in his chest. All the changes he'd made on the surface when Casey came to live with him had suddenly embedded themselves deeply and truly into his soul.

Facing his own mortality had given Cal Sullivan a much truer picture of what was really important in the all-too-short life he'd been given.

He pulled on his T-shirt to give himself a moment to erase the anxiety from his face. "Okay. So it's no big deal. Then why should I have to broadcast it to your mom the minute she shows up in Charlotte?"

Casey rolled her eyes and exchanged a glance with Tory. "Are they all like this?"

"Mostly."

"Do you want me to tell her? I think we're going to have lunch tomorrow, so I could just..."

"No, I do not want you to tell her. If and when she needs to know, I am perfectly capable of telling her myself."

Casey once again looked at Tory, this time silently mouthing the word Tory had spelled out earlier. "Chicken."

She suddenly leapt up as if she had lost all patience with inactivity and jumped onto the stepper machine Cal had abandoned. "So, how is she?"

"Your mother?"

"Yeah." Casey concentrated her attention on the digital monitor. "I mean, how does she look? Did she seem ... any different?"

"She looked ... fine. Great. She looked great."

"And?"

"And what?"

"And how did she seem? The same as always?"

The last time he and his daughter had discussed her mother—after Trish flew back to Chicago following Casey's high school graduation almost a year ago—Casey had asked solemnly if Trish had ever been any fun. Or had she always, as Casey put it, been wrapped so tight she squeaked?

"No, Casey, I don't think she's much different."

"What did she say about me?"

Cal screwed up his lips, searching for the right thing to say. Casey's steps slowed, the rhythmic squeak of the machine stilled.

"It's okay, Daddy. You can tell me. She's bound to tell me herself, anyway."

His daughter grinned wryly; he joined her.

"Yeah. I guess so." Nevertheless, he chose his words carefully. Deep in his heart he agreed with Trish and wished there was some way to convince her not to harden Casey's resolve by coming in on the attack. "She's worried you're a little young."

"I'll be older than she was."

"By four months."

"And I'm not even knocked up."

"Casey!"

She giggled. "I don't mean that in a bad way, Dad. It's just a fact. I mean, I was about twelve when I figured out that I wasn't *really* born four months early. I weighed, like, nine pounds. How early could I have been? So, anyway, it's not like I'm getting married because I have to, right?"

"Maybe I'll go make us some tea." Tory backed away from them.

"So she thinks she's going to talk me out of it, huh?"

"I didn't say that."

"You didn't have to. But she looked good, huh? I mean, really good? She looks great on TV. Does she still look that good in person?"

Cal smiled. "Better."

Casey smiled, too, and stepped off the exercise machine. "Yeah? That's nice. I mean, I know she's pretty serious about stuff, but she's still a real babe. Right?"

"Right."

"You still sweaty?"

Cal patted himself for moisture. "Mostly dry."

"Good." She put an arm around his waist and they followed Tory's path, pausing while Casey retrieved her shoes. "It'll be fun, won't it? The three of us planning a wedding?"

"You mean the four of us?"

"Oh, yeah. Will, too."

Cal had always been careful not to let his daughter get wind of his fatherly paranoia: He had learned early on, from watching Casey and Trish battle, that that only served to make his daughter dig in her heels. So he hadn't made a big deal of the fact that he had never even met his daughter's fiancé, Will. He was away at school, she said. It didn't add up for Cal, but he knew better than to act suspicious.

Casey chattered as they climbed the stairs from the basement he'd converted into a workout room. "So, where should we go for dinner tomorrow? Somewhere Mom'll like that isn't totally stuffed shirt. Or maybe we should just blow her out of the water. She might as well get used to it, right? Say, can you pick her up? We could meet you."

Finalizing their plans for the next evening, they entered the red-and-black kitchen he and Casey had designed together. Neon light fixtures and textile wall art created a look Tory had once teasingly called Nouveau Nightmare. Cal agreed with Casey; it was simply eye-opening, which seemed appropriate for the room where you ate breakfast. Like the rest of the house, it was modern in a kinky, art deco sort of way that reflected the adventurous spirit he and Trish had passed on to their daughter.

In fact, Cal sometimes thought Trish had spilled all of her wild, quirky nature into their daughter. She had changed so completely after Casey was born.

Cal watched his daughter as she helped Tory pull down teacups and browse through the fridge for snacks. He knew plenty of middle-aged parents who would bemoan the kind of young woman Casey was, who would be praying for the day when she outgrew her outrageousness and became more like the sensible, level-headed Tory.

But Cal loved Casey the way she was, and doubted she would ever be any different. From the moment she was born, she had made it clear she had no intention of making life easy on them.

1974

LONG BEFORE she made her appearance, Casey Hilton Sullivan was making her mother miserable. Many times during the nine months of his young wife's pregnancy, Cal had pressed his hand protectively against the swell of Trish's belly as their unborn daughter kicked and flailed and and protested her confinement.

"Call the Washington Redskins. He's going to be a placekicker," Trish had grumbled more than once, her cheeks beautifully plump with the extra forty-nine pounds she'd gained.

"Or the Joffrey," Cal had always countered. "She could be practising her pliés."

Labor was long and hard and left Cal feeling help-lessly, hopelessly unnecessary. His last useful act had been driving them to the hospital. And once there, Casey seemed determined, now that the time had come to escape her prison, to do just the opposite of what was expected of her. She obviously hadn't counted on her mother's determination. Cal watched with growing ap-prehension as Trish grew more stubborn with each new contraction.

"Okay, here comes another one." His left hand now numb and crushed from Trish's grip, Cal watched her sweat-drenched face and forced himself to remember his role here. Calm, supportive; not afraid and panicked and ready to call the whole thing off, which was how he really felt. "Okay, now push, Trish. That's it. Push."

"I...am...pushing!" she grunted between clenched teeth. "Push yourself if you can do any better."

And an hour later, her hair pulled off her neck and back and streaming over the pillow in wet strands, Trish vowed, "If he doesn't come this time, tell him I'm coming in there after him."

After twelve hours that had seemed more like twelve days to Cal, Trish set her jaw and growled, "Now, dammit! Now, you little brat! This is your mother speaking. Now!"

And with an endless, deep, primal scream, she pushed with much more strength than Cal had left at that point, and a tiny head was forced into the world, soon fol-lowed by a tiny body struggling to remain safely curled.

Looking down at the wrinkled, grimacing face of his newborn daughter—could that possibly be dimples just like his—and the drained but satisfied face of his young wife, Cal had struggled to fight back tears. He was part of something real now, something enduring. Like the stories of death, when they say your life flashes before you, he felt as if he could see this small being's life unfolding before his eyes.

Quaking, he took the already squirming body offered by the doctor and laid her on Trish's belly.

He leaned close to her ear, one hand on the baby, the other on Trish, to whisper, "It's a girl, Trish. A girl."

She smiled, her swollen, weary eyes gazing down at the wiggling bundle, then up at him. "It's about time."

CAL SMILED as he watched his daughter putter around the kitchen. In all his forty-one years of memories, the memory of her birth was his favorite: better than the memory of his first one-man show at the age of ten on the stage of the Stanley Elementary School; better than his memory of Trish, a delicate wreath of baby's breath and purple ribbon circling her head, walking toward him at Latta Park, mouthing her vows so she wouldn't forget; better than the offer of his first TV job; better than the first day he realized he could earn a comfortable living training business execs on management style and leadership techniques.

Yes, the day he watched Trish give birth was Cal's favorite memory. Often these days he regretted those early years when Trish had done most of the parenting; he only hoped he had made up for it in some small measure during the last four years.

He only wished he hadn't been so blindly immature about what Trish had needed out of life in those days.

Casey filled three teacups and thrust one at him. "So, when are you on the road next?"

"Three days next week. Denver, then Boise, then Phoenix."

"I thought you were supposed to be taking it easy."

"That is taking it easy. I used to do six cities in five days."

"And we know where that got you."

To the top of his profession, one of the most in-demand speakers and trainers in the country, he wanted to say, but didn't. "Tip said—"

"Doc Tipton said you came right out of the hospital acting like nothing had happened. No change in diet, no change in habits. Classic denial. Three months later you were still smoking, for criminy's sake, and..."

"I know. I know. And that's what Tory is here for, to..."

"To keep you in line."

"To oversee my recuperation. Which, if I do say so myself, is now complete and I am perfectly capable of looking after myself like any other grown man." He saw the apprehension in Tory's eyes and was surprised to realize how dependent on this relationship she might be, too. "Almost. Soon."

Casey snorted her skepticism. "And perfectly capable of ending up right back in the hospital with tubes stuck in your nose. What a bummer! Daddy, do what the doctor says."

"I am. I am." He looked at Tory for support. "Tell her."

Tory studied him, then nodded. "He is. Mostly."

"Mostly." Casey threw up her hands. "Mostly, Daddy? If I'd done *mostly* what you told me to do when I was growing up..."

"It would have been quite a victory."

She grinned impishly and passed him the platter of tasteless but politically correct—cholesterolwise—cookies that Tory had insisted he buy. "Yeah. I guess neither one of us is very obedient. Guess we both need somebody to keep us in line, huh?"

Cal had only a moment to ponder that comment before she breezed right into a discussion of her new plans to check out the welding program at the local community college. But he promised himself he would bring her back around to it sometime.

CASEY SAT ON THE bare wooden floor, one leg curled under her, the other bent so she could reach her toes with the brush from one of the five bottles of polish sitting at her side—Purple Passion, Big Apple Red, Flamingo Pink, Neon Coral and Gold Dust.

She dabbed her big toe with purple and held it at leg's length to examine the effect, wiggling her long, skinny appendages. "You'll like them, Will. You'll see. They're excellent. Especially Dad. He's cool. And Mom, well, Mom's cool, too, in a different way."

Will Henderson draped a long leg over the edge of the lopsided armchair that was the only furniture except for the psychedelic-print futon in Casey's studio apartment. "I can't believe I let you talk me into this. It's not too late to call the whole thing off, you know."

"You let me talk you into it because you don't want your mother to know that you're majoring in architecture and not business," she said, recapping the purple and studying Will before pulling the tiny brush out of the red.

"You wouldn't really tell her."

Will's dismissal of her blackmail was nonchalant, but Casey knew he knew her well enough to harbor enough doubt to go along with her crazy schemes. Besides, she suspected he got his kicks just being close to her antics. Because Will did not have one wild bone in his body. That much was obvious at a glance. From his short, smooth brown hair to his neatly creased jeans, he was the closest thing to a nerd she had for a friend. The only thing that saved him from total nerd-dom was that he was good-looking in a straight, Prince Charles kind of way, and his brain was a computer programmed with every detail anyone would ever want to know about popular music in the twentieth century. From Bessie Smith and Billie Holiday to those little geeks all the teenyboppers loved, he knew it all. It blew her away.

She touched the brush to the red polish again. "Don't sweat it, Will."

"Don't sweat it, she tells me. This from the woman who drove my car to Myrtle Beach last month and rode back with someone else."

Extending her leg as far as it would stretch across the room, she studied her toes. "I forgot, okay? But we got your car back, didn't we?"

"Doesn't your dad think it's weird he's never met me? And what about all these expenses you're going to rack up? You know, people want deposits on stuff, Casey. You have to think about these things."

"So we'll plan a very low-budget party. What a swell way to announce their engagement. Or maybe we can figure out a way to get a marriage certificate in their name and..."

"We?"

"Will, I'm telling you, it's going to be okay."

"But what if something goes wrong? What if..."

She gazed up at his concerned face. "Sometimes I can't even remember why I like you. You are *so* straight. Don't worry, Will. You aren't going to have to marry me."

"You can say that again." He grinned. "But what if they find out what you're doing?"

"They won't. Trust me." She fanned her toes and opened the hot pink for her third toe. "I've done this too many times. But this time it's going to work."

Now Will sat straight up in his chair. "You've gotten engaged before?"

Casey giggled. "No, goof. But there was the year I was fourteen, when I had appendicitis at summer camp in West Virginia."

Will looked dubious. "You don't have a scar."

"Precisely." She grinned smugly. "But by the time the doctors discovered I didn't need surgery, Mom and Dad were already rallying at my bedside. Then there was the time I ran away to Boston and called them both to come after me. And you remember two years ago, when I shaved my head and threatened to join that weird religion?"

"That was all a trick, too?"

She nodded, finishing up her pinky with a coat of clear gloss flecked with gold sparkles.

"But none of it worked," Will pointed out, as practical as ever.

She refused to give him the satisfaction of worrying about his pessimistic pronouncement. Now that her mom was successful and her dad was out of TV, there was no reason for professional jealousy to keep them apart.

She didn't dwell on the real reason for her conviction that this time her plotting would finally work—

their pain-in-the-butt daughter, Casey Hilton Sullivan, was now a grown-up and no longer a reason for disagreement.

"This time it's going to work." Casey leaned back and waved her foot in the air. "This time I've got them together for two whole months. They need each other, and it's going to take time for them to realize it. This time they *will* fall in love again. I guaran-damn-tee it."

CHAPTER FOUR

THE MOMENT THE FRONT DOOR of the tattoo parlor whooshed closed behind her, Patrice forgot every vow she'd made to herself while parking the rented Mercedes.

I will be calm, she had said, dropping the keys into her taupe leather bag. *I will smile and smile and I will not be a villain.*

Then she had seen the storefront at 1821 Seventh Street, where she had arranged to meet Casey. There, over the side porch entrance to a down-at-the-heels, 1920s cedar-shake bungalow, was the name of the shop, emblazoned in psychedelic letters: Body Designs.

A retro clothing store, she had decided, preparing herself for the worst.

I will not disapprove.

Then the door closed behind her and she saw the cracked, yellowing plaster walls, painted white too many years ago to calculate and now covered with illustrations like the walls of a T-shirt shop. Snakes twisted around daggers, and motorcycle insignia surrounded butterflies poised for flight.

Patrice decided her reportorial instincts must be failing her. This could not be what it appeared to be. *I will not jump to conclusions or lose my cool.*

Then she saw Casey. She saw the hand-held machine in her daughter's hand and the pot of colors at her daughter's elbow. She saw the buzz-cut hair and the shiny vinyl jeans, but decided to let both go for the moment. She concentrated instead on the bearded man with the red-white-and-blue eagle wings unfurling on his back.

"With you in a nanosec," said the daughter who had tortured Patrice from the moment she had been yanked, headfirst and kicking, into the world.

Casey didn't look up. For which Patrice was grateful. It gave her time to compose herself. To wipe the chagrin off her face. To...

Compose myself, hell! I'll get a court order. She moved warily into the room, thinking it amazing that an international reporter who had spent the night spitting out dust in the desert while missiles exploded overhead had never before set foot in a tattoo parlor. *I'll have her removed from the premises and handcuffed to my wrist and we'll board the first plane for Chicago.*

But not before I pulverize Cal Sullivan and every single dimple on his charmingly boyish face.

Casey stood back, wiping the tip of the beastly little tool she had been using and studying the bird on the man's beefy back. Nodding, she handed the man a mirror. "Totally excellent. Here, lay eyes on the masterpiece."

The man took the mirror and held it over his shoulder to get a look at the reflection of his back in the full-length mirror on the wall. He grunted in what was clearly appreciation.

Only then did Casey turn toward the door. The moment she saw her mother, her angular face blossomed into a smile, the wide, engaging, heart-stealing smile that had battled for control of Patrice for almost twenty years, first in the person of Cal, then in the person of her wayward child. Nothing—not the year since they had last seen each other, not the tough and ugly clothes her daughter wore, not the GI haircut or the studded collar around her neck—could dim the magic of the smile that was pure exultant devilment.

Patrice melted.

"Mom!"

And Casey had her surrounded. All long, spindly arms, she wrapped herself around Patrice. Patrice wrapped back, squeezing away the moisture in her eyes as she absorbed this person who was the best part of her soul. Taller by inches now—they had been the same height less than twelve months ago—but still all bones and angles. She smelled of sandalwood incense. She was warm, beautiful and outrageous.

Patrice was happier than she knew it was wise to be.

Casey stepped back and swept her arms around the compact shop.

"So, how do you like it? Isn't this too cool?"

Patrice tried to fashion an answer. An unantagonistic answer. But truthful. She couldn't be untruthful here. Just a bit of dissembling, perhaps, to keep the peace. After all, she and Casey had more important things to disagree over.

An answer wasn't necessary. Casey barely paused for breath.

"Of course, I'm just in training. But Hoss says I have good instincts. A natural artist."

Hoss. The name conjured images of someone swarthy and hairy, bulging in unsightly ways on the seat of a Harley-Davidson. Patrice shivered.

"I'm even working on some of my own designs. Look."

Casey turned, yanking her leather vest down to reveal a skinny, tie-dyed tank top and a wild orchid on her right shoulder. It was lovely, Patrice noted. But burned into her baby girl's delicate flesh?

If only she were the kind who could faint.

"And here."

Casey hiked up her jeans to reveal the multicolored peacock on her ankle. Then she paused and Patrice knew she had no choice. It was time to speak.

Calm. Composed. Not the villain.

What chance had the child had? She had been raised by Cal.

And it *was* a lovely peacock. "Casey, I had no idea you were so talented."

Casey all but jumped up and down in delight. "You think? I mean, really?"

The love swelled up in Patrice's throat again. "I mean, really. What a wonderful eye for color. For design."

Now put it to good use, lectured the voice of motherhood inside her.

On the outside, she continued to smile.

"Wow." Casey was momentarily silenced by the praise. Then she pranced to a back wall. "Listen, I know you'll think my mind has been seized by aliens, but I was looking up here the other day and I saw this and I thought how cool it would look on you. I mean, it's just *you*. The essential Patrice. Know what I mean?"

Maintaining her control, Patrice strolled back for a polite look at the tattoo design. It was a moon, a sliver of silver blue, with a teardrop of brilliant light spilling from its lower point. It was lovely. Mysterious. As well as a bit cool, a bit aloof. Patrice felt a quiver up her spine.

"Is that how I am?"

"Sometimes. But you know what? On the other side..."

Patrice watched as her daughter went in search of something else.

"On the other side of what?"

Casey giggled wickedly, a look in her eyes that was disturbingly familiar. Cal's look of mischief.

"Well, it's up to you, of course." She pointed at a starburst of fireworks. "There. That's the rest of you. We could do one on each shoulder. Or on your backside. Although, if we did that, they will tend to droop out of shape after a while..." She paused. "Well, not for a long while, of course."

"Of course." *As long as the money for the fat farm holds out.*

"Dad said you looked sensational. Or terrific, maybe. He said your hair is smashing. He said he doesn't know how you stay so young looking and he just keeps getting older."

"He did?"

Instantly Patrice could have kicked herself. She sounded too eager for the compliment. Who cared what Cal thought?

Who, indeed?

"But he doesn't, does he? I mean, I don't think he looks old at all. He is *such* a hunk. For a dad. Don't you think?"

Patrice smiled and nodded. Her daughter wasn't the only young woman who thought so. She wondered how Casey felt about Tory of the Megacleavage. Or perhaps

Tory was simply one of Cal's many Insignificant Others.

"So, are you hungry? How about some lunch?"

Although the paraphernalia of the art of tattoo had driven any thought of food from Patrice's mind, she agreed simply to get them out of the shop. At Casey's suggestion, they walked down the street to a nearby restaurant. Along the way, Casey pointed out the high spots of the neighborhood as they stepped over the feet of an aromatic congregation of street people. Patrice took a perverse satisfaction in the fact that more than one of the people knew Casey's name and spoke to her warmly.

Casey might act like a ditz, but she had heart. Patrice was proud of her in spite of everything. Proud to bursting. So proud it ached to think of her daughter throwing away all her opportunities for a brilliant future, on the art of tattoo and a marriage doomed by her youth.

Casey waved an arm toward a shabby, twenties-era two-story.

"They sell Caribbean clothes and artifacts there. They have the coolest collection of antique sexual aids. Do you suppose they really used those things?" Without pausing for a comment Patrice couldn't have managed anyway, Casey pointed to another old house, its cedar shake siding painted a vibrant coral color. "And that's a co-op for artists—one woman makes handmade jewelry and there's a potter and a fabric artist. I got this tank top there."

She stopped in the middle of the sidewalk and took Patrice by the shoulders, scrutinizing her carefully from top to bottom. "They have this killer bodysuit that is to die for, if you have a body. It's totally sheer. I mean totally. All I'd have to show is bones sticking out in all the wrong places, but you would be such a babe in it. Want to check it out?''

"I'm not sure it would work for on the air."

Casey laughed. "No. But Dad would swallow his golf clubs if he saw you in it."

Patrice doubted he would notice with Tory clinging to him.

Next was the New Age center, which sold incense and crystals and books on herbal healing. A visiting psychic from Atlanta had recently told Casey that years of determination would soon pay off. Patrice was positive she didn't want to know what the payoff would be.

"Dad loves it there."

Dad. Always Dad. They were close. Patrice was jealous. She looked at the bright yellow frame house. A young man with a ponytail was exiting. Faceted light catchers hung in the front window. "He does?"

"Oh, yeah. I brought him here for the psychic fair last month."

"I'm sure he enjoyed that." She didn't dwell on the fact that Cal could enjoy himself at almost anything; for Cal, life was a lark. That had been only one of the many reasons they'd done nothing but fight in their last years together. Patrice had grown weary of feeling like the only adult in their family.

And when she had taken that role seriously anyway—by deciding to carve out a successful career in TV news—Cal's lack of support had been the final blow.

1985

PATRICE'S HANDS trembled as she unpacked. The job was hers. Hers! All the years she'd struggled to learn the business, working her way up from co-hosting a morning show to co-anchoring the late news, were finally paying off.

The skirt of her raw silk suit slipped out of her jittery fingers and she didn't even bother to bend and retrieve it. She simply shoved her suitcase aside and sat on the bed.

Atlanta. Millions of viewers. A shot at the big time.

If only she could count on Cal to be proud of her, to share her excitement. If only...

When she heard him come in from picking Casey up at school, Patrice's outer trembling stopped. An inner quaking started in its place. She waited, listening to Casey stampede through the house, calling out the unconcerned greeting of an eleven-year-old with TV on her mind.

Cal was slow in joining her. When he did, she saw the guarded look in his eyes. Her enthusiasm waned.

"You got the job." There was no congratulations in his blunt announcement.

"I hoped you would be happy."

He yanked at his tie. "How can I be happy? What happens to me if you go to work in Atlanta?"

"You can come with me. I'm sure it won't take..."

"Won't take long? Six months, maybe? A year? Or maybe not at all."

She knew what he was thinking, although he'd never spoken the words. He was afraid he wasn't good enough for the Atlanta market. Afraid he wouldn't make it.

"Cal, you'll see..."

"Stay here, Trish. You've got a good job. Charlotte's a good place to raise a family. We've got roots here."

"Come with me, Cal."

But she knew from the uncertainty in his face that he would let her go without him before he took the risk.

WITH CASEY'S CHATTERING to distract her, Patrice drew herself out of the memory that weighed her down every time she relived it, every time she second-guessed her decision and wished she'd been mature enough to cope with Cal's insecurity in the face of her success.

"I'm telling you, Mom, Dad almost went ballistic when the tarot card reader told him a long-lost love would come for him soon."

Patrice didn't want to hear about Cal's long-lost love, either. She'd made it a point to avoid news of her ex-husband's social life, especially after his short-lived engagement a few years back.

Although why it should matter that her ex-husband chose to dally with women barely released from day-care was beyond her. Especially after her dalliance with Truman.

But Truman was—had been—a momentary diversion. An aberration. A fling of minuscule proportions. Truman had been a few weeks of attempted passion; Tory was erotic felony.

Nevertheless, Cal's playthings shouldn't matter, any more than it should matter to her that the execs at ICN thought Lettie Gundersen was getting too old to cut it on the air.

But replacing her best friend? Could she do that? Issues of aging and office politics aside, could she take the next big step in her already spectacular career at the expense of the woman she called mentor and friend?

The restaurant Casey selected was a juice bar and health food store. Patrice ordered something with sprouts and sunflower seeds, determined to remain

faithful to everything she'd learned at the fat farm.
Casey ordered a carrot-and-alfalfa-juice shake and a
pestomato pizza. The waiter wore ballet slippers and
purple leggings imprinted with the likenesses of the
Mount Rushmore presidents. His head was shaved, except for a long, wavy tendril over each ear.

"So, Ma, I wondered what you thought about a
wedding dress."

"A wedding dress?"

"Yeah. I was thinking of something . . . not ordi-
nary."

No kidding. "Well, Casey, are you . . . that is, I've
been wondering if . . ."

"There's a little shop just around the corner. Maybe
we'll stop by after lunch."

"For a wedding dress?" *In this neighborhood?*

"Yeah. Dad and I stopped in a few weeks ago. It's a
riot."

Patrice felt a headache coming on. Cal again. They
were inseparable, it seemed. And, yes, she was definitely jealous. As she had been so many times when
Casey had preferred staying with her father over summer vacation to visiting her mother in Atlanta or Chicago. Jealous and left out.

She had done everything but beg Casey to come
home. Casey had let her know she felt she *was* home.

Maybe she should have begged.

Patrice sipped chamomile and rose hip tea, wishing
for a vodka, straight up. The last time she'd had a vodka
straight up had been in a crowd of protestors and cele-
brators in Red Square, the week of the aborted coup
that had ultimately brought Communist rule to an end.

This visit to Charlotte threatened to be at least that
significant.

"Dad said a girl only gets married the first time once, so I should make this one whatever I want it to be."

There wouldn't be a better opening. And it wasn't like she'd be spoiling the best lunch she'd ever eaten. She pushed the sprout sandwich to the edge of her plate and leaned her arms on the table.

"Your father is right about that." *For a change.* "About doing it only once, I mean. And I'm . . . well, it occurs to me that you might . . . that is, these days a lot of young people seem to be waiting. To marry. Until they're certain. Of who they are. What they want to do with their lives. I . . . it occurred to me that might be very wise."

Casey carefully placed her slice of pizza back on her plate and stared across the table.

"Mom? You mean you think I should make absolutely sure that marrying Will is the right thing to do before we make it legal?"

Good. She sounds rational. Almost adult. Patrice allowed herself to breath again. "Why, yes, Casey. I think that would be exactly the right idea."

Casey merely stared, openmouthed. But Patrice saw the glitter in her gray-green eyes; a maddeningly familiar glitter. Patrice had the sinking feeling something had happened here that she didn't understand. Only two people in her entire life had ever made her feel so adrift. Cal and Casey.

"You should experiment with life. While you're still young. Before you tie yourself down."

"Mom. I do not believe you're saying this." Casey lowered her voice and looked around, as if in fear that someone would overhear. "Are you suggesting that I *live* with Will? *In sin?* Just to make sure we're *right* for each other? Or maybe you think I should play the field a little first.''

Patrice gulped chamomile and rose hip. It was cold. Was she actually going to say this? ''Well, perhaps you *should* live together first. It makes sense, Casey. If you take the proper precautions, of course. You know, marriage requires a great deal of maturity and...''

''Mom! I can't believe you're saying this. Do you know what year this is?''

''Well, of course I...''

''This is *not* 1974.'' Casey wiped her hands on her paper napkin and leaned across the table, her voice low and desperate. ''Attitudes toward sex have changed. My generation is far less casual than yours was. I hope you know that. You aren't doing anything foolish, are you?''

Patrice thought of Truman and felt her cheeks grow hot. ''No. Well...no. Of course not. But that's hardly the point. We're here to discuss your situation and...''

''And I have no intention of being promiscuous.''

''Now, wait a minute. I'll have you know I was never promiscuous, either.'' She lowered her voice as the waiter slipped their check onto the table.

''You weren't?''

''I most certainly was not.''

''Good. Then I know you'll understand that all I'm really after is stability. A secure *family* situation.'' On the word ''family,'' Casey tossed her paper napkin onto the table and stood. ''Now, let's run around the corner. You'll love this place.''

Dropping a ten-dollar bill onto the table beside their check, Patrice managed to stand and follow her daughter, although Casey's mention of family had knocked the wind out of her. Yes, maybe this whole disaster was her fault after all, because she hadn't provided a secure family for her only daughter.

She followed Casey around the corner in miserable silence, contemplating all her shortcomings, every way in which she had failed to be the perfect mother.

Actually, Patrice did love the little shop. Seedy and dark and run by two young men with the limpest wrists she'd ever seen, Oh, Dahling was, in Casey's words, a hoot. The once-elegant rooms of the old house were jam-packed with vintage clothing from the thirties, forties, fifties and sixties.

"We're just getting into psychedelic," one of the proprietors confided to Casey as she whipped through a rack of cocktail dresses in satin and net. "I have a pair of bell-bottoms in the back with patches all over them. This is authentic, I kid you not. Worth a fortune."

"Here it is." Casey gently pulled a pink dress off the rack. "Isn't this *too* perfect, Mom?"

Patrice managed to get her daughter out of the store without purchasing the strapless cocktail dress, a body-skimming pink satin with net flouncing over the trim skirt.

"Well, there's plenty of time to settle on a dress," Casey said as they headed back to Body Designs. "Although that one would pick up the colors in the orchid tattoo on my shoulder, don't you think?"

Patrice pretended to study the tattoo while doing her best not to look at it directly. "Truthfully, I think the shades are just a bit off. They might clash."

"Oh. Well, listen, there is something I really need your help in deciding. Some of my friends think we should have a hot air balloon wedding. Although Pete and Frankie had their wedding on a roller coaster last summer, which was a riot, no question about it. But I'm thinking a hot air balloon just isn't right. Not for me, at least."

Right in the center of each temple. Throbbing. Definite throbbing. Patrice was in serious danger of grabbing her daughter by the shoulders and shaking her. Not hard. Just enough to rattle her brain back into position.

"I had something much better in mind." Casey drew a long, deep breath and her face blossomed into a wide grin. "Mom, don't you think it would be absolutely stellar to have a bungee cord wedding?"

THE SELF-ASSURED young face stared coolly back at Patrice from the TV screen. She couldn't believe it! Young, brunette Cinda Reisling was already filling in on her weekend anchor spot. Already! After four lousy months at the station.

And the worst of it was, she was good.

Of course she's good. You trained her.

Patrice's disgruntlement distracted her only momentarily. As soon as the doorbell of the condo rang, she remembered what really had her tied in knots tonight. Dinner with Casey and her fiancé, Will.

And Cal. Her date. Who had arrived.

She cast about for a mirror and realized there was no place in the living room for last-minute scrutiny before she opened the door. She smoothed the sleek black dress over her hips. She raked her fingers through her hair to fluff it up. Then she remembered the black pumps she had kicked off under the coffee table. She slipped her feet into them and marched to the door.

Cal filled the door frame. With his broad shoulders and thick, wavy hair and that overwhelming smile, he seemed to shrink his surroundings. Patrice remembered how he had always insisted on a king-size bed, and even then he had seemed to fill it....

"You're on time."

"And you thought I hadn't changed."

She laughed. Nervously, it seemed to her. While Cal was whipped-cream smooth. Her heel snagged on the carpet as she stepped away from the door. She stumbled slightly, just enough to make her feel clumsy and awkward, the way she used to feel before she became the cool, efficient network news star.

Back when she was Cal's wife.

"I'll get my wrap."

Cal stepped into the condo. Patrice grabbed her brocade jacket from the back of the couch. No lingering. Not here. Alone. With Cal.

He closed the door behind him. He was in. And they were alone.

"You look lovely." He stepped close to help her into her jacket, which felt far too warm at the moment. "I still can't get used to you."

"What do you mean?" She swallowed. He was close. The couch was against her knees. She was trapped. He was warm. She was warmer. This was not good.

"So sophisticated. I guess I'll always remember you the way you were. Barefoot half the time. Jeans. All that hair swinging loose. And now..."

"People change, Cal. It's not 1974 anymore." *And I don't feel that way about you anymore. I don't, I don't, I don't.*

Do I?

The phone saved her from answering her own accusations. Cal stepped back and she slid past him to pick it up.

It was Casey. Running late, of course. "Why don't you guys just have a glass of wine there and we'll meet you at the restaurant in about an hour."

"An hour?" The words barely escaped Patrice's tightly clenched jaw.

She heard Cal chuckle, then from the corner of her eye saw him settle onto the couch. After listening to a few more of her daughter's loosely offered excuses, Patrice hung up and squared her shoulders.

"I gather our daughter is not as punctual as her old man tonight."

"You gather correctly."

She paced around the room. An hour? What in heaven's name was she going to do with Cal for an hour?

"Calm down, Trish. It won't do a bit of good to get worked up. You know what she's like."

"Yes. I certainly do."

Cal chuckled again, completely ignoring the fact that she was condemning him for Casey's irresponsibility. How like him. He'd always been like that. Never taking anything seriously. Especially her. Especially her career.

She ignored the tiny voice that told her she wasn't being fair, that she hadn't been the model of understanding at the time herself.

"I'll bet there's basketball on TV. The Hornets are in the playoffs. Wanna watch?"

"You want to watch basketball?" She whirled on him. Here she was, able to think of nothing but the botch they'd made of their marriage, and he wanted to watch hoops!

He shook his head. "Nah. Come to think of it, I'd rather watch you. Did you know your eyes turn to absolute ice when you're angry?"

"You are not taking this seriously."

"Not taking what seriously, Trish?"

"Any of it!"

Us. The fact that we were both so young and self-centered and immature that we couldn't reach a compromise. Wouldn't even try.

No, no, no. That's not it.

"Casey. You aren't taking Casey seriously."

"I take her seriously. I wonder if you do."

"What's that supposed to mean?"

"It means that I respect the fact that she is ... Casey. She's a person, her own person. She isn't an extension of me or you and she can't be bent to our wishes."

"She's a child!"

"She's a young woman."

"She needs guidance."

"She won't be shackled, Trish. You ought to know that."

"Did you ever try to ... did you ever once ..."

Cal stood and walked over to her. Once again he put his hands on her shoulders. Now there was no wicked gleam in his eyes, just a solemnity she could never remember having seen before.

"I did the best I could, Trish. It probably wasn't the best that could have been done, but it was the best *I* could do. I was scared to death of making mistakes and I'm sure I made plenty."

She wanted to snap back that he certainly had, but his eyes stopped her. They were...vulnerable. They were the eyes of a Cal she couldn't remember having met before. A Cal she couldn't quite bring herself to hurt intentionally.

"She's the best of both of us, Trish. And maybe the worst of both of us, I don't know. But the time is long past when we can push her into performing the way we want her to."

Patrice felt a lump in her throat. She remembered how headstrong she had been at Casey's age and she knew Cal was right. She also suspected, for the first time, that he might have done a better job of raising Casey than she had wanted to believe.

"If you don't get off her case, you'll push her away again, Trish."

Patrice tensed under his hands. *Again?* As if she had pushed her daughter away before. As if she should have sacrificed discipline for the sake of being buddies.

"I think it's time we left."

All the way out to the car, Patrice couldn't help but wonder if Cal was more right than wrong. Casey may have once needed more control, but perhaps that time was past.

But admit it to Cal? Never.

No more than she would dream of admitting that his hands on her arms had reminded her of too many things. His unerring ability to arouse her, for example, as if his touch were the magic wand, the sprinkle of fairy dust, that brought her alive.

That magic had died in her the day she drove out of Charlotte and left him behind; it was a magic no one had been able to resurrect in her since.

Until now. Until the moment when Cal's hands on her arms had generated a compelling thrum. Her body was alive again. Electric.

And that was something she would never, never, never admit to Cal or anyone else.

CHAPTER FIVE

DOOMED. PATRICE KNEW instantly that was the fate of
any marriage between her helter-skelter daughter and
the straight-arrow young man sitting beside her in the
black-and-white-tiled bistro they had chosen for dinner.

Will Henderson was tall and lean and wearing the
unofficial uniform of the University of North Carolina
at Chapel Hill—khaki slacks with a crisp, well-starched
pleat, a blue oxford cloth shirt with button-down collar and slightly worn but freshly polished Top-Siders in
cordovan. He wore tortoiseshell glasses and had close-
cropped brown hair that would someday recede to en-
hance the high forehead that gave him a serious, intel-
lectual look. He was also polite and well-spoken and a
clear candidate for an upwardly mobile position in
someone's conservative firm.

Casey, on the other hand, wore a yellow-and-pink op
art print, subdued only slightly by the soft lighting and
softer jazz of Café Society.

Hoping she didn't sound like the stereotypical, pry-
ing, prospective mother-in-law, Patrice smiled her
Emmy-award-winning smile and asked, "What are you
studying at Chapel Hill, Will?"

"Architecture."

Not philosophy? Or Middle Eastern religions?
Something he and Casey could share? Patrice resisted

raising her eyebrows and pressed politely for details. As Will told her about his abiding love for the infrastructure of buildings and the interdependence of function and flair, Patrice glanced at Cal for his reaction.

Surely even Cal could see storm clouds in the distance. The not-too-distant distance, even.

He was smiling benignly, draped casually but dashingly in his chair, occasionally sipping from his glass of mellow merlot. She had forgotten how breathtaking Cal looked in a suit. Although casual dress was more his style, the charcoal suit and crisp white shirt were stunning against his sun-bronzed skin.

Realizing he had caught her looking, she snatched her eyes away from her ex-husband and returned her attention to Will and Casey.

"Will might want to be an architect," Casey was interjecting, "but he's got his good points, too. His mind stores about one megabyte of RAM on music."

Of course. Casey would not see the pluses of a man with an interest in anything as stable as architecture.

"He knows everything there is to know about music. All kinds of music. Jazz and Dixieland and blues—you should hear some of the early blues. That stuff was, like, X-rated. Did you know that? Will, what's that song about the woman who says the only thing she sells is barbecue, but..."

Will laid a hand on Casey's arm. "Put a lid on it, Case."

Casey dimpled. Will looked uncomfortable. Patrice liked him. He seemed levelheaded. Maybe, if she couldn't talk sense into Casey, she should talk to Will. Persuade him to take this a little more seriously.

She sat back in her chair, feeling more relaxed now that she saw a way to regain control. Yes, there might be a solution after all. She listened absently as Casey and Will engaged in a heated discussion about whether or not Frank Sinatra was really the greatest popular singer of all time. Will voted for Old Blue Eyes. Casey was making her case for the lead singer of a group whose trademark was strategically padded spandex jumpsuits with genitalia printed in place.

"I'm for John Lennon. What do you think?" Cal's voice was low, meant just for her. He leaned close. She inhaled bayberry memories again.

Perhaps she could avoid breathing for the next several moments. Ration the air in her lungs until he pulled away. How long before she passed out? Already she felt light-headed.

She forced herself to whisper back. "I think listening to this discussion is all anyone needs to know about the likelihood of an amicable future together for those two."

Cal chuckled. "Opposites do attract."

"And look where it gets them."

He leaned closer yet. Their arms brushed. The soft blond hairs on her forearm stood up.

"As I recall, the polarization of opposites creates quite an electrical field."

She turned her gaze on him and tried to freeze him with a look.

He only smiled. He lowered his voice yet another octave. "They still work, you know."

"What works?"

"Your eyes. They still have the same effect. After all this time."

Patrice caught her wayward eyes straying to his lap to confirm his words. She almost huffed out a stuffy, outraged comment before she realized how much Cal would enjoy knowing he had flustered her.

Instead, she smiled. The sultry smile they never let her use on the air. "Oh, come now, Cal. At your age?"

He laughed out loud, which brought the debate across the table to an instant halt. Unexpectedly, Cal reached for her fingers and brushed them gently with the ends of his own. "Got any money you want to put on that?"

Patrice stared at him. His eyes gleamed with mischief, but the wicked gleam couldn't hide the barely banked fire in his dark eyes. Patrice tried for a cool response despite the steam rising in her.

"Save your demonstrations, Cal." She slipped her fingers away from his.

"I will."

Patrice looked up and across the table. Both Will and Casey were staring. Cal reached for the bottle of wine.

"Seconds, anyone?"

Patrice wondered if she could get her foot in position to bring the spike heel of her pump down solidly onto the arch of his foot.

"Dad, did Mom tell you her idea? About Will and me?"

Cal cocked one dark eyebrow quizzically at Patrice. "Why, no."

"She thinks we ought to live together. Instead of getting married. Until we're sure."

Will shifted in his seat, his cheeks growing pink. "Casey—"

"Why, Trish, I must say I'm surprised."

Like father, like daughter. Always goading. "I think there's a certain wisdom in waiting."

Cal clucked in mock disapproval. "But to suggest that our Casey—naive little Casey—live in sin. Trish, that's hardly like you."

"Cal, try not to be insufferable." She smiled as sweetly as she could manage. "Could you do that? Just try?"

"I'll try, dear." He winked at Casey. "So, Casey, what do you and Will think about that?"

Will looked prepared to speak up, but Casey jumped in first. "Oh, Will's mother would never hear of it. I believe she would cut you out of her estate, don't you, Will?"

"Well..."

"Although, actually, she may do that anyway. She lives in the Myers Park neighborhood, you know. Old Charlotte money. I think she keeps hoping the neighbors won't have to meet me." Casey delivered a look to Will that said they shared a wonderful joke, but Will didn't look amused. "Speaking of living in sin, Daddy, how's Tory?"

The wind rushed out of Patrice's lungs. Of course, she'd known. She hadn't thought for one moment that their relationship was platonic. Cal was handsome and wealthy and well-known, all powerful aphrodisiacs for young women. And Tory herself was ample aphrodisiac for a man of any age. No question about that.

Still, it bothered her.

And that fact bothered her more than the idea of young Tory McIntyre sharing her husband's— ex-husband's—bed. And his shower. His kitchen. His laundry room.

She remembered that time on the fluffy pile of blankets still warm from the dryer....

The warning signals in Cal's deep voice captured her attention. "Casey."

"Just kidding, Dad." Their daughter dimpled again. If her mouth hadn't been so dry, Patrice might have smiled to see Cal getting such an unappetizing dose of his own medicine.

But she didn't feel like smiling. She felt like smashing the bottle of merlot over her ex-husband's charming head. But jealous fits had never been her style. Even in those last months, when she had seen with her own eyes that Cal's relationship with the station manager's secretary had to be something more than... what had he called it? Professional but friendly?

Right.

And calm, collected Patrice had let it go. Maybe a little jealousy would have been in order, after all.

She was surprised to realize that, eight years and a couple of lukewarm relationships later, the memory of the petite little brunette named Jeanine still rubbed against something raw and unhealed inside her.

Yes, a little overt jealousy might have been better than the two-can-play-at-that-game routine she had employed.

But she had thought Cal would never let her go off to Atlanta alone after she'd hinted she was on the verge of fooling around with the general manager there. Not if he really loved her. But then, if she was right about Cal and the brunette, he would let her go.

And he had.

The son of a bitch.

She glared at him. He smiled at her, a bit uncomfortably, she thought. *Squirm, you rat.*

"... involved in Tory's personal problems, Daddy."

"Casey, I don't think this is the time to discuss Tory's personal life."

"But after all that's happened to you in the past few months..." Casey faltered. "I like Tory, Daddy. Don't get me wrong. But she's been through a lot, too. And..."

"So it works for both of us right now. Wouldn't you agree?"

"Mom, what do you think?"

"Well, I..."

"I don't really think it's any of your mother's concern."

Patrice couldn't remember the last time she had seen Cal actually grow defensive. Tory the Terrific must be a lot more important to him than just another meaningless tumble.

She felt empty. She wondered if they could bypass dessert. She wondered if it wouldn't be smart to pack her bags and head back to Chicago.

"Daddy, you're not..."

But before Casey could stir things up any further, an imposingly rotund man walked up behind them and stood between Cal and Patrice. He placed his hands on their shoulders and his bassoon of a voice cut through the quiet restaurant.

"Well, if it isn't the Sunny Sullivans. I'll be a hog on the porch."

Everyone who had been in Charlotte since the old days recognized the folksy voice of Ralph Walters. A veteran broadcaster since radio dominated the airwaves, Ralph was the voice of Charlotte television. A newsman, a talk-show host, the spokesperson for countless local and regional products, Ralph had given

Cal his big break. And later, he had been the master-mind behind the pairing of Cal and Patrice.

Patrice had never been certain whether to be grateful or not. But it was, after all, impossible not to adore the round-faced, aging legend. Tall enough to hold his own on a basketball court, Ralph had grown portly and gray haired, but the broad slash of his smile hadn't dimmed.

They hugged. Ralph mentioned Patrice's career. He bemoaned how much local broadcasting missed Cal. He expressed astonishment over Casey, whom he had last seen when she was on the brink of adolescence.

"But listen, I can see you folks are in the middle of a family dinner here, so I won't keep you. Just wanted to hit you up to emcee this year's Carousel Princess activities, Cal. Can we count on you?"

Patrice was surprised when Cal hesitated. Cal had always reveled in events like the week-long activities leading up to the annual Thanksgiving parade.

"I'm... I don't know, Ralph. Don't you think you'd be better off with somebody else—somebody who's better known these days?"

"Now, Cal, you've been in hibernation enough lately."

"He's right, Daddy. You should do it."

"Come on, Cal. It'd be a great boost to the pageant."

"I'm not sure what's on my schedule . . ."

"I'll call your office. If you're free, you'll do it, then."

Cal in hibernation? Patrice could hardly believe it. Something weird was going on here if Cal was trying to avoid the limelight for a change. *What had Casey said? After all that's happened . . . ?*

"Sure, Ralph. Just call the office."

TORY SWAM UNTIL her arms ached. Her body churned through the heated water, which glistened aqua blue in the floodlights from the deck flanking the back of the spacious Sullivan home. She poured all her energy, all her frustration, all her bitterness into the battle with the water.

And when her arms would no longer move, she thought for one brief moment about slipping quietly beneath the surface into watery oblivion.

She hoisted herself sluggishly out of the water and sat on the edge of the pool, dripping.

As soon as her body stilled, she felt the uneasiness rise in her chest again.

"Go away," she whispered. "Swallow up somebody else's life."

She lay back on the cool, hard tile, letting it bite into her shoulder blades, inviting the acute awareness of her body. It was strong again, muscles no longer flaccid, but firm, the long red slash up her thigh starting to fade. All organs functioning efficiently. Appetite good. Not great, but good.

Only her heart was still broken.

And sometimes, like tonight, something in her blood—something she feared she would carry the rest of her life—started begging her.

A little pill, Victoria? One little pill? What could it hurt? Who'll ever know?

Cal would know, when he came home. And she couldn't let him down. He depended on her, just as she depended on him. He had faith in her. And she wouldn't let him down, even if she had sniffed out his interest in his ex-wife. She hadn't realized how much that bothered her, taunted her and all her half-formed notions, until she was alone here tonight with all the ghosts. All the urges.

Yes, she reminded herself, Cal would know.

And Whitney would know. Maybe not now, when she barely knew one color from the next or one letter of the alphabet from another. But later, when she was six or eight or thirteen. Later, when she wanted to know why her mommy had never come for her. Then she would know.

Tory rolled over and pressed her cheek to the tile. She prayed the hunger in her body would stop. Just for tonight. That's all she asked. She would worry about forever some other time. All she wanted was one more clean night.

And to get her baby back.

PATRICE WISHED she was heading for her condo alone, instead of tucked into the front seat of Cal's Bronco.

"What's it like coming back to Charlotte?"

Cal's voice came to her intimately in the darkness, cushioned by the soft sounds of a classical symphony resounding from the CD player.

"I haven't come back."

"Ah. Of course."

She didn't look at him. She didn't ask what he meant. She knew how he would look, his mustache bushy over pursed lips, his forehead puckered in a frown. And she knew what he was thinking. That she cared more about her career than anything, even Casey.

It had never been true. And was even less true now. But she had no intention of telling Cal that.

"So Chicago is home now?"

"Yes." *Not really.*

"And you're happy there? With ICN?"

"Who wouldn't be?" *Lettie, perhaps? Or any other woman staring middle age in the face.*

"You could always come back, you know."

To you? Patrice kept her eyes on the road and pondered coming back. To Cal.

"To Charlotte, I mean. Not as glamorous, of course."

"ICN is not glamorous," she snapped. "It's hard work."

He braked to a stop at a traffic light and turned toward her. She was aware of his scrutiny but still stared straight ahead. He reached out and closed his fist gently around a handful of her champagne-blond waves. Patrice almost jumped at the contact. She steeled herself against his touch, letting the tension out only as the light changed and he slowly turned away.

"You make the work look easy."

She permitted herself to think about the touch of his fingers on her hair as he maneuvered the curves of Queens Road. A touch of mastery, of possession.

But he doesn't own me anymore, she argued with herself as he parked in the condominium lot and came around to open her door.

But he could possess you again. One more time. People do it. All the time.

She shivered. He pulled her jacket more snugly around her shoulders.

"You don't have to see me in."

He smiled. "You're back in the South, Trish. You'll have to humor my gentlemanly upbringing."

He acted the part. He unlocked the outer door for her, then held it open while she entered the lobby. He stepped into the elevator behind her and faced her from a respectable distance. But he wasn't totally fulfilling the role of Southern gentleman. He was smiling. And there were things going on in his head. She could tell. She felt the anticipation. His. And hers.

You're crazy, Sullivan.

He unlocked her front door and followed her in. She paused in the entrance hall. He would leave now. She wouldn't lead him into the living room.

He went without her. She followed.

"Tell me about your book."

He leaned against the back of the cream-colored couch, ankles crossed, hands in his slacks pockets. She thought how nice it would be to have a photograph of him looking just like that. So elegant. So confident.

She swallowed. She tossed her purse onto the chair and circled away from him. "My book? How did you know I was writing a book?"

"I read about the advance in the paper. Impressive. I was thinking of suing for alimony, but my attorney told me to back off."

She forced herself to laugh. "Uncle Sam got most of it."

"So how's it coming?"

"Slow."

"As disciplined as you are?"

She roamed the room, looking for distractions. She thought of offering him wine, but she didn't want him to stay.

"I'm not all that disciplined. Not anymore."

"Mmm. That's interesting."

She didn't answer. She walked over to the window. There was very little to see. Treetops in the moonlight. Glimpses of wide sidewalk. The red tile roof of the house on the next block. Nothing as compelling as Cal Sullivan.

"It won't have any kiss and tell, will it?"

"What?"

"The book. You're not going to tell naughty little lies about my sexual prowess, are you?"

She wheeled. "It's about my career, Cal. Not yours."

He had the nerve to laugh. To cover her anger, she kicked off her shoes. They sailed under the coffee table.

"It was just a little joke, Trish."

"Your sex life isn't funny, Cal."

"Ah. So you take that too seriously now, too?"

"Don't you think one of us should take something seriously?"

"Something, yes. But everything?"

"Let's start with something, then. Like Casey. Could we take her seriously for a moment?"

"You're obsessing, Trish. You know that, don't you?"

"Obsessing!" She stalked over to him. "*Obsessing!* All I'm doing is showing the kind of concern a normal, mature parent would show."

"Do you have ulcers yet?"

She jabbed a finger in his chest. "There you go again. Changing subjects. Anything to avoid a serious . . ."

His hands came up. One closed around the wrist of the hand she was using to jab him in the chest. The other he raised to her face and a finger pressed against her lips.

"Shh."

She froze.

"Don't fuss. I really don't want to fuss."

Still gripping her wrist in one hand, he slipped the other around the back of her neck. His fingers tangled in her hair. They pressed into the back of her head, pulling her close.

Stop. Stop now.

She could do nothing but obey his insistent hand as he pulled her face to his.

She opened to his kiss instantly. His lips were knowing, confident, the kind of touch their decade together had taught him she liked. Bold, a little reckless even. Almost rough. She kissed him back the same way. Hot. Hard. Pressed hard against him, trying to find her way into him, through him, all around him. His shoulders, his chest, his arms, all harder and more powerful than they had been in the old days. With a low growl, she tugged at her jacket. He helped. She tugged at his jacket. His tie. His buttons.

When the top button of his shirt snagged and refused to release, Patrice realized what she was doing.

She sprang away from him.

No one rumpled as sexily as Cal Sullivan.

"I want you to leave, Cal."

"You don't mean that."

There was little use in denying it.

"Leave anyway."

He bent over and picked up his suit coat where it had fallen to the floor. Before straightening, he retrieved her brocade jacket and draped it carefully over the back of a chair. Her heart thumped just watching him, and she tried not to imagine telling him she'd changed her mind.

He turned back before he closed the front door behind him. "It's nice to know some things never change."

He was smiling that damnable smile.

CHAPTER SIX

CAL HADN'T VISITED the Lincoln Memorial in years. At one time, a decade or more ago, he had never set foot in the nation's capital without a pilgrimage to the marble shrine to the lanky president. Usually at night. After midnight.

He had visited once after Trish left. And decided, as her laughter echoed in his head and her scent filled his nostrils like a phantom, never to return.

Although speaking engagements brought him to Washington, D.C., at least once a year, Cal never again went back to the monument.

Until now. This time, Trish's low, sultry laughter had beckoned and he had been too weak to resist.

So he stood at the base of the statue, his striped silk tie carelessly folded and shoved into the front pocket of his suit coat, and stared up at the marble-faced man who had witnessed Trish's last act of reckless abandon.

1978

CAL KEPT LOOKING around for the police, certain someone wearing a stern face and a uniform would show up soon to suggest that he and his rowdy wife return to their motel.

Two in the morning was not the time to be gamboling and laughing on the lawn in front of one of the nation's most significant symbols.

"Abe won't care," Trish called back in answer to his cautions. "I'll bet he's not asleep yet, either."

"No, but everybody else in town is."

He dashed after her as she scampered toward the Doric columns.

"Everybody else in town is a stuffed shirt! Including Mr. H. T. Hodgkins and the lovely Mrs. Blue-Haired Hodgkins."

The manager of one of the city's small but growing independent TV stations was, indeed, stuffy, and his wife so artificially pleasant that Cal had spent the entire evening hoping he and Trish wouldn't laugh in the woman's pinched face. About two hours and twenty minutes into their three-hour-and-ten-minute dinner at one of Washington's most starched and formal restaurants, Cal made up his mind. He didn't like Hodgkins and he couldn't imagine working for him and he was quite convinced that, museums and cultural events aside, Washington, D.C., was no place to raise a child.

He was almost sorry Trish hadn't egged him into misbehavior until the check was signed for and the waiter departed with a stiff-backed half bow. She even kept herself in control until after Mr. and Mrs. Hodgkins finally agreed to let the young couple walk back to their motel instead of spending another quarter hour locked in the false heartiness of the white Lincoln Town Car with the burgundy crushed velvet interior.

As soon as the Town Car turned the corner, Trish's facade had crumbled. The prim little bow at the neck of her blouse had unraveled and she had scampered down the street.

She was almost a block away before Cal overcame his astonishment. This was not the Trish he knew. Not worrisome, fretful Mother Trish. No, this was someone else. This was . . . the slightly brassy Trish he'd first met fresh off her Halloween heist at the university.

Shaking his head, Cal followed this woman he barely recognized. "Trish? What's going on with you?"

Lowering her lids to rake him with the sultriest gaze he'd seen in months, she covered his lips with her fingertips and whispered, "Sh. I just escaped. Don't give me away, okay?"

They had walked for hours, stopping on a street corner to call his parents to see how Casey was handling her first long-term visit out of Mommy and Daddy's sight. They had walked past the White House, where Trish tried to convince him that fellow Southerners Jimmy and Rosalynn Carter wouldn't mind a bit if they scaled the fence and dropped in to sit a spell. They had stopped for one more glass of wine at an all-night diner, where they assured themselves that staying in Charlotte was a much better plan than moving to Washington.

And now, Trish's rambunctiousness still not spent, they were making the obligatory tour of historical sites. Much better now, Trish had assured him, than twelve hours later, when they would be elbowed by people from Kansas and Mississippi wearing Bermuda shorts and carrying camera cases.

Cal felt happy following along behind her. He picked up one of the sedate black pumps she dropped onto the lawn and stuffed it into his jacket pocket. Then another. She paused by the edge of the long pool that led up to the monument and leaned over to dip her toe in it.

"You'll fall," he warned.

She turned on him with that heavy-lidded look that always tempted him. "Then I'd catch a cold."

"We'd have to hurry back to the motel to get you out of those wet clothes."

She paused, as if considering his words, then stepped right off the edge and into the pond. She squealed and splashed and Cal had the strangest sense that he remembered her from some other time and place.

He shook off the thought and laughed with her, extending a hand to pull her out of the water.

Then she was off again, dashing toward the monument, dripping and shaking off water like a puppy just out of the creek. He followed her, but she had disappeared up the stairs long before he caught up with her.

When he walked into the darkened hall, he didn't see her at first. Then the soggy jacket she had worn over her silky blouse and simple black skirt caught him in the face. He grabbed it.

"Up here, big boy."

He looked up. She was sitting on Abe's knee, peeling her wet blouse away from her ivory skin.

"Trish—"

He caught the blouse, too. Her breasts swelled above a scrap of satin and lace.

"Trish, I think this is against the law."

She paused and smiled, her hands behind her back, breasts thrusting forward as she reached for the hook. "You wouldn't want me to come down with anything, would you? In these wet clothes?"

She found the hook. He didn't move fast enough to make the catch.

They made love in Abe's lap. And didn't leave their motel the rest of the weekend.

CAL TURNED AND WALKED away from the monument. Hands shoved deep in his pants pockets, he headed back to his hotel.

He wondered if things might have turned out differently if he had been older then, mature enough to recognize Trish's fantasy weekend away from the pressures of motherhood for what it was. When they had returned to North Carolina that Sunday night, the difference in her after they picked up Casey and headed for home had been visible. He might as well have been watching her once again shoulder the burdens of the world.

But he had been young and immature and not quite responsible enough himself to realize how heavily her responsibilities rested on her smooth ivory shoulders.

If he had, could he have saved the marriage? Granted, that was only one of the complications. There was his insecurity when her career took off. And her growing absorption with her work. And his jealousy of her success in a field that was supposed to be his. Jealousy of the time she spent away from him.

And then there was Jeanine.

His stomach grew queasy.

Jeanine Dawkins had been his fault. And he couldn't even explain her to Trish, because the truth was probably worse than what Trish believed.

Yes, the truth about Jeanine would really tick her off.

Tory was already in his suite when he returned to the hotel. She was on the phone arranging for the product—audio tapes of his training sessions and the training manual they had published two years ago—that had not sold at his speech earlier in the afternoon to be shipped back to Charlotte.

"You killed 'em," she said after she hung up. "As usual. They'll go back to the office tomorrow motivated to move mountains."

"Thanks."

She gave him that knowing look she had; he turned away to avoid her eyes.

"Cal, what's wrong?"

"Just . . . tired. That's all."

"Mmm-hmm."

He knew she wasn't convinced. Turning his back on the plush mauve and gray suite, he stared out the window overlooking Pennsylvania Avenue. It was a far cry from the view of the parking lot of the seedy little motel that was the best he and Trish could afford in 1978.

"Thanks for taking care of all those details," he said. "I'll be lost when you're gone. You know that, don't you?"

"You can find plenty of competent people to arrange shipping, Cal."

"Not that. It's the support." And the understanding. And the acceptance despite his failings. All the things he'd missed since Trish left.

Tory didn't answer and he finally turned to look at her. She was staring at his itinerary, her face closed. "Does that mean you're ready for me to go?"

"No. It means I know you'll probably be ready yourself, soon."

She shook her head, a little too vehemently.

"I know you miss her."

Pursing her lips, Tory pulled her legs onto the couch, huddling into a protective ball. "Of course I do. But what if . . . what if I'm not ready? What if I screw up?"

"You're not going to screw up, Tory."

Her eyes focused on the thick pile of the mauve carpet. "I did once."

Cal wished he knew some way to ease her emotional pain, the way she had eased his. But he felt helpless against it, which only made him realize all the more how special Tory's talent was. "It wasn't your fault. Most people would never have recovered from the accident you were in. Most people—"

"Most people don't get addicted to Dilaudid."

An edge of anger came into his voice as she continued to berate herself. "Most people don't mangle a leg and spend eighteen months in physical therapy. In excruciating pain."

"I should have known better. I was trained. I should have realized what was happening."

"The point is, you realized in time."

The sound that came from her throat was part sob, part strangled laughter. "No, Cal. I should have realized before I was addicted. Before the courts had to take my baby girl away."

"It was a mistake. You'll get her back."

She was silent for a long time, then unfolded herself from the couch and walked over to him.

"Cal, I don't know what I'll do without you, either." Unexpectedly she wrapped her arms around him for a quick, self-conscious hug. "If you hadn't been willing to take a chance on me, I don't know where I'd be right now."

Cal only knew where he would be if Doc Tipton hadn't told him about the young therapist and fitness coach who needed a second chance and was willing to work cheap in exchange for a home and a stable environment. He'd be heading at a breakneck pace toward heart attack number two. He smiled. "Tory, if it hadn't been for me, you'd probably be making a lot more money and working a lot less hours somewhere else, I suspect."

"Don't discount what you did for me, Cal. You never give yourself enough credit."

Cal shrugged.

"So," Tory said firmly. "Are you going to tell me?"

"Tell you what?"

"What's really wrong."

No such thing as a free lunch, he told himself. Tory bares her soul, she expects you to do the same. "Nothing."

She leaned against the pickled oak credenza and studied him. "Cal Sullivan, do you realize that your face gives you away every time? Your eyes might as well be a neon billboard. So spill it. Mama Tory's listening."

Cal slipped out of his jacket and started rolling up his lightly starched cuffs.

"I don't know. I guess I'm just like you. Feeling vulnerable."

Hands on her hips signaled she wasn't buying it. "You're in great shape, Cal. You know that."

"Thanks to you."

"Thank yourself. I just snap the whip. You do the hard part."

"But you know, I still don't feel as strong as I used to."

"That's normal. Our psyches are sometimes more fragile than our bodies. And your psyche still feels traumatized."

"My psyche thinks my body is over the hill now."

Tory laughed. "Your psyche hasn't looked in the mirror lately. You should see things from my vantage point. When you're onstage, in front of a group, I see how the women react to you. They gobble you up with their eyes."

Cal looked down at his hands. They were brown and square; they didn't look a bit different than they had looked seven months ago. But he saw them differently; saw everything differently. "Maybe."

Tory's voice softened. "You don't really care what *they* think, do you?"

"No."

"I didn't think so." She hesitated. "Is it Trish?"

Anxiety wavered through him. He wasn't prepared to admit that ever since the night he took Trish in his arms, he'd been unable to shake the feeling that he'd wasted the past eight years of his life. "Trish?"

"You remember Trish. The cool blonde the mere mention of whose name brings fire to your eyes."

Her voice was the least bit tight and Cal wondered if her hip joint was giving her trouble today. She didn't seem herself.

"That's just me getting battle-ready."

He laughed, expecting her to join him. When she didn't, he studied her closely. And thought it odd she wouldn't look at him.

"What happened, Cal? Why'd you break up?"

He slumped back in his chair and covered his eyes with a weary groan. "Why *didn't* we break up? That might be easier to answer."

"Okay. Why didn't you break up?"

"Mmm. Well, we didn't have in-law problems. That was one of the few disagreements that never came up." He slipped lower in the armchair and propped his feet on the edge of the coffee table. "Let's see . . . We were both too young to get married in the first place. Then

Trish grew up real fast—too fast—and I kept holding out. So Trish had two kids to deal with instead of just one. And believe me, Casey or I alone would have been a handful.

"What else?" He paused and forced himself to talk about things he'd never said out loud before. "I couldn't handle it when Trish moved into my territory. I wanted to be the top dog. I felt undermined. And suddenly she was better than me at what I was supposed to be good at. I was nothing but a lightweight local interviewer. She was good enough to do the news."

He looked up into Tory's surprised gaze.

"Cal, you were one of the most talented people on local TV," she protested. "How could you be insecure?"

"Haven't we've talked about this long enough?"

"No. I want to hear this. Cal Sullivan insecure? I don't believe it."

"If you don't get off my case, I might have another heart attack."

"Won't work. I saw your last EKG." She dodged the necktie he balled up and pitched at her. "Well, you've certainly changed. That's all I can say."

Have I? For all Tory's insight, Cal was grateful she didn't seem to realize how much his choice of careers had been—and still was—rooted in his need for approval.

"So, you were an obnoxious MCP and didn't want Trish to have a career of her own?"

"Male chauvinist? No! Well, that's what she thought. Well, maybe it was true. A little. That's why Jeanine..."

He stopped.

Now her eyes registered suspicion. "Go on."

"I think I'm having chest pains."

"You can't have chest pains until you tell me about Jeanine."

"There's nothing to tell. I swear."

"You fooled around with this Jeanine bimbo."

"No!" He shot upright in the chair, feeling guilty about Jeanine just the way he always did. Admittedly, she had fed an ego that was sorely bruised by Trish's success. But he'd never let it go further than a little innocent flirtation. So how could a man remain faithful and still feel guilty?

Because there are other kinds of betrayal? he chided himself. And he had almost committed one of the worst with his boss's administrative assistant.

He'd beat himself over the head with Jeanine for eight years; he wasn't ready for Tory to do the same. "Jeanine was not a bimbo. And I didn't fool around with her or anyone else."

She stared at him long and hard. "Trish didn't believe it, either, huh?"

"You don't believe me?"

"You look entirely too flustered to be telling the truth, the whole truth and nothing but the truth."

"You've got work to do." He stood and headed toward his room. "I'm going to rest."

"And you never even discussed it with her, did you?" Tory's incredulous voice followed him into his room. "You didn't, did you? Oh my gosh, you both just hid your heads and closed down communications central. Right?"

"You're fired."

"You can't fire me. I know too much. And I've always wanted to try blackmail, Cal Sullivan."

He closed the door. Damn right she knew too much. Too bad he hadn't known as much when he was her age.

THE TINY WHITE BLIP on the blank green screen of her rented portable computer winked at Patrice. And winked. Then jeered. Taunted.

Empty screen. Empty screen. Empty screen.

The screen should be filled with words. An entire disk should be filling up with words. Words from Berlin. Words from Moscow. Words from the Middle East. About seventy-five thousand of them, to be exact. All of them insightful and entertaining and due on an editor's desk in New York City in five months, one week and two days.

Patrice adjusted the contrast. The screen darkened. The tiny white blip faded from sight.

"Take that."

Yasser Arafat and Boris Yeltsin were not the men on her mind at the moment. At the moment—and for many of the moments during the past few days—the only man her mind had room for was Cal Sullivan.

His arms were so hard. So powerful. Masterful. That was it. Like his lips. No hesitation.

Patrice liked sensitive men as well as the next woman. But some situations just cried out for a man who had it in him to...ravish.

Cal could ravish. She couldn't forget how well he ravished...

Thanksgiving, 1980

CAL FOLLOWED HER into the master bathroom while all the relatives—all fifteen of them—were gathered in the living room sniffing the air for the scent of turkey and dressing.

Patrice had just slipped on the opal earrings Cal had given her for her last birthday and was catching her long hair in a loose braid. She hadn't had a chance to finish dressing that morning before the brothers and sisters and wives and nieces and nephews and parents started ringing the doorbell. Now, between basting the turkey and unmolding the cranberry sauce, she had a few free minutes to pull herself together.

As soon as Cal closed the door behind him and pressed himself to her, she knew dinner would be delayed at least another ten minutes. She felt the surge of emotions from his body to hers and knew all over again that some things were far more important than overcooked turkey.

"I'm grateful," he whispered.

"So am I." She dropped her hair ribbon and leaned back against his broad chest, which was all she needed to feel secure and loved. "I'm grateful that you keep us smiling. I'm grateful that you've brought me a whole new world I never imagined possible."

He kissed the curve of her ear and their eyes met in the mirror. Cal's hands crept slowly up her rib cage and came to rest on her breasts. Her voice almost failed her as the sweet ache spread through her.

"So what are you grateful for, Walker Calhoun Sullivan?"

His hands played along her curves. "I'm grateful for a wife who thinks I'm worth admiring, even when I'm not always as responsible as I should be. For a daughter who still thinks I walk on water. A home that's a joy to come home to."

The words brought a lump to her throat, while a rush of longing and emotion washed through her. She pressed more tightly against him and felt his telltale hardness. Her eyelids grew heavy and she smiled. "I'm grateful for a husband who can't keep his hands off me."

He chuckled and maneuvered himself even more firmly against her. "And I'm grateful I'm going to have dessert first."

"Do I look like a pumpkin pie to you?" She slipped a hand behind her and flattened her palm against his insistent erection.

"Mmm. I don't know. Let's see what you taste like."

And he had turned her and kissed her, long and slow and hot and wet, using a free hand to raise her skirt. His hand was like fire against her thigh. She gasped and sighed. "Cal, everyone will hear us."

"I can take care of that."

And he had lifted her and moved toward the shower stall, clothes and all. He pressed her back against the wall and reached up to turn on the shower.

"Now, woman. Let's celebrate."

The warm spray showered over them and the certainty of his love filled her.

All the relatives, Patrice decided, as Cal did his usual slapdash job of carving the bird, had noticed that she and Cal had come out wearing a change of clothes after their mysterious disappearance. But only Casey mentioned it.

DAMN CAL! Memories of all the tender moments they had shared had been haunting Patrice ever since he had kissed her three nights ago. At least, that had become her carefully edited version of the incident. Cal had kissed her. She might have kissed him back, but only under duress. And her response, well, it had clearly been more habit than anything. Of course, that was it. Force of habit.

If an eight-year-old habit has that kind of force, she told herself as she pushed away from her desk, *you're in deep kitty litter.*

Deciding once again, as she had many times during the past four months, that her manuscript could wait, Patrice headed for the kitchen. There on the counter she found the small bag of potting soil, the cheap plastic window box and the flat of varied herbs she had bought at a nursery earlier in the day. Sort of her own version of meditation, the mantra of dirt and roots and frail green shoots. The planter, a soft mauve that matched the wallpaper and fit snugly in the sunny kitchen window, would have to be dumped when she left, but at least she would have some dirt to dig in, something green she could watch grow when the words on her computer screen refused to do so.

Her fingers had just slipped into the cool, moist soil when the telephone rang.

"Damn."

She thought about letting it ring. That had been her modus operandi most of the week. But Casey had promised to call, and after all, she could hardly hide behind an answering machine forever.

Brushing the dirt from her left hand, Patrice reached for the phone while she scooped soil into the planter with the other. *If only it's not Cmienski.*

"You're not tied up, are you?"

As soon as Cal's warm voice wrapped itself around her, Patrice almost wished it had been her boss.

"No, but I am doing something dirty."

"Alone or with company?"

"Alone."

"Ah. Good. Then you can talk while you...whatever. Would it help if I talked dirty?"

Actually, simply hearing his voice was more stimulating than risqué language, but she had no intention of admitting it. Even acknowledging it to herself reminded her that a telephone conversation with Cal Sullivan could be dangerous. Cut it short. That would be the best thing to do.

"Is anything wrong, Cal?"

He seemed to hesitate. "No."

She wasn't convinced. "I see."

"I was thinking, that's all."

"Oh, Cal, you don't want to get started on that. It'll ruin your life." Anything to keep him from telling her what he was thinking about. She had a hunch she didn't want to know.

He chuckled. "Do you treat everyone this way, or is it just me?"

"I save all this just for you." That seemed the best way to keep him from believing it was true, which it was. And that disturbed her. She hadn't realized it until he asked. Damn his sorry hide anyway.

"How do you handle being on the road so much, Trish?"

So that was it. He was lonely. And she was probably the last one on his list and the only one he'd found at home. She took some satisfaction from the thought that Tory the Terrific might not be sitting home alone waiting for his return.

"I enjoy it." *Sometimes.* "I thought you did, too."

"Mostly. I guess the same cities get old after a while. I've been to D.C. so many times."

Washington, D.C. City of the Lincoln Memorial. Her hand clenched the dirt. She avoided Washington whenever it was possible to weasel out of an assignment—had never, in fact, returned to the Lincoln Memorial.

She hoped Cal wasn't remembering the same thing she was remembering.

"Have you ever been back, Trish?"

And she knew, somehow, that he didn't mean back to the city. That her job took her there with some regularity, he had to know. He could only be asking if she had ever revisited the site of their early-morning tryst.

"I never go back, Cal."

"You sound awfully positive about that."

"I am."

"If I correctly recall our last meeting, you didn't seem terribly averse to a little jaunt down memory lane."

She didn't answer. She coaxed the tiny mint plant out of its pot and positioned it carefully along one edge of the new planter. Maybe he would hang up. Maybe if she ignored him, he wouldn't have the nerve to keep on.

"I can't get it out of my mind, Trish."

She was ashamed of the cowardice that kept her from admitting the same. She floundered about in her mind for a silencing retort; none presented itself.

"I've been thinking...maybe it's not a bad idea if we...try to see a little more of each other. As long as you're in Charlotte. What do you think?"

"I don't think so."

"Sometimes this happens, Trish. Couples get back together. They find out that...they've changed. Things have changed."

"No, Cal. Things haven't changed. And I don't see any reason to try and kid ourselves."

"Haven't you ever thought we might have made a mistake?"

Only about a hundred times a year. "Never. That's never crossed my mind, Cal."

"Well, now it has, Trish. Think about it."

The line went dead.

Patrice stared at the phone, then slammed it down with enough force to rid herself of the frustration welling up in her.

"I hope you miss your next flight." She hurled the curse of the business traveler at Cal, whose presence lingered. "And the one after that, too."

By the time she had finished transplanting her basil and oregano and fennel, generously watered the planter and positioned it on the bare sill, she felt calmer. Nothing was better for frustration than gardening. Nothing you could do alone, that is.

But as she wandered back through the condo, avoiding the laptop computer and making a face at the aerobics video she had not yet plugged in today, Patrice felt a void where her frustration with Cal had resided.

She was thirty-nine years old and in the past six months all the things that had seemed important were suddenly not as important any longer. Prestige. Money. Making the deadline. Getting the best quotes from the most famous newsmakers.

Big deal.

She checked her wristwatch. Nine forty-five. Lettie would be between broadcasts. Probably at her desk, poring over the reports from other wire services as they fed into her computer, making sure they missed nothing, let the competition scoop them on nothing. An urgent report from Baghdad. Another from

Johannesburg. Then three quick minutes with makeup and back in front of the camera.

Lettie Gundersen had taught Patrice everything she needed to know about broadcasting that she hadn't already learned from Cal. The anchor in Atlanta when Patrice had moved there, Lettie had become not only a friend in need when Patrice was trying to get over Cal, but her mentor. Coaching her. Advising her. And ultimately recommending her for an ICN job just six months after Lettie herself moved to Chicago.

She needed Lettie. Lettie would help her get her head on straight again.

She dialed the number from memory and was rewarded when the familiar, distracted voice answered. "Gundersen. News."

"I hear there's a riot in Charlotte tonight. Can you confirm?"

Lettie's voice instantly lost its distance. "Sullivan! There *is* life after ICN!"

"After? Yes. During . . . ?"

"No, baby, this isn't life. This is purgatory. We're in a holding pattern between hell and . . ."

"If you say heaven, you'll lose all your journalistic credibility, Gundersen. ICN isn't even in the same astral plane as heaven."

Lettie laughed. "So, is it all you remembered down there?"

"Worse." She filled her friend in on Casey and Will and recited the news about Cal and Tory with little enthusiasm. She stopped short of confiding anything that had happened between herself and her ex-husband.

"So, he's having his middle-age crazies."

"He's had the crazies all his life, Lettie. I keep expecting him to grow up." She listened politely as Lettie gave her advice from the deep well of her forty-nine years of experience. But somehow none of it seemed to apply. Not to Cal. No, Cal was a special case and it appeared Lettie knew no more about how to deal with him than Patrice did.

"Anyway, don't make mistake numero uno, Sullivan."

"What's that?"

"Giving him another free ride for old times' sake. You know, fan the old embers. Heartbreak isn't always better the second time around. You heard it here first."

Patrice ignored the little nibble of discomfort inside her and managed an almost convincing laugh. "I'll remember that. So, anything new up there?"

"Nothing you didn't already know. The vicious rumor that Cmienski wants you to cut my throat and slip into my chair has been confirmed."

Her preoccupation with Cal suddenly seemed insignificant. "Confirmed how?"

"He told me. One of those cozy little lunches over at Printer's Row. Very much on the up-and-up. I don't have the right presence for current needs. Not accessible enough for the average viewer. Some BS like that. I spit in his eye and told him I'd nail his butt to the wall with an age discrimination suit."

Lettie's casual retelling of the luncheon didn't disguise her dismay over the episode to Patrice's discerning ear. "What did he say to that?"

"He patted my hand. The slimy snake, *he patted my hand!* But listen, if it's time for me to slide into a supporting role, there's nobody I'd rather have taking over the lead than you, Sullivan. You're the best."

"Did he say that? That he wanted me?"

"Spelled it out very clearly. As soon as you come back to your senses, he wants you moving up."

"Then he'll have a long wait."

"Don't do it, kid. You can't beat Cmienski at his own game. He stacks the deck. And if he ends up replacing me with some babe in her twenties, I'm likely to snap and go right into premenopausal rage and hack everybody in the place to pieces."

They laughed together in spite of their shared disappointment.

"Don't worry, though, Sullivan, I'll give you the exclusive."

"It's just so damned ridiculous in this day and time, Lettie."

"It's my own damn fault. I should play the game and you know it. A little nip. A little tuck. Maybe a chemical peel and I could hang on for years."

"When did it stop mattering whether you were good or not?"

"When ratings got to be more important than delivering the news, maybe? Don't be naive, kid. You've got your shot. Take it."

And end up like you in ten years? But she couldn't say it.

"Speaking of kids, your sweety is about to have a massive coronary."

Patrice wrinkled her nose at the reminder. "Truman?"

"Yeah. He's demanding to know where you're spending your sabbatical. Did you swear him to faithfulness before you left, Sullivan? Celibacy doesn't agree with him. He's climbing the walls. He wants you and he's determined to find you."

"Tell him I'm in Tahiti."

"He's a reporter. He'll find you."

"He's not a reporter. He's a pretty face."

"Why don't you let me send him down? Let Cal know he's not the only one who can still commune with the younger generation."

The thought of Cal and Casey looking on while tall, lean, blond, pretty Truman Matthews hovered over her, flashing his straight teeth and taking care to maintain the crease in his Dockers, gave Patrice a touch of heartburn. If Truman was an example, she couldn't imagine what older men saw in younger women. It was fun for about twenty minutes, then you started longing for someone who remembered the same things you remembered. Someone who remembered the night the Beatles first appeared on Ed Sullivan and staying up late to watch the first moon walk.

Someone like Cal.

Except not Cal.

That was all it took to make up her mind. She had to steer clear of Cal. No ifs, ands or buts. Cal Sullivan was dangerous territory. Mistake numero uno. Beirut, no problem. Cal Sullivan, big problem.

CHAPTER SEVEN

AS SHE DRESSED for another outing with Casey, Patrice knew that if she heard, "Mom, you're not going to wear *that,* are you?" one more time she was likely to go ballistic.

She studied the clothes hanging in her closet. Surely *something* would pass muster with Casey. Not the gray linen suit; Casey had already banished that. Not the black linen skirt that was one of her staples in Chicago. Hoping her red raw silk slacks and a red-and-black-striped cotton tunic sweater were acceptable, Patrice finished dressing.

Today they planned a trip to the printer to discuss invitations. Patrice only prayed she wouldn't have to put up with another cozy family outing that included Cal. Did the man never work?

When the doorbell rang, she was confident she wouldn't embarrass her daughter. She had even replaced her sedate pearl studs with a pair of red wooden earrings that dangled. Somewhat.

Casey—resplendent in a clingy jersey micromini skirt in leopard print over a bronze bodysuit—looked her mother up and down but said nothing about her clothing. Patrice consoled herself with the reassurance that lack of criticism was a step in the right direction.

Casey clanged all the way out to the car. Her ears, her arms, even her ankles and waist, were adorned with brass and copper. Tons of it. Enough to give plenty of advance warning of her arrival.

"Sorry Dad couldn't make it." Casey popped her gum as Patrice pulled the Mercedes onto Queens Road.

"So am I." Patrice didn't normally advocate fibbing to offspring, but this seemed to be a special case. She was bending over backward to get along with her wayward daughter.

"But he said he definitely wants to go with us to the bakery. You don't think we have to have one of those disgusting white cakes with little pink flowers squirted around the edges, do you?"

"So traditional? Why, of course not."

"Cool. Maybe we'll have peanut-butter volcano instead." Patrice refrained from requesting details about peanut-butter volcanoes. She was certain she would learn all she wanted to know in due course. "Anyway, if we call the Pop-meister in about an hour, he might be able to meet us for lunch. So let's don't forget, okay?"

Patrice had hoped for a day just for the two of them. A day when they could talk about things, maybe begin building a bridge over the past four years, when the gulf between them had widened. But Casey seemed equally determined to keep her father around as a buffer whenever possible.

Is it that difficult for her to be alone with me? Patrice wondered, swallowing the melancholy the thought prompted.

The printer Casey had selected was, as Patrice should have expected, a family operation owned by an aging hippy who looked as if he were still wearing his favorite bell-bottoms from 1972. He looked as if he hadn't cut his hair since then, either. But as they talked, Patrice discovered that Waco Stephens was soft-spoken and

imaginative, and his long silver tresses smelled of the
herbal shampoo she herself had favored twenty years
earlier.

"So, do you have your copy ready?" he asked after
Patrice had talked her daughter out of the sky blue paper preprinted with a rainbow. The gold-embossed
sunburst was not much of a compromise, but it was
something.

Casey pulled a slip of folded paper out of her fanny
pouch and thrust it into Waco's hands. He read.

Patrice cleared her throat. "May I?"

Casey squirmed.

"I'd just like to see what I'm paying for, if that's all
right with you?" She smiled to soften the firmness of
her words.

"Okay." The reluctance in Casey's voice was marked.

Waco handed over the paper, which was scripted in
Casey's flamboyant hand with words crossed out and
revisions written above.

New families are strongest built on the foundation
of old families. Patrice and Cal hope you will join
them as a new and loving family is created with the
help of Casey and Will.

The date and time followed.

"Casey, this is a lovely sentiment, but it's not very
complete. Shouldn't it have Will's and your full names?
There's not even a location."

"Oh. Well, I haven't decided on that yet. Maybe I'll
just make up a map and photocopy that and slip it in
the envelopes."

"A map? A photocopied map?" She tried reminding herself of her own wedding in Latta Park. The only

invitations had been last-minute phone calls. *This is Casey's wedding. Chill out, Mom.*

If they were truly lucky, Casey's preparations would be so haphazard the wedding wouldn't even come off. She wondered if she was the only one who had thought of a licence.

She decided not to mention it. Not yet, at any rate. Plenty of time for that. And if they ran out of time, well, so be it.

"But your last names aren't even on here."

"Mom," Casey started in that voice Patrice had come to recognize as the voice of youthful impatience with the shortcomings of doddering adults. "If they don't even know our last names without being told, why in the world would I want them at a wedding?"

"But you don't even say it's your wedding."

"Well, what else could it be but a wedding?"

"Your grandmother..."

Casey raised her chin with smug confidence. "Grandma knows exactly what I'm doing. And she approves."

"She does?"

"She certainly does."

Her own mother had given her blessing? Her own mother, who had said by telephone just the week before Patrice flew out of Chicago, "Darling, you know that daughter of yours has a wild streak. I wish you better luck talking sense into her than I had with you."

If her own mother had given her blessings, Patrice knew it must be time to unbend a little.

When they finished at the printer's, Casey insisted on calling Cal to see if he would join them for lunch. And as irritated as Patrice was at Casey's insistence, she was hard-pressed to explain her reaction when Casey learned that Cal was tied up. It felt suspiciously like disappointment.

Not possible, she told herself as she let Casey drag her into a boutique in the Dilworth neighborhood before heading for lunch.

"You won't believe these clothes. We are talking killer. And they're just...*you.*"

"Me?"

Casey was already whipping through a rack and pulled out a pair of black stretch jeans. "Here. Try these."

"Jeans? Casey, I haven't worn jeans since...since..."

"Get back to your roots, Mom. Jeans are at the center of your cosmic essence."

Patrice looked up from the jeans in time to catch the teasing gleam in her daughter's eyes. "I know what's at the center of your cosmic essence, Cassandra Hilton Sullivan."

"Yeah, I know." Casey shoved the jeans into Patrice's hands and turned to a display of tops. "But you can't talk that way in front of your daughter."

And they laughed together, a rare laugh of understanding between two people who had seldom shared understanding or laughter. Patrice decided to try on the jeans—and the shoulder-hugging sweater Casey discovered.

"Awesome!" Casey pronounced as Patrice viewed herself dubiously in the mirror. "Major babe-dom."

"Really?"

"Oh, definitely. You'll slay 'em."

"Slay whom?"

"All the dudes. Personally, I wouldn't let you within a block of a guy of mine dressed like that."

"You mean Will?"

"Right. Will."

Patrice turned for a back view of the jeans, which molded snugly to her recently firmed backside. Actually, Casey was right. She looked great, if a little out of character.

"Dad will, like, truly flip out when he sees you in those."

"They really aren't me, though." She wheeled away from the mirror and headed back to the dressing room.

"Sure they are. You're a babe. They're babe jeans. Trust me. I think I'm psychic."

Patrice bought the jeans. And two verging-on-funky sweaters, including the one that slipped off her shoulders.

"Wear a camisole under it," Casey advised. "Drives 'em wild when they think they're seeing your intimate apparel."

"And how do you know so much about what drives them wild?" Patrice asked as they returned to the car.

"*Mo-om,* I'm nineteen. I'm hardly a child anymore." She flopped into the front seat and folded her long, thin legs into the seat. "Besides, I used to watch Dad."

"Of course."

"Not that he was...I mean, he wasn't what you'd call...that is, I think before I came back to live with him, he'd been pretty...loose." Casey punched buttons on the stereo, bypassing everything with a tune in favor of something loud and raucous that necessitated raising their voices. "But once I came back to Charlotte, he really cleaned up his act."

"I'm sure he was a shining example."

"No, truly. He was. I swear. He even got engaged. That's how straight he went."

Patrice remembered the engagement. She had permitted herself anger, because anger had been the least threatening emotion she had experienced upon hearing that her ex-husband planned to remarry.

"But I knew he'd never marry her."

"You did?"

"Sure. She was just like you. Why should he settle for second best?"

THE LIGHTS WERE OUT in Cal's workout room. Tory lay on the vinyl-covered exercise mat, one arm over her eyes, breathing steadily.

Cal had canceled their workout. Again. It wasn't the first time in recent weeks that he had had something more pressing to do. Something related to Casey's wedding.

Tory knew what that meant. It had nothing to do with Casey's wedding. Wedding plans equaled one thing. Time with Trish.

Ignoring the tension in her leg that was threatening to become an intermittent throb, Tory pictured Cal's ex-wife. Blond and sophisticated and cool. Perfect. The only mistake Trish Sullivan had ever made, the way Tory figured it, was giving up Cal without a fight.

Tory sat up, sudden insight filling her head.

She was jealous. Jealous of Cal's ex-wife. Jealous of the way he felt about her.

"You're nuts," she muttered.

You've been with Cal for months. He's like ... like a father to you.

And he makes a great father, doesn't he?

The sly little voice in Tory's head took her breath away. Yes, Cal Sullivan made the perfect father figure. And she did love him, in her own way. And she knew he sincerely cared for her. She also knew how much easier it would be to bring up a child with him in the picture than it would be alone.

Cal in the picture might even make it easier to ensure that she was the one who would be bringing up her child, instead of some court-appointed guardian.

Was she willing to make the same mistake Trish had made, letting the perfect father and—she swallowed hard—husband get away? If she wanted Cal, and she would be crazy not to, she would have to be willing to fight for him.

She would have to seduce Cal.

Seduce Cal?

What an intriguing thought.

CAL HAD NO DEEP HUNGER to be involved in the planning of Casey's wedding. He had no abiding interest in whether she wore satin and lace or Lycra and leather. He had no stake in the wording she chose for the invitation or the style of type. It was Casey's wedding; if it made her happy, he was glad to write the checks.

What he was interested in was Trish. Seeing her. Talking to her. Being with her whenever he could work it out. He told himself Casey wouldn't mind his ulterior motive and made himself part of their outings whenever possible.

And it was obvious from his ex-wife's attitude that he had no alternative if he wanted to see her. Staying away from him seemed to be her number-one goal.

He wondered who would win this particular battle of wills.

He made up his mind, as Patrice strode out of her lobby to join Casey and him in his Bronco, that he would. There was nothing sinful, nothing even unethical, in wanting to seduce your ex-wife. Especially when she stepped into your car wearing second-skin jeans and a sweater that drooped off her shoulder.

"Is that supposed to show?" He pointed at the narrow black straps clinging to the hollow of her shoulders.

From the back seat, Casey giggled. "See. I told you."

"I'll never doubt you again." Trish's voice was smug. "Just drive, Cal. Over to Central, then right to the little house with the green gingerbread trim."

"Green gingerbread?" He turned to Casey, who was sprawled with one leg on the seat, the other foot propped on his headrest. Both shoes were on the floorboard. "You're not planning green gingerbread in the place of a wedding cake, are you?"

"Just drive, Pop. I don't know, I might have purple macaroons. You never know."

He drove.

He also inhaled enormous lungfuls of Trish, who wore a scent that was exotic and musky and made him wish he could bury his face in her. Anywhere. Everywhere.

He also permitted her voice—as deep and musky as her scent—to envelope him as she and Casey chattered. Her voice came from deep in her chest, somewhere behind the round, full breasts that had once fit perfectly in the palm of his hands. He forced himself to return his thoughts to her voice, which was sultry and self-assured. A voice that had once been the first to reassure him when he needed it, the first to spring to his defense, the first to promise understanding when he shared the anxieties that came with success and fatherhood.

The voice that shook with low, husky laughter right after a truly satisfying climax.

"Cal!"

"Daddy, the light's red!"

He slammed on the brakes. "Sorry."

"Daydreaming, Daddy?"

He focused his attention on the light.

"Perhaps I should drive, Cal."

"I don't need back-seat drivers."

From the corner of his eye, he saw Patrice turn to look at Casey over her shoulder. Her creamy, round, bare shoulder.

"At your age, maybe your eyes are failing."

"You've gotten pretty cheeky for an ex-wife. You've been hanging around your daughter too much, I'd say."

She acted as if she hadn't heard him. "I'm surprised you haven't bought a sports car yet. Isn't that part of the syndrome, Cal? New young girlfriend. Racy car. Or is that racy girlfriend, new..."

Although he knew he had only himself to blame, Cal was outraged at her assumption and jumped in to defend himself. "I do not have a young girlfriend."

"Oh. Sorry. If she isn't young, Tory must push her cosmetic surgeon into a higher tax bracket every year."

"What?"

"I said..."

"I heard you. Tory is not my girlfriend."

"Oh. Of course not. What a foolish mistake. I can't imagine how I got that idea."

"Why? You're not jealous, are you?"

"Daddy, tell her."

"I told her. Tory is not my girlfriend."

"Tell me what?"

"She's not his girlfriend. She's his..."

"Trainer."

Now Trish laughed right out loud. Not the sultry laughter he had been daydreaming about but a big belly laugh. He wondered where it came from; in those jeans it was a distinct certainty that she had no belly to speak of.

Thank goodness for Tory; he would have hated for Trish to look this good and see him looking the way he had looked before Tory started badgering him to work out. Not old and flabby exactly, but . . . fortyish. A little soft around the edges.

"Cal, I didn't recall that you needed that type of training. Perhaps you've gotten rusty over the years."

Casey snickered. Cal felt his face growing warm.

"Why, thank you, Trish. That's the nicest thing you've said to me in decades."

"Credit where credit is due."

He pulled into the parking lot and killed the engine, and they all climbed out. Cal waited for Casey to dash ahead of them to the front door of the small bakery before he eased closer to Trish.

"If you'd ever like a demonstration of what I've learned . . ."

She sucked in her breath and kept her eyes pointed straight ahead. Her chin came up a notch.

"Why, thank you, Cal. But I'm confident that I'm already well-versed in whatever it is you're just now learning."

He faltered and watched her step briskly to catch up with their daughter. He was irritated to think she had spent the past eight years learning new techniques, and yet eager to find out just what they were.

An erratic flutter in his chest diverted his attention and he immediately ordered his thoughts to stick with butter-cream icing and raspberry filling.

"I HAVEN'T HAD SO MUCH FUN needling your father in years."

Casey hid her smile as she and her mother claimed a table for three on the patio of a Spanish restaurant and sat back to wait for her father, who was parking the car.

I can tell, she wanted to say. *It's working and you'll have me to thank for it.*

"I know you're making an effort just for me, Mom," she said, hiding her grinning face behind her menu to avoid raising any doubts about her sincerity. "And I really appreciate it."

"He's as impossible as ever, but I *am* trying."

Casey frowned and dropped her menu. She was pleased to note that in spite of her mother's words, her face held a distracted look that was uncharacteristically insecure.

"What's good?" Cal asked as he slid into his chair.

"The vegetarian combo," Casey said. "Hold the sour cream."

"Hold the sour cream?"

He looked unconvinced. She nodded once, a nod that brooked no opposition. Tory needed all the help she could get.

"So, I've got a terrific idea," she announced after their orders had been taken.

Her parents exchanged glances. Casey was enjoying this whole charade so much more than she had ever dreamed. Imagine their surprise when they discovered that every check they had written, every charge slip they had signed, had been for their own wedding party. Well, engagement party, she supposed, since she hadn't yet figured out a way to get a marriage license in their name. Although she hadn't given up on that yet. If she could get her hands on the proper ID, she was certain she could figure out a way....

She reined in her scheming. Right now, her biggest concern was to keep them both off balance. If she could manage to do that, they might just fall into each other's arms. She smiled at the thought.

"I think the two of you should put together a grand-parents' book. Like a scrapbook for your first grand-child. I think it'll be a granddaughter, don't you?"

Satisfied, she settled back to enjoy the explosion.

CHAPTER EIGHT

CASEY HAD NEVER HEARD her mother come so close to shrieking even in private, much less in public. And she knew her father only bellowed under the direst of circumstances.

She'd had no idea they could be toyed with so easily. This was downright addictive.

"Trish, I thought you told me she wasn't..."

"How am I supposed to know! You see her every day, not me. You're supposed to be the one who knows what she's up—"

"Guys."

"She's your daughter, too, Trish. And you ought to know that even the best parent..."

"Best? If she'd lived with the best parent we might not be—"

"Guys!"

They turned toward her. Such a good-looking pair. But so childish sometimes. If they could just learn to hold their tempers. She could teach them plenty, if only they would listen.

"Guys, what are you so upset about?"

Her mother drew a long, deep breath. Her father swigged back half his glass of water in one quick gulp.

"Casey, your father and I simply weren't aware that we needed to prepare for grandparenthood."

"Hey, take a chill pill," she said. "You don't *look* like grandparents. Besides, it's not like you have to be ready for it, like, right away or anything."

"We don't?" Her father's voice had that threatening edge.

She smiled brightly. "No. Why, I may not want to be a mother for years. But I thought you'd want to be ready. And since you're both here in town right now, this seemed like the perfect time. You could go through pictures of the old days and write down all those corny old stories that grandparents like to tell about the first time you met and the first time . . . well, you know."

Her mother glared at her father once again. "You know, Cal, this is your fault."

"*My* fault? How the hell is it my fault?"

"By example. You taught her by example that it's okay to yank people's chains a little. Lead them along. You never could resist and now she's doing it to us."

"Casey, tell your mother that all the examples I set were good ones."

"Oh, he's right, Mom."

They both glared at her, then at each other. Casey smiled. This was awesome. Anybody knew that two people who worked this hard at acting like they hated each other just had to be in love. Probably even the waiter could tell when he set their steaming plates in front of them.

"So, will you do it?"

Her father, as usual, was the first to recover. "Of course, sweetheart, if that's what you want."

Her mother thumped his forearm with the fist she had closed around her fork. "I don't think that's a very good idea, Cal."

"You don't?"

"Aw, Mom."

"No, I don't. I'm busy right now. I have a book to write. I really don't have the time to sit around on the living room floor and wade through a lot of sentimental claptrap."

"But think of all we could preserve for little Casey, Junior."

"Maybe some other time. Or maybe we could each do one of our own. How does that sound? One from me. One from Gramps."

Her father winced at the word.

"We'll want her to know about that Sunday morning you stormed into my dorm and..."

"I doubt that, Cal."

"Then how about our trip to Washington?"

"I didn't know you guys had been to Washington together. When? You never told me about that."

"You were far too young to remember," Trish said in her most crisp tone. She then turned her frostiest look on Cal. "It was a long, *long* time ago."

"You didn't know this, Casey, but your mother is a tremendous fan of the Lincoln Memorial."

He was smiling that absolutely wicked smile that gave him dimples as deep as the Grand Canyon. Casey knew there must be a delicious story behind her mother's affection for the Lincoln Memorial.

She also knew she wasn't very bloody likely to hear it. At least not from her mother.

"Eat your spinach, Cal."

Patrice turned all her attention to her plate of paella. Cal sliced off a bite of his spinach enchilada, his dimples unfaded.

"You know, Trish, I think our daughter has an excellent idea."

"Daddy, I have so many good ideas. And I just know you're going to love them all."

TORY STARED AT HER daughter through the two-way mirror. Whitney was banging a bright yellow plastic puzzle piece against a red puzzle piece in the room full of toys and games at the Department of Social Services. She was laughing.

She doesn't even miss me, she thought. *She's thirty-four months old and she doesn't even understand I'm her mommy.*

Eleven months was a long time in the life of a baby. Long enough to forget the person who loved you more than anyone else in the world.

Tory tried to tell herself things were looking up. Today was her first unsupervised visit with her daughter in eleven long months. Four whole hours to do whatever they wanted instead of one meager hour under the watchful gaze of a social worker.

The door opened and Tory turned reluctantly away from the mirror. Before she could take Whitney, she had to endure another session with Helen Shepherd, the judgmental social worker who had been assigned to her case. Portly and officious, Helen Shepherd closed the door behind her and leaned on the edge of her desk with its tidy stacks of paperwork, clipboard under her arm.

"Well, Miss McIntyre, I see it's been determined that you might be ready for an unsupervised visit."

Tory was certain the woman had placed undue emphasis on the "miss."

"I was hoping for longer. Four hours—it isn't long enough."

"I'm certain you understand. It's difficult for little ones to be away from their secure environments for long periods."

"When can I take her home with me? For good."

Ms. Shepherd leveled a long look that was doubtless intended to be intimidating. Tory didn't lower her own gaze. The social worker consulted her clipboard, pursing her lips and perusing the pages carefully.

"I think we'd better wait and see how these unsupervised visits go first, Miss McIntyre."

"I don't want to wait."

The smile she bestowed on the room was bland. "We could, of course, schedule a court date."

"Court?"

"Yes. The courts removed the child from your custody. The courts will have to decide whether or not it is wise to return the child to you."

A flurry of fear and outrage surged through Tory. For a fleeting moment she thought about the satisfaction to be gained from smashing this woman's clipboard into her face, then grabbing Whitney and leaving.

A short-lived satisfaction, she knew. She forced herself to appear calm, to sound calm.

"Then schedule it."

Again, Ms. Shepherd seemed to give the matter thoughtful consideration.

"I *can* do that, Miss McIntyre. Are you certain it's wise?"

"She's my daughter. I want her home with me."

"Yes. I'm certain you do." She walked around her desk and sat. "Are you still drug-free, Miss McIntyre?"

"I am not a drug addict, Ms. Shepherd. I was in an automobile accident. I almost died. I spent months in physical therapy. I was in severe pain. I..."

"And you turned to drugs to alleviate that pain." She thumbed through the pages on her clipboard once again, as if to ascertain that she had not made an error. "Is that not correct?"

"I took what the doctors gave me. It was all prescription drugs." She turned back to the mirror so the woman's hard eyes couldn't study her too closely. Despite her protestations, Tory knew where the blame lay. Because her work as a therapist was often closely linked with the local hospital's pain management program, she had known exactly how to manipulate the system. Exactly how to get what she wanted, long after she had realized she had a problem.

Ms. Shepherd's voice didn't soften. "I do understand. And you became addicted to those medications. I believe that is what our records indicate."

Tory clenched her fists at her side.

"And the baby's father is..."

"Gone." *Back to his wife.*

Tory hadn't even realized he wasn't divorced until she discovered she was pregnant—about the same time he discovered his loyalty to his wife. *Good riddance.*

Ms. Shepherd raised the sharp arch of one eyebrow....

"Then, let's see, I believe there was the problem of neglect. Neglect, if prosecuted, does carry a prison term, Miss McIntyre. How fortunate for you the decision was not to prosecute. The child *was* left alone, I believe?"

"She had a sitter. I had hired a sitter." Tory would always be haunted by the moment of horror when she had returned home to find her apartment full of strangers. Social workers. Police officers. She had been so relieved when she learned that nothing had happened to Whitney, then enraged when she learned that the high school senior she had hired to stay with her daughter had gone out, leaving her baby alone.

At first she had been grateful to the neighbor who called for help.

Then the people who came to help had discovered Tory's problem. Had discovered that she still hadn't been able to break the dependency on painkillers that she had developed during her months of recuperation and physical therapy following the four-car collision that had almost killed her.

Ms. Shepherd tapped her pencil on her clipboard. "Yes, I do understand your problems, Miss McIntyre. If you're positive you're...ready...I'll schedule a court date."

Tory's breath trembled in her throat. "How soon?"

"A few weeks. A month, perhaps."

A few weeks. In a few weeks she could take Whitney in her arms and never let her go again. They could get their own place. She could teach her to say mommy again. She would give her so much love that Whitney would never remember the long, hurtful months of their separation. She would be the best mommy in the world. She would make it up.

Ms. Shepherd's voice stopped her as she turned to leave. "I'd be well prepared, Miss McIntyre. If everything isn't in order, the judge may well decide to make this arrangement permanent."

CAL'S MORNING HAD BEEN wild and threatened to get wilder. It was the kind of morning that made him glad he'd never had to work behind a desk in somebody's office, with piped-in music and carpeting to muffle the uproar.

The fax machine was on the fritz, and the new leadership techniques manual he would be using with many of his seminars had arrived from the printer. Boxes and boxes and boxes of them lined the entrance hall like sentinels, towering waist high. Reminding him that someone should have taken a leadership role in getting them delivered to their storage facility instead of to the front door of the home that did double duty as his office.

And Tory had dashed in at 9:43 a.m. Cal remembered the moment precisely because it was the last minute any work had been accomplished all morning.

He had been rehearsing a new segment of his seminar, developed to tie in to an individual leadership evaluation form in his new manuals. He heard the putter of Tory's VW in the front driveway. He heard the front door open.

And he heard the unmistakable sounds of a toddler careening through the house.

The surprise Tory had promised was a visit from her little girl, Whitney.

Dropping his notes, Cal had dashed out of his office and into the living room, where a chubby-faced toddler in pink corduroy overalls and a T-shirt adorned with balloons was scampering from table to chair to bookcase.

Tory stood in the doorway. She looked nervous and proud and close to tears.

"What a little doll." Cal gave Tory a hug. "I'm so glad you brought her out here so we could see her."

Tory nodded.

"What's wrong, kid?"

At first Tory said nothing. Then she drew a ragged breath and said, "She's not in diapers anymore."

"Now there's something to be grateful for." But he knew for some reason that Tory was anything but grateful.

"I guess. It's just... I wanted to be the one. The one who trained her."

He took her hand. There was nothing he could say to make the loss of those eleven months less painful. He remembered only too well how much it had hurt to lose years out of Casey's life. He had seen the same hurt in Trish's eyes over the past few years. He understood. But he knew better than to say so. All Tory needed now was love, and a chance to heal.

"And she talks better every time I see her. She can say all kinds of things. Except..."

They watched as Whitney pulled herself onto the couch and attacked one of the tapestry pillows.

"Except mommy. At least, she doesn't remember to call me mommy."

He thought she might break down and cry, something he wasn't certain he could handle coming from his staunch and stalwart Victoria. But she merely wiped the tears from her eyes and turned a wobbly smile in his direction.

"So I guess I'll have to teach her all over again, huh?"

"You'll have her saying it in no time."

"Yeah..."

"Do I hear a 'but'?"

She stared at the floor. "The social worker. She said... she said the courts might take her away... permanently. They wouldn't do that, would they, Cal?"

Cal felt his mouth go dry. "Tory, the courts do all they can to keep families together. You know that."

"I guess. Still, I can't help thinking—well, I worry I won't be able to manage. Alone."

He put an arm around her shoulder. "You can manage. Believe in yourself, Tory."

"But alone? I keep thinking . . . it would be so much easier . . . if she had a . . . father, too."

"How about a grandfather? One slightly reconditioned grandfather?"

Tory gave him the strangest look and he hoped he hadn't overstepped his bounds. She never did answer him.

They played with Whitney, finding the Koosh ball in his desk drawer and teaching her peekaboo with the designer throw pillows, until he heard his office phone ring and his manager came out looking for him.

"I don't care who it is," he told Anne Winfield, the young woman who worked for him half days and studied for her business administration degree at night. "Tell them I'm in a very important, high-level meeting."

"It's Patrice."

Cal dropped the pillow away from his face and dodged Whitney's pudgy fist. "Oh."

"I'll tell her you'll be right there."

Tory pulled Whitney into her lap, her face settling into a frown. "First things first."

Although his heart beat faster all the way back to his office, Cal told himself Trish probably had a perfectly legitimate, platonic reason to call. Nevertheless, her first words disappointed him.

"I'm going to talk to Will. I think you should come with me."

"Will?"

"Our daughter's fiancé."

"I know who. I don't know why."

"Because Casey is in the process of ruining her life and I am not willing to let her do it without putting up some kind of fight. I think Will can help us. He seems levelheaded. I'm sure if the two of us sat down with him, adult to adult, and appealed to his common sense . . . don't you think that would work, Cal?"

He passed a hand over his forehead and dropped into his desk chair. "I thought you'd mellowed a little on this topic, Trish."

Silence. "I had."

"What happened?"

An even longer silence. "I suggested to Casey that it might be nice for us to get together with Will's family. Have dinner. Get to know each other."

"And?"

"And she refuses."

Cal had his first strong moment of doubt. He really would hate admitting Trish might be right about this whole wedding business. He really would hate that. Maybe he didn't have to yet. "She could have a perfectly good reason."

He could almost see Patrice narrowing those hazel eyes into threatening slits in the long silence that followed.

"She had several. They were all flimsy. His mother's busy social calendar—she's on the Heart Ball committee, don't you know, and she's absolutely swamped until February 15."

"I see."

"That's ten months from now, Cal."

"I can count."

"Besides, Will and his mother aren't very close. Never have been."

"Now, Trish, you know those things happen. It's perfectly plausible that . . ."

"I think he's an ax murderer. He probably chopped his whole family into little pieces and buried them in the azalea bed."

Cal laughed.

"Okay, Cal. You're right. I don't think he's an ax murderer. I think he's a very mature young man. And that's why I think we should talk to him. He'll see reason, Cal. I know he will."

"Trish, you're getting yourself wound up over nothing."

"I am not wound up. I am simply acting in our daughter's best interests. If you don't want to come with me, fine."

She hung up.

He spun around in his desk chair to face his forty-gallon aquarium. The African cichlïd was after the angelfish again. They'd told him the two didn't mix well, but he'd been too cocksure to listen.

He picked up the phone and dialed his ex-wife's condo. It rang ten times before she answered.

"When do you want to go?"

"NOT THAT THERE'S anything wrong with a man your age dallying with a woman her age," Patrice said as she looked for a parking spot on the narrow residential street. "Personally, I don't object at all. I just have trouble imagining what the two of you have in common. What *do* you talk about, Cal?"

She maneuvered her Mercedes in behind a pink seventies-vintage Lincoln with a rusted roof. Needling him about Tory felt a tad hypocritical with the image of Truman lurking in the back of her mind.

"I told you already, Trish. There's nothing personal between Tory and me. She's my trainer."

Patrice turned off the ignition and turned to give her ex-husband a skeptical look.

"Tory is a fitness coach. Honestly."

That was the thing about Cal. He could never lie convincingly. And right now, there was enough veracity in his face to be downright convincing. At the same time, there was a little something around the edges of his eyes that told her he was fudging the truth at least a little bit.

"I'm forty-one, Trish. You may not need help staying in shape, but I do. And looks are important in my job. I need to look young, vigorous."

"And you really expect me to believe your looks are so important that you'll spend the money to hire a full-time fitness coach?" She remembered the fat farm and felt a moment of shame for her badgering.

"It's not my looks, Trish. It's...it's my job. Besides, it's not that expensive. Tory...this arrangement works out for her, too."

"I'm sure it does."

They got out of the car and walked toward the address Will had given them.

"And there's nothing personal between you?"

She looked at him and caught his moment of hesitation.

"Not...no."

So much for Cal's credibility.

The apartment, which Will shared with his brother when he wasn't in Chapel Hill, was in a dingy building, circa 1930. They walked up the crumbling sidewalk. Patrice noted the tangle of weeds and bare spots that was the lawn. She spotted the broken light fixture on the porch and the fat gray cat curled up in the porch swing at one end of the concrete-slab porch.

She wondered where Will and Casey would live when—if—they tied the knot.

If the outside of the building was gloomy, the inside was even worse. The long, narrow corridor was lit only by a bare overhead bulb and what little sunlight shone through the grimy window at the end. The bank of gray metal mailboxes was dinted and mangled. The apartment doors had been painted muddy brown. The building looked and felt and sounded deserted.

Patrice pulled a note out of her jacket pocket and glanced at it. "Fourth floor." The stairs leading up were steep and narrow.

She and Cal grimaced at each other and started up, single file. On the landing between first and second, Cal spoke.

"Are you absolutely, positively positive this is what you want to do, Trish?"

She didn't look back. "Absolutely."

"You realize Casey will be furious."

"Only if you tell her."

"What about Will? Suppose Will tells her."

"I hadn't thought of that. An open and honest relationship. What a novel idea."

"Now wait a minute. We had an open and honest relationship."

From years ago, an image of Jeanine Dawkins fluttered through her consciousness. "Oh, really?"

"Of course we did. At least *I* did."

Now on the third-floor landing, she whirled to face him, only to discover that he was much closer than she had realized. He was on the step below. His face was inches from hers; his body so near she measured the distance in the subtle brush of blouse against shirt, skirt against trousers.

"That better not mean you think I *wasn't* honest." The words she had turned to hurl at him came out on a breathy huff.

He seemed to sway in her direction. "And open. You forgot open."

"Right." She was barely aware of Cal's motion. His arm moved; his hand rose. "Honest. And open."

His hand brushed her waist. The touch jolted her, but she remained stock still. Only her insides became a source of frenzy. His hand swept slowly, softly up, molding itself fleetingly to her ribs. Front. And back. Then down, his fingers dipping into the curve of her back, drawing her infinitesimally closer.

Their bodies met, and then their eyes. His were deep, captivating brown and absolutely devoid of the teasing humor they usually held. She wondered if she looked as mesmerized as he did.

His fingers traced up her spine, then down again between her shoulder blades, along the inward dip at her waist and on to the fullness of her buttocks. He cupped her only briefly before allowing his hands to continue their journey down, along her thigh, which started to quiver, to the back of her knee.

He toyed with the hem of her slim skirt. His fingers caught under the edge of her skirt and started traveling. Up. Along her inner thigh. Up.

With a small sound that was half gasp, half moan, Patrice backed away until his outstretched hand slipped from beneath her skirt and she was beyond his reach.

She dashed the rest of the way up the steps.

CHAPTER NINE

BY THE TIME Cal reached the fourth floor, where Patrice waited outside the peeling brown front door of apartment 416, he was winded and his heart was racing. He wasn't sure what to blame his condition on, the climb or his encounter with Trish.

From the look on her flushed face, Patrice had also been affected. Nevertheless, she turned cool eyes on him right before she knocked on the door. "You're certainly out of breath for a man with a personal trainer."

He didn't answer.

She smiled. "I hate to be the one to say this, but it appears your trainer may not be delivering your money's worth."

He studied her mercilessly. "You seem a little breathless from the...exertion...yourself, Trish."

For a split second he was damned certain she was going to haul off and wallop him right across the cheek. He prepared to make a lunge for her wrist, but the apartment door opened before either of them had a chance to move.

As Will welcomed them and escorted them to lumpy armchairs in the sparsely furnished living room, Cal chastised himself. He really had let this thing about Tory get out of hand, but what could he do now? Trish wasn't about to believe him, no matter what. Besides, getting Trish to believe the truth would doubtless involve telling her an awful lot more of the *whole* truth than he wanted to share with her.

And why is that? he wondered as Trish and Will engaged in stilted small talk.

Because I'm fine now. All I want to do is put that incident behind me. The last thing I want is for Trish to make a joke out of that, too. Or feel sorry for me, decide I'm a broken old man.

He looked at her sitting across from him, long, shapely legs crossed, a hint of knee showing beneath the hem of her prim skirt. Laughing at something Will had said, she was gorgeous and regal. And most amazing of all, she seemed as susceptible as ever to the fire that had once smoldered between them.

Trish was the one. Always had been. Always would be, he had to admit to himself.

But physical attraction aside, she seemed to have little use for him. She seemed to believe he was still the same immature, self-absorbed, insecure fellow he had been at thirty.

He had to find a way to convince her he had grown up.

The conversation between Trish and Will had died. Will's angular face was rigid and his skittering eyes revealed tension. They flickered from Trish to Cal and back again. Cal tried to catch Will's eye with a reassuring smile, but most of Will's tension seemed directed at Trish.

Astute young man, Cal decided. Actually, he would likely be good for Casey. In about ten years.

Trish recrossed her legs. He couldn't remember another time when she'd been so reluctant to say what was on her mind. He supposed everyone changed over the years.

"Will, I hope what we're going to say here will be just between the three of us," she said.

Cal supposed he was the only one in the world who knew her well enough to detect the uncertainty in her voice.

The color vanished from Will's face. "Oh. Um... well, I don't know..."

Seeing how disconcerted Will was seemed to calm Trish. She leaned forward and reached out to put a hand on the young man's wrist. When she spoke, her voice was warm with reassurance. "We're not trying to interfere, Will, and we're certainly not trying to cause problems. Are we, Cal?"

She turned to him, her eyes pleading for support. His first impulse was to respond that he, at least, was not trying to interfere. But if he was out to convince her that he had matured, he might find no better starting place.

"She's right, Will," he said, striving for the best fatherly expression he could muster.

Trish rewarded him with a grateful smile. This might not be so tough after all.

"But we're not that much different from all parents, I suppose," she continued. "We're concerned about our daughter's future. And we thought...that is, you seem levelheaded and responsible, so it only made sense that we speak to you."

"Oh." Will sank deeper into the threadbare cushions of the couch with every word Trish spoke.

"I'm going to be straightforward, Will. We're not fully convinced that Casey is ready for marriage. You may be levelheaded, but Casey is...not."

Cal couldn't be certain from across the length of the coffee table, but beads of sweat appeared to dot Will's high forehead.

"We feel she should wait before making such a commitment. And we wondered, I guess, if you would consider..." Trish faltered. "If you would consider talking to Casey about slowing things down a little. A postponement. That's all."

"Postponement?" Will's voice cracked.

"Yes. Solely to give everyone a chance to. . ."

Cal jumped into the awkward silence. "Grow up."

No one spoke for a long time. Trish pressed her lips together and smiled expectantly at Will. Will stared at his knees. Cal was afraid the young man would either bolt or lose his lunch. He decided to help. Leaning forward—earnestly but nonthreateningly, he hoped—he spoke in his newly cultivated father tone.

"What do you think about that idea, Will?"

Will looked up, his soft brown eyes filled with trepidation. "I'm not sure. Casey wouldn't like that a bit."

"Why are the two of you so eager to marry?" Trish asked.

Will hesitated for a long, electric moment. "Look, I'm not sure it's such a good idea for us to be having this conversation."

Cal's respect for the young man grew. "Trish, maybe he's right."

"I don't think that's an unreasonable question," she said, a bit testily it seemed to Cal. "You're both young. There's plenty of time. What's the rush?"

"Listen, I'd feel a lot better if you'd just talk to Casey about this."

Cal stood. Hurriedly Will stood, also. Trish glared up at Cal and he knew he'd lost the ground he'd made only moments before.

This whole maturity business would take some fancy footwork, apparently.

"Will, thanks for letting us interrupt your day." He reached out and shook the young man's hand, almost smiling at the abject gratitude and relief he saw in Will's face. Poor sap. Trish was probably right. This wedding was a disaster in the making. But what the hell could they do? Put their foot down? With Casey?

Trish stood. "Just think about it, Will. That's all I ask."

They walked to the door. As Trish stepped out into the hall, Cal hung back for a moment. "Listen, Will, I know this isn't a fair request, but if you can find it in your heart, maybe it would be just as well not to mention this to Casey. I'd hate to have a major explosion this close to the wedding."

Will nodded. "So would I. Believe me, so would I."

Cal followed Trish out into the hallway and down the stairs, keeping a safe distance, especially on the landing between the third and fourth floors.

Keeping his distance wasn't tough all the way home; Trish seemed to have the same idea.

BOYD CROSBY WALKED into Cal's office with just the idea Cal was looking for.

He didn't realize it at first. He was tired from two days on the road—Denver and Omaha. Looming over his head were a million calls to return and a meeting with his business manager to discuss marketing strategies. The request from Boyd, a longtime friend and former co-worker from his TV days, sounded like one more obligation he wished he could wiggle out of gracefully.

"I'd be glad to do it, Boyd," he fibbed. "But there are so many others who could do it better."

"Cal, you never used to be modest," Boyd said. "You're closer to Ralph Walters than any of us. And we know how you feel about him—he gave you your first break on TV. The committee thinks it would mean a lot to him if you emceed his retirement roast."

Cal couldn't quite figure out his reluctance to do this kind of thing. There had been a day when nothing thrilled him more than being in the spotlight. He had basked in it, soaked up the exhilaration. And he still enjoyed working with the audiences at his training sessions. But he knew there was substance to what they took away. He didn't enjoy being fluff anymore. He enjoyed educating; he didn't enjoy entertaining.

Still, this was for Ralph Walters. Cal owed it to him.

"You could get bigger names, Boyd. Bigger draws."

Boyd rubbed his hands together and dropped his eyes for a moment. "Actually, Cal, there's sort of a part two to this whole request."

"There is?"

"Yeah. We heard . . ." He hesitated. "Aw, hell. We heard Trish was in town. Ralph told me he saw you two at dinner a week or so back. And we thought we could really turn this into a major event if we could bring back the Sunny Sullivans. Trish is such a big name now, Cal, and the two of you were always so good together. It would be just like old times. We could sell a thousand tickets, Cal. And all the money goes for the station's broadcast scholarship, you know."

Boyd rambled on. Cal barely listened.

So that was the truth of the matter. Hometown celeb Cal Sullivan wasn't the draw. ICN's Patrice Sullivan was, plus the novelty of seeing the divorced partners on the dais together again. Once upon a time that would have rankled. Right now, Cal found it pleased him.

Who would have thought that day about fifteen years ago, when a blushing, timid Trish first joined him on the set, that she would go so far.

He was proud of her.

And best of all, Boyd had given him the perfect excuse for spending more time with the woman he was determined to win back.

"You've got a deal, Boyd."

After Boyd left, Cal got on the phone to Trish right away. They had only a few weeks to prepare for the retirement roast. The basic script was being written by one of the station's copywriters, but he and Trish would have to rehearse. Might even plug in a few bits of business of their own. You know, play on their former relationship. People loved that kind of thing.

All he got was her answering machine. He left a message and spent all day expecting her return call. It never came. He called Casey to see if they were out. They weren't. He tried again after lunch. Trish's nononsense recording ordered him to leave another message. He did so. But when she hadn't called back by late afternoon, he was growing impatient.

With a trip to the golf shop as his excuse, Cal decided Trish's condo was right on the way. A quick stop couldn't hurt. She might be working on her book; if so, it was time she took a break.

PATRICE PRESSED the store key on her laptop computer. There! Chapter two, finished. She sighed and leaned back in her chair, flexing her stiff back muscles. How long had it been since she'd moved? She looked up at the crystal clock on the oak-finished shelf. Five-thirty. The last time she'd budged had been noon, when near starvation drove her to scavenge for a container of low-fat yogurt and some stale melba toast.

She remembered the country ham, gravy and biscuits she had watched Casey devour at a recent breakfast. She wondered if Anderson's, the old-fashioned diner that was a tradition for longtime Charlotteans, served breakfast all day.

And she wondered if Cal would enjoy indulging in a little high-calorie, high-fat sin.

Forget Cal.

She had almost managed to do that for the past two days. At first he had haunted her as she tried to clear her mind and concentrate on starting this damnable manuscript. She remembered the way her flesh had sizzled when his hand whispered up her thigh. She turned to lava inside just thinking about it.

And when she wasn't trying not to get worked up over her physical reaction to Cal, she was battling to forget all the ways she enjoyed being with him. How good it had felt to have him at her side with a little moral support—very little, as it turned out—when she talked to Will. How much fun it was to spar with him verbally—too many men were threatened when a woman matched them barb for barb.

How satisfying it was to look into his eyes and read his understanding of her. It had been too long—eight years too long—since a man had really understood her. And she craved that.

Just as much as she craved the whisper of Cal's touch along her thigh.

She had tried not to think about it. But every time she had managed to muster her concentration and get a couple of uninterrupted paragraphs down on the screen, the telephone rang.

First it was her editor.

"Just wanted to check the progress, Patrice," said Hilary Seinfeld, the disembodied New Yorker whom Patrice knew only by telephone. "I heard you'd disappeared from the face of the earth and thought I'd better make sure you hadn't thrown yourself off a cliff. Writers facing deadlines start thinking along those lines sometimes."

"It's going well," she lied, refusing to gaze at the puny output reflected on her computer screen. "How'd you find me?"

"I bribed thirteen people at ICN. Lettie Gundersen finally caved in. Said to tell you she'd split the take with you. I'd take her up on it if I were you—my boss is going to make me pay for it out of your advance, I think."

Next it was Truman.

"You knew how much a little intrigue turned me on, didn't you?" he murmured. "I hear phone sex is the hottest ticket going. Wanna try?"

She frowned into the receiver. Why was risqué talk from Cal a little provocative, when from Truman it just seemed tacky? "I have a headache, Truman."

He laughed. "Take an aspirin. It'll be gone by the time I get there."

"You're not coming here, Truman." She figured Lettie owed her Hilary's entire bribe, because only Lettie could have spilled the beans to Truman. Unless someone overheard Lettie and word got back to Truman and . . .

"I can't stay away, love. I'm only human. If I don't hold you in my arms soon, I'll revert right back to barbarian."

How had she ever let herself fall into this younger-man trap, no matter how much that wicked look in his eyes had reminded her of Cal? And why hadn't a few weeks of ravenous romping been enough to satisfy Truman, when it had more than convinced her that May-September romances should be wiped off the calendar completely. What young men brought to a relationship in enthusiasm and endurance they more than made up for in immaturity.

"I'm busy, Truman," she said, hoping she didn't sound too brusque. Brusque enough to get her message across, not brusque enough to wound. "I came down here to get away. I don't have time to see you."

"You'll change your mind," he had purred.

Third, her boss called.

Cmienski growled into the phone and suddenly Patrice really did have a headache. "Sullivan. Get your ass back to Chicago. I've got decisions to make and I can't have you sitting around on your butt down there."

"I'm on sabbatical, Cmienski. You approved it."

"Then I'll disapprove it. Now is not a good time for you to pull a vanishing act. Next year I'll give you four months instead of two. Just be back here by tomorrow."

"No."

"No?"

She knew the sound. It was the sound of his blood pressure soaring to the danger point. His face was now the color of rare rib eye.

"I'm warning you, Sullivan, if you don't get up here, I'll find somebody who takes their career a little more seriously."

Patrice knew Cmienski liked to toss around threats. But she also knew she wasn't quite ready to pitch her career; close, maybe, but not certain she wanted to walk away from everything she'd worked so hard for.

"Give me some time, how about it?"

"Okay. You've got till tomorrow."

"I mean some real time, Cmienski."

"A week, then."

"How about a month?"

"A month! A friggin' month? Sweeps Week, Sullivan. You've heard of Sweeps Week, I trust. It's coming up. And I want you on the air. I want good ratings, Sullivan."

"Lettie's good. She's well liked." *She's not old enough to pitch out with last week's garbage, you rotten jerk.*

"She's not right. Not anymore."

"I'll call you."

"You'd better call. One week. I'm telling you, Sullivan. One week."

However the leak about her location had started, it had become a torrent in no time.

She turned off the ringer on the phone. She turned down the volume on the answering machine. And she made herself a promise not to answer another phone call until she had completed a minimum of fifty pages.

It had taken two days.

She stared at the blinking light on her answering machine and wondered if it would take her the next two days to return all her calls. Before she could get up and walk over to the machine with her notepad, the doorbell rang.

She groaned. When she hoisted herself out of the chair, she groaned again. Her back was protesting her lack of movement for most of the past forty-eight hours. She stretched again on the way to the door and peered through the peephole.

Cal.

Grateful there wasn't a mirror over the brass-and-glass library table, Patrice knew she was in totally unsalvageable condition. Her hair was swept up in a clip, with unruly waves escaping around her temple and neck. Her face hadn't seen makeup in two days, and the bridge of her nose bore the imprint of the eyeglasses she wore for close work. She'd rolled the legs of her warm-up suit up over her knees and pushed her athletic socks down around her ankles when she'd grown too warm a few hours earlier. Hastily she shoved her pant legs back into place.

She jumped when the bell rang again as she reached for the door.

"I know you're in there, Trish. Let me in or I'll break the door down."

She opened the door. "What makes you think I'm even in here?"

"Lucky hunch." He sauntered in, sweeping past her.

"What is it, Cal?" Crossing her arms over her chest, she followed him, peeved to realize she wasn't at all sorry to see him. She made up her mind not to let that fact slip.

"I've been calling all day. You didn't answer."

He sprawled on the couch. His arms and face and neck were dark against the soft mint color of his shirt. She found herself studying the solid delineation of muscle in his forearms.

"Did it occur to you I was busy? Or out? I might've been out." She started to sit in the chair across from him, but the twinge in her back stopped her. She'd been sitting too long already.

Instead, she paced back and forth in front of him.

"It did. It also occurred to me you might simply be avoiding me."

"But you didn't care whether you were welcome here or not."

She stopped and tried intimidating him with a glare. The deepening of his dimples told her she was singularly unsuccessful.

"I wanted to see you."

He grasped one of her wrists and pulled her toward him. As her body swayed in his direction, something in her back seized. Halfway onto the couch she froze, back bent, knees bent, bracing herself against Cal's chest. She cried out in pain.

"Trish? What's wrong?"

She hazarded a cautious movement. The pain was sharp and unrelenting. She gasped.

"You've broken my back," she said between gritted teeth.

"Your back went out?" His arms went up and he grasped her rib cage to support her.

She saw the gleam of humor in his eyes. Terrific. Here she was, after spending a small fortune to impress her ex-husband with how terrific she still looked despite her thirty-nine years, and he caught her at home in wrinkled workout clothes, no lengthening and extending mascara and a catch in her back.

As soon as she could move again, she might just inflict some permanent incapacitation on him. Something lingeringly painful.

"This is not funny, Cal."

He swallowed a chuckle. "I didn't say it was funny, Trish."

"You don't have to say a word. Your laugh lines are showing."

"Sorry." He tried to assume a stern expression, but his mustache still twitched. "What can I do?"

She tried to back away. "How about leaving before you do any more damage? That would be a nice gesture."

"I can't leave you like this."

He stood, providing her with an excellent view of his crotch. She was not in the mood to stare at Cal's crotch.

"Yes, you can, Cal. Just walk over to the door, open it, walk out, close it behind you and . . ."

"Don't be ridiculous. Let me help you to the bed."

And he took her by one hand, the other hand braced against the small of her back.

"Just leave, Cal. I've been sitting for most of the last two days and I'm a little stiff, that's all. If you'll leave, I'll be fine."

"Can you walk?"

"Yes, but . . ."

He led her away from the couch, toward the bedroom, moving slowly and hovering over her solicitously. But when they got to the bedroom and Cal swept the comforter back, Patrice wasn't at all certain that lying down was part of her current repertoire.

"Here. Let me."

And he lifted her, gently, and placed her on the bed on her side.

"Trish, now may not be the time to say so, but aren't you a little heavier than you were the last time I picked you up?"

She heard the smile in his voice even though her back was to him. "No, dammit. You're just old. Don't you know men lose one percent of muscle strength every year after the age of thirty-five? *I'm* just like I was at twenty. But you're not."

He chuckled. She smiled, too. As long as she was still, there was no discomfort.

At Cal's insistence, he rummaged through her cosmetic bag for a bottle of extra-strength painkiller, then stood in front of her while he bullied her into downing three.

"If I overdose on this stuff, you'll never beat the rap," she muttered.

"You wear all the stuff in that bag on your face?" he asked as she swallowed. "You never used to."

"Why do you think I look so devastatingly sexy all the time?"

He took the glass from her and shrugged. "Nature's little dirty trick on the rest of us?"

"Right."

She didn't want to risk another gripping pain, so she didn't follow his actions as he returned the painkiller to the bathroom, then walked around behind her once again. Before she realized what was happening, he had raised her top.

"Where does it hurt?"

"None of your business," she snapped.

The smell of liniment filled the room.

"You can't put that stuff on me!"

"What on earth do you have it for if you don't use it?

"For warm-ups. When I work out."

"Well, now we're going to use it the way old fogies have used it for generations. Quit being a pain in the rear and tell me where it hurts."

"Low."

No immediate response. "How low?"

"Too low."

"Hmm. This should be interesting. Would you like to be a little more specific, or shall I just explore the area until I get it right?"

She reached around gingerly and pinpointed the area just below her waist and above her hip. "There. Not one inch lower. Precisely right there."

"I'm going to have to make a few adjustments in your warm-up pants to get there, Trish. I wouldn't want you to think for a moment that I have anything lascivious in mind. This is purely therapeutic. So you're not going to karate chop me, are you?"

"I make no rash promises. Just keep it clean."

Within seconds he had slipped her warm-up pants lower on her hips and was working the cool liniment into her lower back. Working it until it grew warm. Working it until Trish felt some of the tension in her muscles release.

"Better?" he asked.

"Much," she murmured, hoping he wouldn't stop. He didn't.

She dozed off with Cal's big, broad hands moving tenderly but surely over her lower back. In that fuzzy fog of presleep, it occurred to her that Cal had been the soul of propriety—not once had his hands strayed into dangerous territory.

How disappointing.

CHAPTER TEN

PATRICE SNUGGLED into the warmth at her back, sighing audibly and preparing to sink back into sleep.

Before sleep reclaimed her, she realized the warmth at her back was much more substantial than the feather pillow she sometimes burrowed against in the night. This warmth was much larger even than a king-size pillow; it stretched from the top of her back and curved around her buttocks, molding itself to her legs. This warmth was also hard, not soft.

And it was breathing on her neck.

"Cal, that had better not be you taking advantage of my drugged state," she murmured.

"I'm keeping your back warm," he whispered. "Now go back to sleep."

The tenderness of his words stirred a longing that frightened her, one that went far beyond mere physical longing. For the sake of her sanity she had to keep this light. A romp was one thing. But beginning to care again...

"That's what blankets are for, Cal."

"You've never had a blanket this warm. And we don't want your muscles to go cold and seize up again. Do we?"

She started to move away, but his arm was anchored firmly around her waist. Actually, just under her breasts.

"Now, now. Dr. Sullivan recommends no sudden movements. Except, of course, under doctor's supervision."

She wiggled around to face him. It was a mistake. His merry brown eyes lured her back to a time when waking up to Cal had been the best part of her day. Her breasts began to renew their intimate acquaintance with his broad, hard chest.

"Thank you, Dr. Sullivan, for your care," she said, already seriously doubting she could do anything but give in to the tightening in her belly, the aching in her thighs. "But I believe I'm fully recovered now and ready for release."

Would he be able to tell she was already anticipating her surrender?

He merely smiled. She noticed something she hadn't been close enough to notice in years—the renegade auburn hairs in his sable-colored mustache.

She reached up to smooth the hair edging the corners of his full mouth without realizing what she was doing. Then she saw his pleasure at the intimacy and her hand froze. His lips caught the tips of her fingers before she could pull them away.

"Cal..."

"In fact, before your recovery can be considered complete," he whispered, "the doctor recommends beginning a regular routine of gentle, rhythmic movement."

No safe place for her hands existed. Everywhere they roamed they encountered smooth, hard muscle. Or heartbeat. She let her palm absorb the rhythm before continuing her search for something...safe. Only to find heat. Everywhere, heat.

What was it he had said?

"Movement?"

"Designed to keep your muscles toned."

"Rhythmic?"

"Shall I show you what the doctor has in mind?"

"I don't—"

"Who's the doctor here, Ms. Sullivan? You or me?"

She laughed softly. It was hopeless. He laughed with her, then rolled her slowly, gently onto her back.

"First, Ms. Sullivan, this warm-up suit is entirely too confining." His eyes locked with hers. He grasped the pants by their elastic waist and began to slowly tug them down, past her waist, dragging her undergarments with them. Below her hips, past her thighs, over her calves, onto the floor. Then he tugged her top in the opposite direction.

Patrice didn't make a move to protest.

"Much better. I wouldn't be a bit surprised if we've solved half the problem right there."

His eyes left hers and travelled down her naked body. She felt them linger over her breasts, her belly, the triangle of soft curls. She came alive wherever they lingered.

"Now, if you don't object, Ms. Sullivan, the doctor will need to do a more thorough examination."

"I hope the doctor will hurry," she whispered. "The patient is beginning to experience some . . . physical discomfort."

"Ah, by all means. Let's get on with it."

He started with her breasts, cupping her in his palms, brushing the taut pink peaks with his thumb. His hands traversed her midriff, sending sensations rippling over and through her belly. His fingers whispered down the outside of her thighs to her knees, then back up along the sensitive inside.

His touch held the intimate knowledge of one who well remembered all the right spots, all the perfect motions.

Wherever he touched, she prayed he would linger forever. Wherever he touched, the rest of her body craved attention. A hunger eight years in the making escalated, intensified with his caress.

He groaned. She cried out softly.

"Oh, Ms. Sullivan, your condition is far more serious than I ever dreamed."

"Walker Calhoun Sullivan," she said raggedly, "get your clothes off. Now."

He grinned. She could barely see him through her half-closed lids. But she saw enough as he shed his clothes and rummaged through his wallet for the small foil packet to realize that some things did age to perfection.

She wanted to tell him how beautiful his lean, strong, familiar body looked to her, but she didn't dare.

He knelt between her knees. She felt him, as she had so many times before, seeking her heat. Felt him hesitate and knew he would go no further until she looked him in the eye.

"No regrets, Trish," he warned, his eyes demanding more from her than a casual mating. "I don't want any regrets."

Intimacy had never been a mere physical thing for Cal; that was the danger here. *Keep it light. Got to keep it light.* "The only thing you're going to regret is making me wait this long."

He didn't make her wait any longer. But there was no frenzy, no raging passion as their bodies joined and moved together. Only a tenderness, a searching for something beneath the surface of their warm flesh. The tenderness alarmed Patrice as thoroughly as it satisfied her.

CAL TOOK TWO WINEGLASSES from the cabinet and the bottle of mineral water from the refrigerator, enjoying an unaccustomed rush of strength in his body. Still unclothed, he took pleasure, as he returned to the bedroom, in the feel of cool air on his skin and paid attention without fear to the pulse and thump and push and pull that was his body at work.

He had made love. Once gently, almost cautiously, he acknowledged. And once again, after they awoke a second time, more vigorously. His chest hadn't tightened. He'd felt no erratic skip in his pulse. His body had not betrayed him in any way.

It was the first time since his heart attack; despite everything the experts said, he had been afraid to tempt fate. But Trish, as always, had emboldened him, had given him the courage to risk more than he would have been willing to risk alone.

It felt good to be a man again.

It felt good to be with Trish.

After pouring two glasses of the fizzy water, he slipped back into bed beside Trish, an action so familiar he couldn't believe it had been eight years. Still, something was missing. Or perhaps there was something that hadn't been there before—an uncertainty.

Trish pulled the sheet up and tucked it under her arms to anchor it over her breasts as she sat up and took the glass he offered.

"I'd heard divorced people did things like this," she said, casting an oblique look at him from eyes that were heavy with satisfaction and seduction. "I just didn't realize otherwise *sane* divorced people did it."

He wondered what it would take to tear down the wall of smart retorts they had hidden behind for the past eight years. Tapping the rim of her glass with his, he smiled.

"To insanity."

She tapped back. "The temporary kind, I trust."

He wanted to ask for more than the wary distance she'd put between them. He wanted to take advantage of this fragile intimacy and build on it.

He leaned closer and savored the feel of her small, perfect mouth. She put a hand on his chest; her fingers wound themselves through the hair. Cal considered the wisdom of pushing the limits of his endurance. Healthy he might be, but was he *that* healthy?

He pulled back and breathed deeply, inhaling the scent of the liniment along with the fragrance of their lovemaking.

"Mmm. Eau de locker room. I may never feel the same about liniment again."

"All the chic women wear it," she said. "*Très* alluring."

"I remember."

And she dared to look at him, long and openly. "I remember, too, Cal."

He knew that she, too, remembered much more than the night just past. She remembered good and bad. He wasn't ready to open up the bad for discussion.

"Yes, but do you remember strip Monopoly?"

They laughed. Cal wondered if she found it as difficult as he did to believe they had once been young enough to sit on the living room floor stripping off articles of clothing at a roll of the dice.

"You always cheated," she said.

"I did not. You had no business sense. I bought *lots* of property. You saved up for the high-rent district. So naturally, my rent came due more frequently."

She grunted skeptically. "I never did like your interpretation of Community Chest."

The memory made him want to reach out and pull the sheet away from her pale flesh, but he was still wary of taking too much for granted. He wasn't ready for this to disintegrate into nothing more than one of those sudden impulses, soon forgotten.

"It was more fun before Casey came along."

She was silent. Then she said, "A lot of things were."

He had known that, somewhere deep inside, from the beginning. But she had never said it and he had never asked; they had been too young to know what harm could come from hiding their feelings. Sadness touched him for all they had lost, simply by default it sometimes seemed.

"Why?"

She looked almost surprised at his question. Then, for a brief moment before she looked down at her glass, he saw the reflection of his own sad realizations.

"Because I had to... be the grown-up."

"And grown-ups can't have fun?"

"Not the ones I'd known."

He thought about the solemn Trish who had lurked behind the outrageous, fun-loving girl he had first met in college. He caught fleeting glimpses of her, especially the few times she took him home to meet her family. Family life had been grim for Trish. A divorced mother who barely made ends meet with the two jobs she worked. Three younger brothers. And only big sister Trish to make sure they stayed in line.

"I should've figured it out."

"Maybe. Maybe we were just too young, too naive. I'm not sure I realized what was happening to me. How could I expect you to?"

"But later..."

"By then it was just who we were. That was our pattern. I was controlling, no-nonsense Patrice and you were bound and determined not to become no-nonsense Cal."

He listened for reproach but heard none. "You mean bound and determined not to accept any of the responsibility, don't you?"

"I'm not sure anymore."

"Maybe it doesn't matter. Now."

She looked and sounded skeptical. "Because we've both changed?"

"Don't you think so?"

"How have you changed, Cal?"

As much as he wanted to tell her all the hundreds of ways he had changed, all that had happened to turn him into the man he was today, Cal found himself weighing what he was prepared to reveal.

"Well, some men lose hair. I've lost a good bit of ego, instead."

"Oh, really?"

"Really. I don't need the strokes. Not the way I did. I have confidence without that." *At least, I did until seven months ago.*

"Right. Which certainly explains why you're in the business of getting onstage and gobbling up the applause."

"Which is why I got out of TV. I like training. I like feeling that I'm doing something substantial. Not fluff."

"TV is fluff?"

"The kind of TV I did was fluff. At least that's how it felt when I compared it to the kind of TV you do." He saw the tiniest hint of withdrawal on her face. "What's wrong?"

"Nothing."

"You're not happy with your work?"

"Mostly."

"I could hold you down and torture you until you tell."

She smiled. "I can take it."

"Trish..."

She set her glass on the bedside table. "What's the matter, Cal? Afraid you can't dish it out?"

"I can dish it out. But..."

Casting aside the sheet, she jumped on top of him, pinning his wrists to the bed and grinning wickedly. "Prove it."

If she wanted to play instead of being serious, who was he to resist?

NEITHER OF THEM remembered to turn the telephone back on. They romped like kids, as if twenty years had suddenly rolled back and they were once more light-hearted and free.

They fed each other pancakes, until they discovered better places from which to lick the syrup.

She reminded him of the long-forgotten pleasures of making love in the shower.

They didn't have a Monopoly game, an omission Cal vowed to rectify at the first opportunity. But they found a deck of cards and played strip poker—until Trish discovered that Cal had slipped an ace under the floor pillow he was leaning against.

He rubbed her back again, this time with one of the fragrant lotions she had in her cosmetic bag.

She proved to him that even men his age were capable of multiple orgasm, given proper stimulation.

And they both fought against the ever more pressing urge to say the three little words they hadn't uttered to each other in more than eight years.

THE MORNING OF THE SECOND day, Patrice woke to the unwelcome sensation of being alone in the bed.

Eyes still closed, she frowned and swept her arm across the sheets. Empty. Cold. She didn't open her eyes.

What in heaven's name have I done?

You made love with your ex-husband.

I had sex with my ex-husband. There's a difference.

Mmm, hmm.

She groaned and rolled over, burying her face in her pillow. However you phrased it, she was guilty. But even as she tried to chastise herself, she found herself stirring again to the memories of the past thirty-six hours.

They were more wonderful together than they had been years ago. Sex with Cal was fun. Explosive. Unpredictable.

And, sometimes, an almost spiritual experience.

She thought of Cal hovering over her, their bodies joined, looking her straight in the eye. He had said nothing at first, but simply held her eyes with his until she felt what he was trying to show her.

"Feel that?" He put his hand on her chest, then his own. "In here? Do you feel that, Trish?"

She hadn't wanted to admit it, but she couldn't lie. "Yes."

"But you've never felt it with anyone else, have you, Trish? I haven't. And you haven't, either. Have you?"

Tears had misted her eyes. "No, Cal. I haven't."

Patrice rolled over in bed and stared at the ceiling. Now, what was she going to do about it?

With the wishful thought that perhaps she could simply ignore it, she got out of bed and pulled on her robe. She found Cal in the dining room, a glass of juice in one hand, a page of notes for her book in the other. He smiled and looked ready to approach her for a lazy morning kiss that might turn this into their second full day of playing hooky from life.

She smiled tightly in return and moved away to put the dining room table between them.

Cal raised an eyebrow. Then he turned his attention back to her notes. "Looks interesting. How's it going?"

"Fine."

His mustache twitched. "That's what really came between us, Trish. You were such a blabbermouth."

"I said it's going fine. What do you want? A page count?"

"Yeah. How many pages is 'fine,' Trish? A hundred? Two hundred?"

She wasn't about to tell him "fine" was barely fifty-two pages. She turned away and noticed the furious blinking of the answering machine.

"Oh my gosh. I don't think I ever turned the telephone on."

She reached underneath the phone to click the ringer into place, then pushed the button on the answering machine. Most of the messages were days old. Cal, sounding excited. Casey, sounding excited. Cal again.

Then a less familiar voice. It was only after she iden-
tified herself that Patrice realized the caller was Cinda
Reisling, the young reporter at ICN, the one she had
been assigned to train.

"I'm so glad I found you, Patrice. I really need to
talk to somebody and you're the only one...well, I
thought you might know how to handle this. Mr.
Cmienski, I mean. He's...well, it's nothing serious, of
course, but I'm just not sure.... Anyway, could you call
me sometime? I really would like to see what you think
I ought to do."

As she listened, Patrice remembered all the things she
had been running from when she left Chicago. They had
begun to seem far away, but Cinda's voice brought them
back.

"Who's Cmienski?" Cal asked while the machine
was reciting the day and time of the call, then spinning
forward to the next message.

"The boss."

"You don't look very happy about the call. Who's
the woman?"

Patrice was grateful when the next message on the
machine came up. She wasn't ready to discuss her
problems at ICN with Cal. Not when he had made it
clear that he, at least, had come to terms with some of
his insecurities. How, then, could she let him know that
she had more than she'd had at twenty-five?

"Ms. Sullivan, this is Tory McIntyre. I wondered if
you've seen Cal?"

Patrice stiffened. After making love with him for the
past thirty-six hours, the last thing she was prepared for
was hearing from his roommate.

"He just walked out and didn't come back
and...well, I did drive by your condo and I saw his

Bronco was there. But I . . . well, just tell him I need to see him.''

A wave of betrayal surged up in Patrice. This woman had driven by here, looking for Cal. The fact that Tory McIntyre even knew where she was staying outraged Patrice. She wondered how much Cal talked about her to the young women in his life. She wondered how this young woman could be so lacking in pride that she could leave a message like that.

''I guess you've missed your training session,'' she said, trying for lightness, fearing tightness.

Cal walked around the table and took her shoulders in his hands. ''Now, Trish . . .''

She pulled away and moved into the kitchen. ''Don't.''

''Don't what?''

''Don't make feeble excuses.''

''I'm not going to make excuses. I just want you to believe me. Tory is my trainer. She works for me. That's all there is to it.''

His words didn't ring entirely true and Patrice felt something inside her shrivel up and withdraw.

''Then perhaps you'd better go train, Cal. I think she's worried that you're losing your muscle tone.''

CHAPTER ELEVEN

NEVER BEFORE HAD Tory seen Cal angry. But he was angry now. And he was angry at her.

"Cal, I'm sorry but..." Once again he cut off her explanation.

"You had no right calling around after me." He let the weights slam back into place and sprang up from the bench press machine. "What am I, on parole? Out on good behavior?"

Tory knew her barely formed strategy had just received a major setback. He had been with Trish. And he wasn't happy that Tory had interfered. When he stormed in the front door earlier, he had refused to talk. He had stalked into his room and changed into his workout clothes. When she followed him down to the basement, he had glared at her.

"Satisfied?" he had barked. "I'm giving the old ticker a workout."

She was going to have to do something and do it soon, before this thing with Trish grew any more serious.

Crouching in front of him, she stared him in the eye as he bent to adjust the weights on the squat machine. "You can't just disappear and expect no one to worry, Cal Sullivan."

"I'm all grown up now, Tory. I don't need a keeper."

"I'm not so sure." Why was he making this so tough? Why had she been so worried? Was it all concern or had there been an ounce or two of jealousy mixed in, as well?

He slammed the pin into position ten pounds heavier than usual, then stepped into place. "Well, I am."

She watched him rise from the squat position, the muscles in his legs working, his face red from exertion and anger. And she was afraid. He might not need her any longer, but she still needed him.

She studied Cal's rigid jaw. "We were worried, dammit! And I won't apologize for that. You could've been in a ditch somewhere."

He hazarded a sideways glance at her, then stopped in the squatting position. Dropping his hands between his knees, he stared at the floor.

"I'm sorry. That was thoughtless."

Her apprehension didn't diminish at the return of the caring Cal she knew. "It certainly was. Almost as thoughtless as storming in here and taking things out on me."

Heaving a big sigh, Cal sat back on the platform, knees bent, elbows propped on his knees. "You're right. I'm a jerk."

She sat on the floor beside him, feeling guilty for making him feel guilty. After all, she probably had no right to try to win Cal for herself. *But it's not just for me,* she reminded herself. *It's for Whitney, too.*

Guilt spurred her to soften her tone. "Not a total jerk."

He smiled. "Thanks for the vote of confidence."

He stood and started on the stepper machine. Staring at the polished wooden floor, Tory told herself to get off her duff and sweat away some of her own stress. But her thigh was throbbing, and she sat back instead and watched as Cal finished and sat on the bench press. He looked as troubled as she felt.

"So, Cal, you want to explain what I did that set you off?"

He shrugged.

"Where were you?"

"Tory—"

"With Trish? The whole time?"

He didn't say anything. His cheeks grew red again, this time from neither anger nor exertion, and Tory felt the thread of anxiety work its way deeper into her heart.

"A little fling with the ex, huh?"

She didn't think that was the case at all; she had lived with him for almost half a year and he wasn't the type for flings.

"Maybe." He sounded uncertain. "No, not exactly."

"Then what, exactly?"

He looked up. His dimples deepened. She wondered what he would do if she got up and kissed him, then decided she wasn't ready to find out. Besides, she needed a little preparation herself. Needed to psych herself up. Not that Cal wasn't attractive. Of course he was. She just . . . well, she needed time to start thinking of him in that way. Soon. She would work on that soon.

"I think I can win her back, Tory."

Apprehension slithered up her back. She wondered once again if she shouldn't forget this little scheme of hers. Then she reminded herself how precarious her own position would be if Cal brought Trish back into his life. No woman would want another woman hanging around, living in the same house with her man. Where would that leave Tory, especially now that she had insisted on setting a court date for her custody hearing?

Somewhere deep inside her, the thought of Cal pursuing his ex-wife worried her for his own sake, too. She'd seen them together. She'd heard the tales from Casey. The truces were always armed and tense, and they had hovered on the brink of annihilation more than once.

So far, no one had pushed the red button.

But Cal's new strategy might be just the catalyst that would put the Sullivans under a mushroom cloud once and for all.

Yes, perhaps in saving herself she would be saving Cal, too.

She decided to move cautiously; this conversation was bound to be littered with mine fields. "Win her back?"

"We should never have split up in the first place."

"Oh."

"I've always loved her. And I... it seems to me that she still loves me, too."

The conversation was making Tory feel squeamish, but what could she do? "Because she... let you stay a couple of days?"

"No. Because of... the way it felt between us. And I don't just mean... it was more than just physical."

"Did she say so?"

"Trish? Of course not. But I can tell. And I know how I felt."

Desperation gripped her. "Cal, things like this happen. The heat of the moment, that kind of thing. Maybe you should..."

"I know what I'm talking about, Tory. This was more than grabbing a little diversion."

She knew the sound of determination in his voice, recognized it in the deepening furrow between his dark, arched brows. Stubborn man.

"Okay, okay," she said impatiently. "You still love her. Maybe she still loves you. But you couldn't make it work before. What makes you think you can make it work now?"

"Because we've changed."

"Have you? How have you changed? Do you even know why you couldn't make it work before?"

She saw the hint of belligerence in his face, covering the fleeting moment of vulnerability she'd seen while he absorbed her questions.

"All that was eight years ago."

"That doesn't make it ancient history, Cal. Maybe it's still current events. And it's not going away simply because the two of you have rediscovered great sex."

She stood and looked down at him, sorry for the confusion and dismay she saw on his face. Sorry for the confusion and dismay she felt in her own heart.

"Face it, Cal. The last thing you need is more heart trouble."

She hated herself for what she was saying but told herself her reasons were perfectly valid. She was justified in trying to scare Cal away from Trish. It was better for him. Better for her.

Better for Whitney.

HIS WORKOUT COMPLETE, Cal sat at his desk and stared at the messages and mail that had piled up in his absence.

His absence. As if he had merely been off on another of his business trips, away on some pursuit of little consequence. The fact was, the past two days had changed his life.

And everyone seemed determined to convince him it wasn't so.

First Trish, her trust in them so fragile that any little thing could disrupt it. Her withdrawal had been visible when Tory's voice came on her answering machine. But all his instincts told him Tory had only been a handy excuse. Trish had already been withdrawing when she walked into the dining room that morning.

Then Tory. Tory, who knew him backward and forward. She had encouraged him to start dating again these past few months. Why not now? She seemed convinced that reestablishing things with Trish would cause him nothing but heartache.

Heart trouble, as she put it. Which raised another issue. He had to stop dancing around this business of his health with Trish. He had to come clean. After all, what was she likely to do once he told her he'd had a heart attack? She could hardly hold it against him. The worst that could happen was that she might look at him a little differently. Think of him as not quite as youthful. Which was true. Or not quite as virile. Which didn't seem to be true. But if she thought that, it wouldn't hurt any less for being inaccurate.

Soon, he promised himself.

As soon as he was certain she wouldn't use that as another handy excuse.

Right now he needed to get back to her before she stewed over Tory's call long enough to build up a federal case against continuing what they had started. The phone rang just as he was about to pick it up.

"Cal? Boyd here. Wanted to see if you'd had a chance to talk to Trish yet. My copywriter's standing on her head wanting to know how to script this thing."

Cal had the wildest urge to send Boyd Crosby at least two dozen long-stemmed roses. After all, he owed the past two days to his quickly forgotten mission on Boyd's behalf.

"Sorry, Boyd. Things have been so...wild. It completely slipped my mind. Let me call right now and see what I can do."

PATRICE COULDN'T WAIT for the housekeeper. She needed to wipe every reminder of Cal out of the condo. There was no other way to get him off her mind.

She hand-washed every glass, every spoon, every plate and stacked them neatly in their places. She snatched up their towels and hand-delivered them to the bins in the basement, where the laundry service would pick them up later in the day. Then she returned to her condo, only to walk into the bedroom, where she was overwhelmed by the sight of the rumpled sheets.

She made another hurried trip to the basement, arms stiff to keep the sheets as far away from her body as possible. They still carried the faint scent of bayberry and lovemaking and the liniment that had started it all.

Once upstairs, she almost shoved the offending tube of liniment down to the bottom of the garbage can.

"Come on, Sullivan, get a grip."

Instead, she buried it in the bottom of her cosmetic bag.

The remainder of the morning she paced.

Cal was everywhere she turned. She heard his voice, she saw the crinkled eyes and the deep dimples. She felt his soft hair crushed between her fingers. She was haunted by his concern and his warmth. She was terrified by the way she had wanted to surrender to the lure of his unspoken promise that their emotional ties could be rekindled just as easily as their passion.

The second time she picked up the phone to call him, she knew she was in real danger of screwing up royally. That was when she clicked off the laptop computer, stalked into the bedroom and yanked her suit bag from the closet shelf.

"If you don't get out of here right now, Patrice Hilton Sullivan, you'll be sorry."

Before she could get the first thing out of her closet and into the bag, the doorbell rang. She froze. Closing the bedroom door behind her, she walked over and peered through the peephole.

Casey.

Stifling a groan, she opened the door. Her daughter erupted into the room, cutting a flamboyant swath through the subdued furnishings.

"So, what's going on?" Casey stuck her head around the door into the dining room and kitchen as if looking for something.

Her reporter's instincts told Patrice that her daughter's question wasn't casual.

"Not much."

She tried to steer them toward the couch. Casey wasn't ready to sit. Fuchsia and lime-green gauze flowing around her, she continued to case out the room, examining the impersonal details. Then she came to the closed bedroom door and stared at it, hands on her hips.

"Is he in there?"

Patrice's face grew warm. "Is who in there?"

"Dad." Then, without waiting for an answer, she threw open the door.

"Casey!" Patrice sprang off the couch.

Casey looked disappointed. "He's gone already?"

"I don't know what makes you think he was even here."

Casey merely smiled, that wicked grin she had inherited from her father.

"Now, Mom, you always told me there was nothing to be gained from not telling the truth. Besides, I saw his truck late last night."

"Then you no doubt noticed that it was no longer here when you drove up just now."

"Yeah. But wasn't it swell of me not to bust in last night? Now, that would've been a real trip."

"Casey, whatever you're thinking, I want you to know..."

"Mom, don't. Don't start making up stuff, okay? Just don't do that."

Patrice stared at her daughter, seeing a vulnerability and disappointment she couldn't remember ever seeing before. She dropped onto the couch again. Casey took another quick look through the bedroom door, then came and draped her long, lean body into the armchair, tucking her skirt between her legs as she bent them under her.

"So, I didn't really think you were the type."

"The type?"

"You know. To fool around. Casually, I mean."

Patrice had absolutely no defence. She struggled with a number of responses, all of them too flimsy.

"I want you to know, Mom, that I'm not going to let this change my perception of you. I mean, I know none of us is perfect. And if you fell into a little meaning-less..."

"Casey! It's not like that."

"It's not?" Casey's eyebrows rose. "Are you trying to say that you and Dad are, like, serious about each other again?"

"Well, no. Not exactly. But..."

"I didn't think so." She got a particularly smug expression on her face. "Don't bother with excuses, Mom. I've heard them all."

If she'd been in a better position to protest, Patrice would have objected to having her own lines used on her. But she hadn't a leg to stand on.

"I just hope you aren't making a big mistake."

Patrice had, of course, been hoping the same thing. But she wasn't crazy about hearing her own daughter echo her own fears.

"Believe it or not, Casey, a certain wisdom does come with being thirty-nine. It's nature's way of balancing things out."

Casey chuckled. "Wisdom, huh? Sounds like a bogus trade-off, if you ask me."

"Well, it isn't." *If you really gained wisdom in place of firm thighs and wrinkle-free skin, it wouldn't be a bad trade-off at all.*

"I just want you to know, Mom, if things don't turn out the way you hope they will, you can depend on me. I'll be there for you."

There was no mercy in the world if this was the price she had to pay for two days in the arms of the man... *a* man... who made her feel like a woman.

"Casey, I don't have any expectations. I'm not looking for this to turn out any way. Your father and I, we..."

Care about each other? Try getting that past the daughter who had listened to them bicker and battle for the past eight years.

"Listen, I'm glad to hear that. That you're not really expecting anything. I mean, I think he has *some* obligation to Tory, don't you?"

"He does?"

"I mean, I like Tory. And I know she'd like a stable environment to bring up her little girl. But..."

"Little girl?"

"But I don't think Dad has to be the one to provide that stable environment, do you?"

"Well, I..."

"It's not his responsibility. That's what I think. But you know what a softy he is. I think he could get himself sucked into that before he knew what was going on."

"Well. Yes. I suppose he could." Patrice made herself promise not to ask. But she couldn't keep silent. "You don't think... I mean, you're certain he's not..."

"The father? Oh, absolutely not. No question about that. He hasn't known her that long. But you know Daddy."

As Casey excused herself and headed for the door, Patrice's head was spinning.

"Oh, Mom, where are you going?"

"Going?"

"I saw your bag on the bed. You're not leaving, are you?"

"Leaving? Mmm, no. That is...no."

CASEY'S HEART was thumping as she got into Will's rickety old sedan and pulled out of the parking lot.

After hearing from Will about her parents' visit, Casey had stewed for two days about what to do next. Should she make a scene, which would certainly be her first impulse if this wedding business were the real thing. Or should she pretend Will had kept his silence?

Deciding a scene offered the perfect opportunity to force her parents into the same room yet again, she had opted for creating a minor explosion. But when she showed up at her mom's the morning before, planning to demand an audience with both her busybody, meddling parents, she had been stunned to see her father's Bronco parked in the front of the lot.

Maybe they didn't need a scene after all.

She had driven on. They didn't need her sticking her nose in. Then she had returned last night, hoping to pump her mother about what had happened.

The Bronco hadn't moved.

Things *were* going well. Extremely well. At least she'd thought so until she saw the suit bag sprawled out on her mother's bed. Then she had panicked. Just when things were looking up, it appeared her mom was once again poised for flight.

That had called for drastic measures.

She just hoped she wasn't off base in assuming that jealousy would work. She also hoped Tory never got wind of what she had said. She liked Tory and knew Tory wouldn't be very happy that Casey had used her and her relationship with Cal—even if there might be a little bit of truth to the idea that Tory saw a chance for salvation in Cal Sullivan. A chance she would never act on, Casey believed, and her father certainly didn't suspect how Tory felt.

But the element of truth in what she'd hinted to her mother had made her ruse just a smidge explosive.

She decided to light a stick of incense to the Goddess of Remarriage when she got home. And another in penance to the Goddess of Small White Lies.

CHAPTER TWELVE

CAL'S VOICE PURRED in Patrice's ear. "What can I do to change your mind?"

Amazing how seductive he could be, even over the telephone. She set down the watering can beside the planter in the kitchen window and leaned against the counter to muster her defences.

"Nothing, Cal. I am not going to flaunt our divorce on stage, not even to make Ralph's retirement dinner a big hit."

"Trish, our divorce has nothing to do with it. He gave us our big break. And it'll be fun."

She envisioned, for just a moment, standing on the dais with Cal, shoulder to shoulder, trying to sound witty and scintillating.

Entirely too much déjà vu for her taste.

"No."

"You're not afraid, are you?"

"Afraid? I should think not." *Terrified is more like it.* She surprised herself by smiling at her weakness.

"I'm not that much better than you, Trish. I think you could hold your own."

She heard the teasing in his voice and could see that damnable smile.

"You're not *any* better than me, Cal Sullivan," she razzed him with easy confidence. Funny how much her faith in herself had been restored with her exposure to

Cal. She remembered how capable she was and had always been, how talented. Even how attractive she still was.

"Ah," he said, "then it's the personal angle. You're afraid you can't spend that much time with me over the next few weeks without succumbing to my infinite charm."

"Cal, your charm is quite finite." *Who are you trying to convince, Sullivan?*

"Then risk it."

"It has nothing to do with risk."

"Actually, I'm flattered."

"You flatter yourself."

"I could come over right now. We could discuss it in person."

Her shudder of excitement told her she had to avoid that at all costs.

"No."

"I'll be there in five minutes."

"I said no."

"Unless you want to come by tomorrow. The copywriter would like some ideas from us and I thought we could get together and talk about it. My place or yours, Trish?"

Battling a determined Cal Sullivan was like throwing yourself in the path of military tanks. You would only end up flattened and Cal would feel nothing more than a minor bump.

"Your place, Cal. Tomorrow morning."

"Not tonight?"

"Don't push your luck, Cal."

He chuckled. "Give it up, Trish. It's hopeless."

"What is?"

But he had already hung up.

PATRICE WAS STILL TOYING with the idea of backing out of this co-starring routine when she drove to Cal's the next morning. She wasn't even certain she could face him anymore, much less spend countless hours in rehearsals with him over the next few weeks.

Cal was perfectly capable of roasting their mentor and former boss all by himself.

And you're perfectly capable of being an unmitigated scaredy-cat all by yourself, she thought as she rang the doorbell.

The young woman who answered the bell was someone Patrice had never met. Wearing a knee-skimming suit and upswept auburn hair, she managed to look fresh faced and professional at the same time.

Cal, it appeared, had quite a harem.

"You must be Trish." The young woman thrust a hand at her while stepping back to open the door. "I'm Anne Winfield, Cal's business manager."

Trish smiled and accepted the woman's firm handshake.

"Cal's told me all about you," she lied, searching the young face for any hint of misconduct. She saw none and it didn't make her feel one bit better.

"Of course, I've certainly heard all about you," Anne said, leading the way down the tiled corridor. Her calves were excellent. Her hips were trim in her pencil-slim skirt.

Patrice followed Anne Winfield into Cal's office. Dark and rich, it was lined with bookshelves and oak paneling. The furnishings were leather and oak, their scents mingling with the heady fragrance of pipe tobacco. Patrice looked for the framed photos of Cal with all the famous people he'd rubbed elbows with over the years; the photos had been among his most prized possessions when they split.

The only photos in the room now were of Casey at different ages. Casey taking her first step. Casey falling off her first bicycle. Casey astride a motorcycle in her high school cap and gown.

At least he wanted people to *think* his priorities had changed. She had to give him that.

Cal was sitting in one of the dark leather office chairs when they entered, looking a bit too studied in his casualness to fool Patrice. Good. He felt awkward, too.

She followed Anne with her eyes as the young woman retreated, leaving them alone. Better she should go directly on the offensive, she decided, than sit back and wait for him to storm the beach. "How many more?"

"How many more what?"

"In your harem?"

She turned to face him with a sardonic grin and was startled to realize he had approached her. He now stood mere inches away. She saw the beat of his pulse beneath the open collar of his shirt.

"There's always room for one more."

"I should have strangled you when I had the chance."

His eyes grew smoky and dark. She felt her own pulse rising to the occasion. "In my sleep?"

"Yes."

"I'll give you a second chance."

"I don't believe in second chances." She brushed past him on her way to a neutral corner, hoping he was acutely uncomfortable with the way her breast brushed against his arm.

She hadn't counted on the fact that she, too, would respond in a way that was distinctly perceptible through her red silk blouse. She sat on the couch, ignoring the telltale evidence, even draping her arm across the back to accentuate the obvious.

Let him sweat it.

"Shall we?" She crossed her legs, a slow, provocative motion that took full advantage of her short skirt.

"By all means." He stole a glance at her legs, getting that glazed look in his eyes that had always made her heart pound. Still did, for that matter.

She pulled out the hand-held recorder she had stuffed into her purse. "I thought we could brainstorm. See what kind of ideas we can come up with and get it all on tape for the copywriter."

He slipped into his leather chair, which turned out to be much closer than she had realized. Their knees almost touched; his heat embraced her. She felt the urge to shift away from him but wouldn't give him the satisfaction. She clicked on the tiny recorder.

"So, Cal, what do you remember?"

"Plenty. I remember you're an absolute pushover if I tickle you behind the knee. And if I. . ."

"About Ralph Walters, Cal." She allowed herself to register no response. "What do you remember about Ralph?"

"Ah. About Ralph." He paused and stroked the line of his jaw. She followed the motion. He was clean shaven; the line of his jaw was still firm, pleasing to the touch. And by three in the afternoon it would be darkened by stubble. Cal always had to shave twice if he didn't want to look like a wild man for the evening.

That's what she remembered. "I remember the day he had the idea to bring the monkeys on the show when the circus was in town."

They laughed at the memory. "And the chimp escaped and ended up trashing his office."

"But nobody knew where the chimp had disappeared to until he started answering Ralph's phone."

Cal leaned closer, looking across her at the recorder. "You're sure that thing's working?"

His scent. Ah, his scent. She held her breath. "Positive."

He nodded. The threat of a kiss was in his eyes. "Trish..."

She jumped in with the first thing that came to mind. "I'll bet no one remembers the time he decided to man the control booth himself on Christmas Day, so everybody else could have the day off."

"Are you kidding? Who could forget that? We were off the air for two hours. Half the station had to come in to straighten out the mess. I remember when we got the call."

Patrice remembered, too. It was midafternoon and nine-year-old Casey had fallen sound asleep with pieces of her new monster-movie makeup kit surrounding her on the bed, exhausted, vampire teeth still in place.

She and Cal had started out cleaning up the mayhem but were making love in the middle of the wrapping paper when the call came from the station.

"You looked great with those little red bows stuck right on the ends of..."

She clicked off the recorder and allowed her gaze to sweep him intimately. "The jingle bells were a nice touch, too, but do we really want to share that with the copywriter?"

"Stick-in-the-mud."

He recrossed his legs, leaving his left knee within a hair's breadth of her right knee. Patrice told herself it was no more distracting than troops rolling into Red Square and continued working.

They unearthed dozens of incidents that would be fodder for a retirement roast. Ralph's inept conversion to computers. His insistence on calling the presidential election every four years, despite making the wrong call six elections in a row. His penchant for plaid jackets and his staff's conspiracy to gradually sabotage each and every one of them.

But keeping their attention focused wasn't easy.

Cal brushed her hand once, when he reached across her to rewind the recorder so they could listen to the segment they'd just taped. Patrice kept inching backward into the leather sofa, but the room was shrinking, drawing them closer. It was her imagination, of course, but it felt all too real.

As they filled most of the tape, she began to think that it was time to retreat. Or risk another surrender.

"We could finish this tonight," Cal said softly, catching her eyes as she checked the tape.

"I think we have plenty."

"Then we could have dinner tonight."

The crazy thing was, she wanted to do exactly that. Have dinner with Cal and let the evening drift wherever it would drift. Right into his arms, if that's where it led. And it most certainly would.

"I don't think so." She clicked off the recorder for the final time and stashed it back in her purse.

"Come on, Trish. The worst is over. You've already admitted that you still want me."

She stood. "I've said nothing of the kind."

He stood. She realized exactly how foolish her last statement must have sounded.

"Yes, you did, Trish. Loud and clear."

The way he hovered, she thought at any moment he might toss her onto the leather sofa and make love to her there. She realized the idea of an ambush held considerable appeal.

"You caught me in a weak moment, Cal. I don't normally do things like that."

"You mean give in to the things you want? Allow yourself to have fun?"

His lips hovered close to hers. Another fraction of an inch and she would feel the silky bristling of his mustache against her upper lip. She wanted to protest but knew her voice was too weak to carry much authority.

"Life isn't about fun, Cal. It's about..."

"What?" He did it. He brushed his lips over hers. Her knees wanted desperately to buckle. "I thought after all these years that you had learned a little something about life, Trish."

"It's you who has a lot to learn, Cal Sullivan." She gasped as his hands brushed against the sides of her breasts as delicately as his mouth grazed hers.

"Be impulsive, Trish. Teach me something."

She teetered for a moment on the edge of deciding to do just that, right here on the butter-soft leather of his office couch. The door opened with a muted creak. She sprang away from him just as Tory walked into the room.

"Oops. Sorry."

"No problem." Cal didn't turn but kept his smiling eyes trained on Patrice. "Trish was just getting ready to teach me some of the things she's learned in the past eight years."

Despite her discomfiture, Patrice caught the disappointment that flickered across Tory's face in the instant before she composed herself. She wondered if Cal had no heart whatsoever. And she wondered how she had allowed herself to forget Tory long enough to fall for Cal's seduction.

She felt like a rat. She decided to make it up to Tory. She just couldn't figure out how. She smiled at Tory and hoped her sympathy didn't show in her eyes.

"I think we're done here, Cal. Let me know when they schedule rehearsals."

She swept past Cal and Tory and hurried down the corridor to the front door, hoping she wouldn't encounter Anne Winfield. Or the upstairs maid. Or anyone else young enough to remind her that she was old enough to know better.

The spring shower sweeping through town suited her mood as she drove back to the condo. When she arrived, she didn't dash through the raindrops, she gave herself up to them. Her hair began to wilt; water streaked her makeup. She felt heavy of spirit. The weight was familiar, and that distressed her.

Maybe they were right, Cal and Casey. If everybody else could shirk their responsibilities and sit back and enjoy, why couldn't she?

She let herself into the condo and slipped out of her wet shoes. She peeled off her wet jacket and left it in a heap. Her skirt came next, puddling at her feet before she stepped out of it. By the time she reached the telephone, she was wearing nothing but the silk teddy and tap pants she had worn in honor of her visit to Cal.

And he didn't even know.

Because I'm too smart to make the same mistake twice.

She grunted at herself and picked up the phone.

Dull, dull, dull. That's what you are.

She was dialing Lettie and trying not to feel guilty that she hadn't returned Cinda Reisling's call and didn't intend to. But when Truman's resonant voice came on the line instead of Lettie's, she made a snap decision.

"Truman!" She made herself sound glad to hear him. *Very* glad. "Fancy running into you here."

"At last! You've finally realized how much you miss me."

She decided not to answer. A little flirting was one thing; an out-and-out lie was something else. "Truman, I'm pining away down here."

True enough, just not for him.

"I can be there by nightfall."

As much as she hated the pettiness of it, there was something satisfying about the idea of having Cal walk in on her and a younger man.

"Actually, I thought you might want to come down for the wedding."

"How soon?"

His eagerness should have stroked her ego. It didn't. She gave him the date and suggested a few days before then; second thoughts skittered immediately around the edges of her mind.

"I could come earlier."

"That should be soon enough."

"Not soon enough to suit me."

For a moment she imagined Casey's reaction to the pretty boy with the square jaw and the fifty-dollar haircut. That wouldn't matter, she told herself, nearly as much as Cal's reaction.

But as she hung up, Patrice saw with disconcerting clarity the sardonic grin that would cross Cal's face the moment he laid eyes on Truman's young, empty face.

That's what impulse gets you, she told herself. *In the middle of something you wish you could get out of.*

CHAPTER THIRTEEN

PATRICE GLANCED at the written directions beside her on the car seat. Turn right at burned-out barn, Casey had said, about two miles past the South Carolina line.

She caught sight of the charred remains of a building and tripped her blinker. The road was gravel.

What in the world was Casey getting her into now? If not for her daughter's call, she would be finishing up chapter four and preparing to tackle chapter five in her manuscript. But Casey—who had called six times in five minutes before Patrice had been curious enough to see who was so frantic to reach her—had been determined.

"Trust me, Mom. Just follow these directions."

"Casey, if you're having me kidnapped in hopes of getting ransom..."

Casey giggled. "We'll be there in thirty minutes, Mom. You'll never forgive yourself if you don't show up."

"We" meaning Cal would be here, too, Patrice grumbled to herself as she searched for the final turn in her daughter's directions. She had been avoiding Cal. For two whole days she had managed to stay away from him.

And he's been beating your door down? she asked herself.

In truth, Cal had made no attempt to get in touch with her since she left him to his harem the day they

brainstormed for the roast. She hadn't been leaving the
answering machine on and had wondered more than
once if she had simply missed his calls while she showered, or perhaps the time she went out to the grocery
store. She found it hard to believe he would abandon his
pursuit of her so quickly.

She saw the red flag tied to one of the young dog-
woods that Casey had told her to watch for and made
the turn. The Mercedes lumbered smoothly over the
tree-lined dirt road, which finally spilled out into the
open. Sunlight glinted off the shimmering blue surface
of a small lake ringed with pink and white azaleas.
Dogwood blossoms made lacy white clouds across the
clearing and green shoots were beginning to stick their
heads up from beds surrounding the dogwood trees.
The soft lavender of wisteria vine was starting to creep
along the larger trees encircling the area.

The vision of growing things brought with it the sense
of peace that it always did for Patrice.

Sitting on the weathered wood of a small pier, feet
dangling in the water, were Casey and Cal.

Patrice pulled her car to a stop beside the battered
sedan Casey sometimes drove and walked toward her
daughter and her ex-husband. Casey waved. Cal smiled,
then turned back to the water.

"So, what do you think?"

"I think you'd better have a good excuse for dragging me all the way out here into the middle of nowhere," she said, smiling and giving Casey a hug as her
daughter rose to meet her. Cal's distinct lack of enthusiasm at her appearance certainly did not bother her.

"Middle of nowhere?" Casey stood, hands on hips,
and turned in a circle, staring at the clearing with an

enraptured expression on her face. "This is somewhere. The most somewhere I've ever seen."

Patrice followed her daughter's gaze. "It is lovely."

"What we'll do is this." Casey pointed to the edge of the pier where Cal was now lying, hands behind his head, staring up at the sky. "We'll have, like, a barge, see, and it'll pick us up right there..."

"Us?"

"The wedding party. If you want to, we can get, like, flowers and stuff and string them around the edges of the barge. Then we'll float out into the middle of the lake—sort of Huck Finn-style, you know?" Casey turned her glowing face from one parent to the other. "Everybody can sit around on the bank and watch. Isn't that awesome?"

"You want to have the wedding here?"

"Yeah. Don't you love it? It belongs to Will's roommate's uncle and he said we could use it."

Although her first instinct was to protest at the unorthodox suggestion, Patrice quelled the urge. For all the weeks she had been in Charlotte, she had refused to think of the wedding in concrete terms. As if refusing to envision it might somehow mean it would never become reality. But the plans were progressing. The date was set. And Casey was growing visibly more—well, agitated seemed more accurate than excited, but Patrice was willing to give her daughter the benefit of the doubt.

If there was to be a wedding, Patrice decided as she looked around her, she was not going to let it drive the final wedge between herself and her daughter.

"I do love it."

She saw the only hint of uncertainty she had ever seen on her daughter's face as Casey smiled at her. "Really? You do? Honestly?"

"Yes, I really do."

"I mean, not just because I like it. But because you like it, too?"

"How could anyone not think it's beautiful out here, Casey?"

Casey flung herself into Patrice's arms and hugged her so hard Patrice couldn't catch her breath.

"Oh, Mom, I love you! I knew you'd like it. I just knew it."

When she released Patrice, Casey leaned and grabbed Cal by the hand, tugging him up.

"See, Dad. I told you!" She faced the two of them on the pier. "Listen, here's what I want you to do. I want you guys to decide just how everything should be, 'cause I've got to run."

Casey started backing away.

"What?"

"I've got a stop to make. Mom, you don't mind taking Dad home, do you? Besides, I want the two of you to plan everything. You know, like whether we should have tents or tables for food, stuff like that."

"Casey, we can't do that. This is your wedding. You have to..."

"Mom, I don't know anything about weddings. Whatever you say will be perfect. I know it will. Later, dudes, okay?"

Then she whirled and dashed to her car, leaving Patrice standing next to Cal on the pier. She shook her head, staring after her daughter. "She's crazy. You know that, don't you? She does not have one practical bone in her body."

"Yeah. Isn't she great?"

For a moment, Patrice felt the energy of Casey's presence. And she was grateful for it. "Yes. She is."

"Thanks, Trish."

"For what?"

He waved his arm to take in the scenery. "For giving this your stamp of approval."

"As if it would make any difference."

"It did."

She thought about Casey's hug and wondered if perhaps Cal might be right. Maybe he was wiser than she realized.

"Well, I guess we should look around. I have a hunch if we don't take some plans back to Casey, she'll ground us and take away our allowance for the next month."

They walked around the clearing. Irises and calla lilies were sneaking above ground; forsythia and clematis shouted in yellow and purple.

"We could have a tent right there for food." She pointed to a level spot between two crepe myrtle just beginning to sprout greenery. "And I suppose we could rent folding chairs and line the lake with them."

"Casey's friends might be happier sitting on the ground."

She nodded. "At least it's low budget."

"But not what you imagined for your only daughter's wedding, right?"

"I suppose not. But..." She struggled with what she had to say. "I've been thinking. Maybe you're right. It's her life. I need to relax and let her live it."

"This must be one of of those moments that define history. You telling me I'm right."

"Don't get cocky. I said maybe. Even a stopped clock's right twice a day."

He laughed and they continued their walk around the perimeter of the lake.

"Trish, did you ever think of...getting married again?"

"Me? Goodness, no."

"Why not?"

What was she supposed to tell him? That no one had ever quite matched the way he always made her feel? Hardly. "Too busy." Partly true, at least. "You did."

He nodded.

"What happened?"

"She...I...she was too much like you."

The words held an unpleasant sting but she kept her smile steady. "Nothing like making the same mistake twice, huh?"

"No. When I realized what I was doing, I knew that wasn't the way to correct the first mistake."

"The first mistake? Marrying me, you mean?"

"Letting you leave."

Nervous laughter bubbled up in Patrice's throat. Casey had said almost the same thing. And this reflective Cal was so convincing she could almost believe in him. This was the same Cal who had made her feel safe and loved; the same Cal who had showed her time and again how easy it was to let herself go and simply enjoy life; the same Cal who had believed in her so much he had patiently taught her all he knew about the television industry.

The same Cal who wouldn't fight for their marriage if it meant confronting his own insecurities.

"We should get back to town."

He stepped forward to face her. "You can't run away from it forever, Trish. We're not the same people we were eight years ago. But these two people still feel..."

"Cal, you don't know anything about what I feel. Quit trying to pretend that you've got the inside track on who I am and what I think."

"I do. You're the one who doesn't know what's going on."

Pulling her key ring out of her pocket, Patrice glared at him. "I'm going back to town. Unless you relish the idea of being stranded two miles down a dirt road in rural South Carolina, I suggest you keep quiet and come with me."

Cal said nothing. He encircled her wrist with his fingers. She tried to pull away, but his grip was too strong. She glared at him. "What are you doing?"

With his free hand, he began to pry her fingers away from her keys.

"I'm stealing your keys. Then I might throw them in the lake. Or, I don't know, I might just take the car myself. Beats listening to you lecture all the way back to Charlotte."

"Cal Sullivan, those are my car keys and I'll thank you to quit playing macho games with me."

With a mighty yank, she pulled her hand free and shoved the keys deep into the pocket of her jacket.

"Oh, wanna play tough, I see." Cal faked one of his favorite gangster imitations and started toward her.

"Grow up!"

But as he advanced on her, flexing his shoulders in gangland style, she couldn't help herself. She started laughing. And when he was close enough to grab her, she did the only logical thing.

She reached out and pushed him toward the lake.

Cal, never one to be taken by surprise, was ready for her. As he stumbled backward, he latched onto her arm.

They tumbled down the shallow embankment and landed with a splash.

"You goof!" She sputtered and laughed as they struggled, arms and legs entangled.

"You bully!"

If she hadn't known better, she would have sworn that Cal was flailing with just the right amount of ineptitude to sink them deeper into the water. The more Patrice tried to pull them out, the deeper they sank, until at last she was firmly anchored between the bank of the pond and Cal's long, hard body.

"Cal, I'm not sure you're doing your best to help us."

"Oh, but I am. I'm doing my absolute, dead-level best." As if to prove his point, he placed his hands securely on her buttocks and tugged her more tightly against his groin.

She felt him stir. Damn him, even at his age apparently minutes were still all he needed. "Then your best isn't good enough."

"How soon they forget."

And he kissed her. A long, slow, wet kiss that distracted her just long enough for him to slip his hands beneath the skirt that had already ridden high on her thighs. She considered protesting but realized she wasn't quite ready to pull her lips away from his.

And while she concentrated on his lips, she pretended not to notice that he had slipped his hand inside her panties. She gasped deep in her throat while he touched and played.

"I'll get you for this," she murmured when his lips left hers to nip at the lobe of her ear.

"I can't be intimidated by threats," he whispered. "Especially idle threats."

"No—" she paused to allow the ripple of sensation radiating out from his thumb to ease over her "—idle...threats...here."

As soon as she was able, she reached for the zipper of his soggy khaki slacks.

"Don't say I didn't warn you." She eased the zipper down and slipped his pants away from his swelling penis.

"I'm at your mercy."

She wrapped her legs around his waist and thrust once and surely to bring them together.

THEY LAY ON THE GRASS, wet clothes rearranged for propriety. His head rested in the cradle of her shoulder and breast; her cheek rested on his soft, damp hair.

"We haven't made love outdoors since Washington," he murmured.

"You've forgotten Grandfather Mountain?"

"Ah, yes. The swinging bridge."

"You always were too impulsive for your own good, Cal Sullivan."

He propped his face in his hand and looked at her. Her eyelids were half-closed, signaling the drowsy afterglow that had always made her so beautiful. "Two level heads in the same family would have been far too many."

She smiled softly. "You were levelheaded when you wanted to be."

"Never!"

"When Casey had the measles."

"That doesn't count. You had the measles, too."

"Exactly my point. You always come through in a pinch."

He noted her use of the present tense and saw the sudden puckering of her brow and supposed she had, too. "You, on the other hand, can be impulsive at the most delightful times."

She glanced at their soggy clothes and caught his eye. "So it appears."

"Well, that, too." She looked twenty again. Except better. Flushed and tousled and fresh, but with a mature sultriness that only years could bring. A real woman, a whole woman. He had never loved her so much. "I was thinking of the time you wanted to slash the tires of the teacher who said Casey was too headstrong for her own good."

She laughed; the throaty sound lurched through his gut. "I wouldn't have actually done it."

"I wouldn't bet on it."

"Being parents together, that was fun, wasn't it, Cal?"

"Just being together was fun."

"I suppose we might as well give in to the inevitable."

"What do you mean, Trish?"

"I mean, as long as I'm here it seems we're simply not going to be able to keep away from each other. So maybe the thing to do is just . . . enjoy it. Go with it."

There was something too casual in her tone to suit him.

"What do you mean, as long as you're here?"

Her eyes opened a bit wider. The somnolent look on her face became more wary. "Just that. I'll be here for another four weeks. You're always telling me to loosen up. So I'm agreeing. I'll loosen up."

"For four weeks?"

Now she propped herself on her elbows and stared at him. "You have something else in mind?"

Now was not the time to press his advantage. She had agreed to four weeks of what she thought would be a casual dalliance. There was plenty of time to turn things around.

He hoped.

He shrugged and leaned close to nuzzle her lips with his. "Four weeks. I hope you can keep up."

"Ha! Are you sure you've still got it in you?"

"I could demonstrate."

"Already?"

"You do that to me."

"You're just bragging." She pressed her thighs to his.

"You're not going to be able to walk out of here if you keep that up."

She chuckled low in her throat, a sound that was half-dare. He took her hand and pressed it to the front of his jeans. Her eyes grew wide.

"Oh, my. I am impressed."

"You should be. I don't do this for just anyone, you know?"

For a moment he saw the seriousness flicker into and out of her eyes. "You don't?"

"No, Trish. I don't."

"Then do it for me."

And he did.

"KNOW WHY I LIKE this place, Trish?" he asked as they once again straightened their clothes.

"Why?"

"It reminds me of Latta Park."

His words startled her. He was right. The water, the peacefulness, the sun glinting through the openings in the trees overhead. The colors and scents and promise of spring.

It was a lot like the place where they had married.

Disturbed to realize it was that memory she had unconsciously responded to the moment she saw this clearing, Patrice brought her eyes back to Cal's. For once they weren't glittering with suppressed humor. They were dark with emotions so deep she could drown if she stumbled in unexpectedly.

"We'd better go now."

Cal nodded. "I knew you'd say that."

She wanted to tell him once again to quit pretending he knew her so well. But she was beginning to fear he did.

CHAPTER FOURTEEN

NOW OR NEVER.

That's the way Tory saw it. If she planned to seduce Cal Sullivan, she had to make her move now. Before Cal managed to charm his way back into Trish's good graces.

She checked the lights. Low. Music, soft. Wine, chilled. Brie, room temperature.

Stomach, unsteady.

If only Trish hadn't backed off after that time she and Cal had spent two days together. Then Tory would have allowed herself to forget this incredibly stupid notion. But Tory had seen for herself, even if Cal hadn't been grumbling about it incessantly, that Trish had decided to put the brakes on whatever was in danger of happening between them.

So you're the consolation prize, Tory thought, looking down at herself.

Silk lounging pajamas? Painted toenails? And a liberal spritz of the fragrance Anne Winfield assured her never failed?

"Wear it at your own risk," Cal's business manager had warned, never dreaming who Tory's target was.

When she heard Cal's Bronco in the driveway, Tory almost ran to her room and locked the door behind her. Reminding herself that Whitney's future was at stake, she stood in the doorway between the entrance hall and the sunken living room. While Cal unlocked the front door, she tried out several smiles.

Suggestive and seductive, à la Mae West. Too hokey.

Naive and seductive, à la Marilyn Monroe. Too phony.

Sultry and seductive, à la Greta Garbo. Too obvious.

Something wasn't working and it must be the seductive part.

"Hi," she said, lowering her voice as Cal turned and saw her.

"Well, hi. What's wrong?"

"Wrong?" She forced herself to walk over to him, then wondered what in the heck she was supposed to do next. Slink right into his arms? Not very likely. She linked her arm through his and led him toward the living room. "Nothing's wrong."

She was no stranger to touching Cal, and it had never before felt in the least bit sexual. She had hoped it would tonight. It didn't. *But he's such a hunk! How many times have you told yourself that!*

"You sure? Your voice sounds...funny. You're not coming down with something, are you?"

She led him to the sofa and pulled him down beside her. Their thighs touched. She resisted the urge to squirm away. For heaven's sake, she touched this man all the time in the weight room. Why was she acting so squirrelly all of a sudden?

"I'm fine, Cal." She softened her voice. "How was your day? Can I get you something? Wine? Brie?"

Cal turned a strange look on her. She tried lowering her eyelids, just for effect. His look grew even stranger.

"Wine? Um, no. No, thanks."

"I think...I'll have some. Definitely."

She poured herself a glass of the wine she had set out on the coffee table, then, on impulse, topped it off with just a bit more. She might need it.

She swallowed deeply, then set the glass down on the table as the alcohol hit her jittery stomach. They sat in silence, her hand still resting on his arm. She felt suspiciously as if she were about to perspire.

"You look tired," she crooned. "Was it a rough day?"

The wrinkle in his forehead disappeared. His smile was satisfied. "I guess you could say that."

"Let me rub your shoulders."

She stood and walked around behind him. Placing her hands on his neck, kneading the tightness in his muscles, helped calm her. This was more familiar territory. Cal, too, began to relax. Yes, this might work.

"Actually, though, it was a satisfying day."

"It was?" she whispered, making her touch gentler, more intimate than usual. "Satisfying is good, Cal."

"Yeah. I think I've got her just where I want her."

Tory's hands grew still. She forced herself to continue the massage. "Her?"

"Trish."

She hadn't needed the clarification. "Oh."

"Yeah, I let her know I was through playing around."

Tory smiled. At last, good news. She ran her fingers through his hair, molding them to his head in a way that was guaranteed to soothe. She leaned down and whispered close to his ear, "That's good, Cal."

"You bet. After that afternoon at the lake, I was afraid I'd scared her away for good. But—"

She straightened. Her hands fell away from his shoulders. "You spent an afternoon at a lake? Together?"

"Hey, don't stop now."

She glared at the back of his head for a split second before launching an attack on his tense shoulder muscles.

"Yeah, where Casey wants to have the wedding."

"How nice."

"After Casey left, Trish and I stayed to...look around. Then I said it reminded me of the park where we got married."

"How romantic."

"Ow! Lighten up, okay?"

She drew a deep breath and continued less aggressively.

"Anyway, I guess that was too sentimental for Trish. Scared her to death, in fact. She's been avoiding my calls ever since."

Tory smiled. "Oh. That's too bad."

"So today I told her I was through playing games." As her kneading grew more gentle, Cal's voice softened to a low murmur. "From here on in, it's serious business."

Tory's fingers stilled. "Serious?"

"Mmm, hmm." His head lolled to one side. "Told her I was going to win her back. She might as well..."

His voice drifted off. After a few seconds, he rallied long enough to complete the thought. "...surrender."

Then he was out. His breathing was steady. Cal Sullivan had fallen asleep in the middle of her big seduction. And the last words on his lips were about his ex-wife.

Well, at least she still knew how to make him relax. At least the shakiness in her stomach was gone.

She shrugged, covered him with an afghan and hurried into her bedroom. She couldn't wait to get out of these silk pajamas and into her cotton nightshirt.

PATRICE WAS HAVING a hard time concentrating on Casey's chatter as they made their way through the light midmorning traffic on Providence Road. Most of the uptown workers had already made their way to the office and the lunchtime crowd hadn't yet surfaced, so the street lined with exclusive shops and trendy restaurants wasn't busy. But Patrice had more on her mind than traffic lights and turn signals.

Cal, for example. Making love with Cal. Feeling the old familiar touches that were more powerful, more evocative than a new, unfamiliar touch could ever be. And remembering all the good. All the closeness. All the ways they had once mirrored each other's soul. All the ways he made her smile; all the times he made her feel secure; all the richness he had brought to her life.

More and more often Patrice had to work hard to remind herself of all the reasons she and Cal hadn't been able to make it work. Their professional jealousies. His immaturity and unreliability. Um . . . there were others. There must have been, because those sounded weak; weak and probably no longer even applicable.

Not true, she argued with herself. Cal was still immature. Why else would a man his age surround himself with women like Tory McIntyre and Anne what's-her-name? Why else would he be trying to seduce the woman he hadn't loved enough to give up his home and his job for eight years ago?

Something about that particular interpretation of their divorce bothered her, so she turned her attention to other matters.

Cal wasn't the only worry on her mind. There was ICN and her old pal Cmienski. Her boss had favored her with another of his tension-producing telephone calls just as she was leaving her condo this morning.

"I want your decision, Sullivan. You taking the full-time anchor job or are you going soft on me?"

"Give me one good reason why you can't keep Lettie in that spot."

"I don't have to give you one good reason for anything. That's why I'm the boss."

She had fumed in silence, unwilling to turn her back on the career she'd worked so hard to build but equally unwilling to be the instrument of her best friend's downfall.

"Decision time, Sullivan. Lettie's on her way out. Are you on your way in or not?"

"And how long will it be before I'm too old?"

A string of profanity spewed from Cmienski. "About ten years and ticking, I'd say. So make up your mind. You've got two weeks. Exactly. Then the job goes to somebody who has twenty good years. Get it?"

Got it.

"Mom! Stop!"

At the urgency in her daughter's voice, Patrice slammed on the brakes, her eyes darting in search of the near tragedy. Casey pointed to a triangular parking lot.

"There. The record store."

"A record store?"

"Sure. You like music, don't you?"

At the worry in her daughter's voice, Patrice vowed she would banish all thoughts of Cmienski and anchor positions and book deadlines—and Cal, definitely Cal—from her mind for the day. Today she and Casey would have fun.

"Absolutely." She pulled into the lot. "How about some heavy metal?"

Casey groaned. "Mo-o-om. Nobody likes heavy metal anymore. Are you a total sleep-case?"

They went into the store laughing and came out with Patrice's credit card nudged another hundred dollars closer to the limit. Carrying a plastic shopping bag filled with CDs of musicians she had never heard of, Patrice said, "I swear, I can learn."

Casey was shaking her head, unable to hide her wicked grin. "I'm not so sure."

"Well, I am. Keeping up with what's new is my life."

"How about ice cream?"

"Ice cream?" She contemplated the hours she had sweated and the broccoli she had eaten and the sizable check she had written to the fat farm.

"I know you remember ice cream. The melty stuff. In waffle cones."

Promising herself that every respectable ice cream store offered no-fat alternatives these days, Patrice followed her daughter the half block to the store. While Patrice studied the alternatives, Casey oohed and aahed over creamy concoctions that featured chunks of pure chocolate and slivers of almond and ribbons of caramel.

She finally opted for a scoop of the regular stuff with real honest-to-gosh cookie dough in it. She felt her hips spreading as she licked the rich, creamy, melty mixture.

Well, her hips wouldn't show behind an anchor desk, anyway.

From the ice cream shop, they walked next door to a boutique, where Casey talked Patrice into buying several outfits that left little room for expanding hips. But the outfits wouldn't fit behind an anchor desk, either, so Patrice wasn't sure where that left her.

Except that she was having fun. And her daughter was having fun. She wasn't certain they had laughed this much since the day at the park when Casey had been afraid to go down the slide alone and would only agree to the escapade while nestled safely in her mother's lap.

"Right, and I'm the one who ended up with my shorts full of sand," Patrice complained after Casey reminded her of the event.

"Yeah, but I've never been afraid to do anything since then."

Patrice started to laugh, then paused to study her open-faced daughter with the bright smile and the happy eyes.

"Really?"

"Really." Casey shrugged and glanced away with the sudden reticence of an adolescent. "I mean, I figured if you weren't afraid, what was there to be afraid of. Right?"

Patrice swallowed hard, grateful Casey wasn't looking her in the eye at the moment. "Casey?"

"Yeah?"

"I am afraid. Sometimes."

Casey looked at her, then lowered her eyes shyly. "But not so much, right? I mean, you never *seem* afraid."

"More than you'd think."

"Like what?"

"Of doing the wrong thing. Mothers... mothers are supposed to always do the right thing, you know."

Casey didn't turn away now and Patrice was more than a little afraid of the fact that she couldn't read the unusually serious expression in her daughter's eyes.

"Mom, you know the only wrong thing you ever did?"

"What?"

"Always doing the right thing." Her smile softened the words.

Patrice pinched the bridge of her nose, where she felt the tears collecting. "Sorry."

"Nah. It's okay. I mean, none of us is perfect." Then Casey threw an arm awkwardly around her shoulder and hugged her close with a quick laugh. "Except you, of course."

Patrice accepted Casey's signal to lighten the conversation. "So when's some of it going to rub off, kid?"

They laughed out loud together and got in the car for their next stop. As Patrice negotiated the traffic in search of the florist Casey had chosen, her daughter closed her eyes and said, "There is one other thing. That you did wrong, I mean."

"What's that?"

"You dumped Dad. Mega-screwup, Mom. I mean, really major."

Patrice was still debating who dumped whom when they pulled up in the parking lot of the florist tucked away on a side street. She winced at the sight of Cal, feet propped on the dash of his Bronco, reading the morning paper.

Had her determination to pursue a real career constituted dumping Cal? Had he dumped her by default when he refused to go along while she pursued that career?

Or, in hindsight, had they simply both been running away from something they had been too immature to handle?

Cal swung his long, lean legs from the vehicle and stretched himself out. She stirred at the sight of the man who had fulfilled all the promise of the boy she had fallen in love with. She was loath to admit it, but Cal still made her feel out of control, on the edge of something risky. The feeling was more than a little delicious.

Cal gave Casey a quick kiss on the cheek, then put his hands on Patrice's shoulders and kissed her, too, but not as quickly. The kiss lingered, grazing beguilingly over her cheek, roaming high onto her cheekbone, straying close to the lobe of her left ear. She felt his breath, the tickle of his mustache. He pulled away and she saw the challenge in his dark eyes.

"Good morning."

He infused the words with all the intimacy of a lover waking amid rumpled sheets. She smiled serenely and ignored the warmth stealing through her. "Hello, Cal."

"I hope you've been rehearsing for the roast," he said as they turned to follow Casey into the small shop.

"I'll be ready." She contemplated a graceful way to wriggle out from under the arm he casually draped over her shoulder but could think of none that wouldn't reveal her discomfort. And her discomfort would reveal the power his touch still held over her.

She stayed within his loose embrace for the few yards remaining to the entrance of the Garden of Temptation.

The florist shop beguiled her the moment she entered. Each room of the converted, Tudor-style home was a garden of a different type. One a dark, steamy jungle, filled with orchids and amaryllis and lush baskets of bougainvillea, accented with wicker furniture draped in mosquito netting. The next a prim but cheery English garden, its carefully manicured boxwood and ivy tracing careful paths between tea carts and wrought iron benches. From an arid desert filled with hand-woven Native American tapestries and spiny cacti to a Japanese rock garden complete with pagoda, the shop was exotic, welcoming and completely enthralling.

Patrice wandered the rooms, barely aware that Cal and Casey followed her in silence. She imagined herself at home here, fingers warmed by the soil, the knots in her neck, shoulders and stomach soothed by the scents and sights of nature that always beckoned to her. She felt not only at home but at peace, something she hadn't felt in almost a decade.

"Lovely," she breathed.

"Thank you, dear." The petite, white-haired shopkeeper who had introduced herself as Caroline Babbington paused and looked around. "It is rather nice, isn't it?"

Patrice stared at the woman, dressed comfortably in a gingham housedress that suited another time, her thick white hair a fluff of cumulus cloud around her translucent, barely lined face. "Much more than rather nice, Mrs. Babbington. I envy you."

A solemn, almost wistful look settled onto the woman's age-softened features. "I must admit, I'm going to miss it."

"Miss it?"

She pointed to the discreet sign in the front window. "It's on the market, you know. I'm retiring to California. My only son is out there now."

And despite the wistfulness on the shopkeeper's face Patrice saw the satisfaction that came with the mention of her son.

"He has three daughters, you know. And—" the elderly woman paused while the glow transformed her face "—the eldest, Margaret, is expecting my first great-grandchild this fall. Well, I can hardly wait. She works, you know. An attorney. I expect she'll need plenty of help, wouldn't you think?"

Patrice smiled. "Absolutely."

"But you're not here to talk about me," said Mrs. Babbington, motioning them through open French doors into chairs on an awning-covered brick patio. "We have a wedding to discuss. I simply adore weddings, you know. Herbert and I were married right here in this garden. Of course, that was many years ago, you know."

And all the while they sat in the garden, talking about ways to complement the natural beauty of the area Casey had chosen for the wedding, Patrice's eyes wandered over the small garden tucked away behind the house. She felt the presence of a young Caroline and Herbert. The placid certainty of their love swept through her just as it filled every corner of the shop.

As Casey and Mrs. Babbington enthused over hot-pink impatiens, Patrice found her eyes captured by Cal's. And improbable as it seemed, the placid certainty seeping to the corners of her being intensified.

"You like it."

It wasn't a question, and Patrice once again found it disconcerting that he could read her so well. She shrugged, still reluctant to give him points for knowing her, even after all these years.

"It's nice."

With the barest touch of his fingers, he brushed the back of the hand resting on the arm of the melon-colored Adirondack chair. "Don't do that, Trish."

His soft voice compelled her and she looked into his eyes again. It was a mistake. They were asking to be let in. When had she grown so vulnerable to his look, his touch, his voice?

"Don't shut me out."

She drew a long, slow breath without breaking eye contact. She felt him rummaging around in her soul, but she was powerless to shove him away, here in this place that offered contentment with the air you breathed.

"Okay. I love it. I feel at home here."

He smiled, not the wicked little smile that always left her breathless. No, this smile was soft. It matched the way she felt.

"You should have it."

The idea startled her. She looked around, trying to imagine herself submerged in this place daily. No more deadlines. No more makeup artists. No more backs to be stabbed. She thought of her book advance and how it could be used to buy her way out of that rat race and into this little bit of paradise. And she thought of admitting that everything she had worked for was meaningless now that she had achieved it.

"A nice daydream, Cal. But not very practical."

"Being happy is practical."

"Cal—"

"Yes, it is. Nothing is more practical."

Patrice was so disconcerted by the exchange that she barely kept up with the rest of the plans for Casey's wedding. She was vaguely aware that Casey was opting for something surprisingly natural and unaffected and distinctly unoutrageous. Patrice didn't even have it in her to argue with Cal when he brought out his checkbook to make the deposit.

She didn't feel like fighting with him.

At least, she didn't feel like fighting with him until they were walking out the door. Everyone had thanked Mrs. Babbington and pressed her slender, fine-boned hand. That was when Cal apparently decided it was time to take over Patrice's life once again.

"Mrs. Babbington, I'm curious. Exactly what kind of investment would it take to buy the Garden of Temptation?"

Cal knew he'd made a big mistake the minute he saw the expression on Trish's face. The look that said he'd just committed a sin far more serious than wearing seersucker before Easter.

Casey, for once, appeared speechless. She simply stared at him, mouth agape.

"Well, Mr. Sullivan, I wish I could give you a specific answer, but you know I just don't know," the florist babbled. "I've left all that to my son and the real estate agency he selected. He's in real estate himself, you know. My son, I mean. Not residential, of course. Some kind of development. But he told me when we first..."

Cal wasn't listening. He was too busy avoiding the venom shooting from Trish's eyes. How could she look both cool and malicious at the same time? he wondered.

"I don't believe Mr. Sullivan's query was a serious one, Mrs. Babbington." Trish's glare dared him to dispute her word. In which case, what else could he do?

"Actually, it was."

"Dad!" Casey warned, her voice recovered.

Mrs. Babbington looked from Cal to Trish, then back again, a look of bemusement on her face. "I see. Well, I have the card of the real estate agency right here if..."

"We're not interested." Trish's voice brooked no argument.

Cal smiled. "Thank you, Mrs. Babbington. That would be very helpful."

Casey groaned.

As Mrs. Babbington produced the card from the deep pocket of her pink-and-white shirtwaist dress, she looked momentarily uncertain. "You must realize, of course, this is a very special place."

Cal took the card just as Trish grabbed for it, and tucked it into his back pocket. Then he covered Mrs. Babbington's hand with both of his and squeezed lightly. "I assure you, Mrs. Babbington, the Garden of Temptation would be in very good hands with Mrs. Sullivan."

Casey jabbed him in the small of the back as he turned to shepherd them all out the door. Trish avoided the solicitous guidance of his hand at her back. Only Mrs. Babbington looked pleased. She beamed at them as they walked outside.

Trish, however, was not beaming. Seething, perhaps. Steaming, even.

"Give me that card, Cal Sullivan," she hissed, marching down the sidewalk.

"I can call," he answered blithely.

Casey jumped out in front of them, smiling weakly. "Maybe we should go to lunch."

"I don't want you to call."

"There's a really cool little sandwich shop right around the corner."

Casey sounded frantically conciliatory; Trish did not sound conciliatory in any way, shape or form.

"And if you ever call me Mrs. Sullivan again, I'll..."

"You never did like haggling over business, Trish. Let me call for you."

"They have salads and, um..."

"You are not my keeper, Cal. And you do not make my decisions for me. Not anymore."

"Anymore? As if I ever..."

"I'll go on ahead and get us a table, okay?"

"Don't use that tone with me, Cal."

"What tone?"

Casey threw up her arms and turned, flouncing down the sidewalk in a flawless imitation of total disgust.

"That tone that says you're absolutely innocent of whatever you're being accused of."

"I am innocent. I may have been guilty of plenty of things, but making your decisions for you was not one of them."

"Oh? Maybe you'd like to clue me in on a few of the things you *were* guilty of."

Cal cursed himself as he felt his face heat up. Surely Trish had never believed that nonsense about him and Jeanine.

"Now, Trish, you know damn well that..."

"I don't know anything. Why don't you tell me?"

This was not going well at all. "Trish, I think we've lost the thread of this conversation. If you could calm down for a minute, maybe..."

"I am calm!"

Then he made his second mistake. He laughed. Out loud. Loud enough, he noted from the corner of his eye, that Casey halted at the corner and turned to face them once again.

"Cal Sullivan, you don't even take me seriously!"

He put his hands on her shoulders and kept them there even when she tried to jerk herself out of his grasp. Then he stared her straight in the eyes until he saw the anger burn itself out.

"That's not true. I take you very seriously. But you, Trish, take everything far *too* seriously."

She opened her mouth to speak but stalled momentarily. "What...I...no, I don't."

"Yes, you do. And it's making you unhappy. I only want to see you happy again."

"I'm not unhappy."

He hurt inside at the weakness of her reply. "No, I was wrong. I don't want to *see* you happy again. I want to *make* you happy."

"Cal, that's just not...you don't...oh, Cal." She sounded on the verge of giving in.

"At least let me try."

"Cal, this is crazy."

"You used to be crazy. I remember." He smiled.

She smiled back. The smile of the lost and unrecoverable. "I'm not eighteen anymore."

"Thank goodness." He put his knuckles to her smooth cheek. "Thirty-nine suits you."

"I can't let you seduce me, Cal."

"Isn't it too late to fight that, Trish?"

"I mean it, Cal. Maybe I slipped up. Maybe we slept together. But..."

"That wasn't slipping up. That was the smartest thing I've done in eight years."

That halted her for a moment. She stared at him, then looked down. "Don't make this difficult."

"You're making this difficult. Just go with it, Trish. That's all I ask. Give it a chance."

"No."

"No?" A hollow, empty sickness opened up in him.

"I wish we'd never slept—"

He pressed her lips with his index finger. "Don't say that. I don't want to hear it."

She closed her eyes and he dropped his hand.

"I didn't mean it."

"Thank goodness."

"But I can't do it again."

Now he grinned, mostly to hide from the emptiness threatening to swallow him. "Sure you can. I'll show you sometime."

"I'm serious, Cal."

"Me, too."

She stopped. He watched her eyes as she debated with herself. He saw a hint of regret replaced by thin-lipped determination. "There's someone else, Cal."

Cal knew at that moment that he must be completely recovered from his heart attack. For if he hadn't been, he would have had another one right then.

"Another man?"

She looked away. "That's right. There's someone...important...in my life."

While Cal struggled to find a response—a flippant reply, a sharp retort, even sincere congratulations— Casey's voice broke into his consciousness.

"What did you say to him, Ma? He looks like you've given him another heart attack."

CHAPTER FIFTEEN

CASEY'S WORDS MIGHT have been gibberish for all the sense they made to Patrice.

Heart attack? What in heaven's name...

She looked at Cal, expecting him to look as perplexed as she felt. He didn't. He looked pale. His usually mischievous eyes were dark with dismay. No hint of a dimple quivered in either cheek.

He shoved his fists into the pockets of his khaki slacks. "Dammit, Casey."

Casey crinkled up her thin face in a comical look she had perfected years ago to take the edge off situations that involved broken glass or permanent stains. "Oops."

"Could someone let me in on the secret?" Patrice stared first at Cal, then Casey, forcing out the words.

Cal glared at Casey but still wouldn't look at Patrice. "I think that's already been done."

"But..."

Patrice stopped. If she said any more, she might cry. If she stood here much longer, looking at the man she...had loved...she might throw her arms around him and clutch him to her.

Cal? A heart attack? She felt cold all over.

"This is a joke, right?" *Please, let it be a joke.*

Cal made a motion to move on down the sidewalk. "Look, I had a mild heart...thing...about seven months ago. I'm fine. Can we eat lunch now?"

Patrice stared after him as he started to walk away. His back was straight and lean, his shoulders broad, his hair dark and crisp. She was struck by an image of him clutching his heart, dropping to the ground. Panic welled up in her chest.

"Omigosh!" She dashed ahead and stepped in front of him to impede his progress. "Are you all right?"

He blew out an impatient sigh. "Do I look all right?"

"Well, yes, but..."

"Then I'm all right."

She looked at Casey, who had caught up with them. "Is he all right?"

Casey thumped her father on the chest, then leaned down to press her ear against his heart. "Sounds all right to me."

"I'm serious!"

Cal brushed past her. "See what I mean. You're always serious."

Her anxiety turning to anger, Patrice dashed after him. "Don't change the subject on me, Cal Sullivan. How bad was it?"

His jaw was rigid and he kept his eyes straight ahead as they turned the corner toward the restaurant. "Not bad."

Casey cleared her throat. "Touch and go for a few hours, they said."

Patrice put her hand on her chest. The organ in question raced out of control. She might have a heart attack of her own. Right now. "Touch and... And nobody called me? Cal, you didn't even call me. How could you do that?"

"It didn't seem important."

She remembered the emotion in his touch when they made love the first time at her condo. She had told herself, in quiet moments when she couldn't shut out the thought, that the act had felt almost like an act of love and not simply an act of sex. But if he cared at all, wouldn't he have called? They had a daughter together. They had lived together for more than a decade. And no one had called her when he might have been dying?

She simultaneously wanted to break his nose and hold him close until the fear subsided.

Cal requested a table for three outside at the café and they were led to a round table under a gold-and-white canvas umbrella. Patrice kept staring at him. He looked so healthy. So tan and fit.

"Stop staring at me, Trish. I'm not going to keel over into the water glasses."

He sounded testy. He must not be as healthy as he looked or he wouldn't sound so testy.

"If you were, would you tell me?"

He hid behind his menu. She did the same. Neither of them spoke until the waitress came for their order.

"Philly cheese steak sandwich," Cal said.

Both Casey and Patrice dropped their menus and stared at him.

"Dad!"

"Is that wise, Cal?"

He glared at both of them this time, then looked up at the waitress with a pleasant smile. "Extra cheese."

"Isn't that just like you?" Patrice said after she and Casey had ordered salads.

"Trish, drop it."

Cal didn't get angry often, and when he did, everyone knew it was better to back off. Besides, the last thing Patrice wanted to do was be responsible for getting him overly excited.

She remembered their lovemaking again. As energetic and athletic as it had been twenty years ago. With a man who had heart trouble?

No more of that. If something happened to Cal...

She couldn't even finish the thought. It emptied her too completely. Life without Cal had been one thing. But a world without Cal? Waking up daily to the realization that he wasn't out there somewhere?

Patrice realized she might cry if she wasn't careful, so she drew her thoughts back to the table as their food was being delivered. Casey and Cal were in the middle of a discussion about his travel plans.

"Don't worry," Cal was saying. "I'll be back in time for the wedding."

"But, Dad, six cities in one week?"

"It's not so bad."

"Cal, are you sure that's a good idea? So much travel is exhausting. I know. Maybe you should slow down and..."

"I did slow down, Dr. Sullivan. But I'm fine now."

"Besides," Casey said, "Tory will be with him."

"Oh. That's certainly reassuring. You know, Cal, I saw a study that said older men who died of heart attacks while having sex were usually having sex with younger women who weren't their wives. Now, don't you think..."

"Mom!"

"Trish, I am not going to have another heart attack!"

"Dad, tell her."

"That's none of her business, either."

Looking ill, Casey turned to Trish. "He's not sleeping with her."

"I said that's none of her—"

Patrice wadded up her napkin and tossed it onto the table beside her barely touched salad. "It is if it kills you!"

For the first time since the conversation began, Cal smiled at her. "Would that bother you, Trish?"

Knowing she had started digging the hole herself, Patrice sought a way out of it. "Yes. I don't want you going out looking like an old fool, Cal Sullivan."

"Can you think of a better way to go?"

"Daddy, you tell her right now!" Casey put her hand on Patrice's arm to draw her attention. "Mom, Tory is Dad's trainer. The doctor made him hire her. That's all. Tell her, Dad. I mean it."

"That's ridiculous," Patrice said. It was bad enough she had let her ex-husband lure her into his arms while he was dallying with a youngster. But she wasn't going to be played for a fool.

"No, really, Mom. After he came out of the hospital, he kept doing all the same old junk. Didn't you, Dad? Doc Tipton said he was going to have another heart attack if he didn't get his act together. So the doc found Tory. Tell her, Dad."

Cal pushed his half-eaten sandwich around on his plate.

"It's true, isn't it?" Patrice felt her anger building to a dangerous level. "It's true, and you let me believe..."

"Now, don't blame me. I told you from the very beginning Tory was my trainer."

"You liked having me believe you were doing...immoral things with that...that..."

"Brick outhouse?" Cal filled in the blank with his most wicked grin.

"You were feeding your own ego, you insufferable egomaniac."

"Mom, don't get all excited."

"It's okay, Casey. *I'm* not the one who has a weak heart."

With a muffled cry, Cal jumped up from his seat so quickly he knocked the chair over. "Neither do I!"

Everyone on the restaurant's patio stared as Cal pulled a wad of bills from his pants pocket, threw them onto the table, then stalked off.

Casey turned to her mother. "Now see what you've done."

"Me? Me!"

With that, Patrice jumped up and followed Cal out into the parking lot. When she caught up with him, she grabbed his arm.

"Don't you run out on me, Cal Sullivan."

Cal whirled, his face red with anger. "I'm not the one who runs out, Trish."

Her first impulse was to lash back with her own angry retort, but when she saw his red face and the pulse pounding at the base of his throat, she grew alarmed. "Now, Cal, just calm down and..."

"And don't give yourself a heart attack," he mimicked, then raised his hands with a roar. "I am not an invalid!"

"Cal..."

Before she could move a muscle to stop him, Cal looked around, then leaped onto the hood of the vehicle right behind him. He stood looking down at her, his arms outstretched. "Cal Sullivan is not an invalid! Cal Sullivan does not need babying! The only thing wrong with Cal Sullivan is that his ex-wife is driving him crazy!"

Patrice almost giggled at the sight of her ex-husband raving on the hood of someone's car, until she remembered that he had, indeed, been near death just a few months ago. She had to do something. Her war-zone experience said the only thing to do was march into the fray.

She hoisted herself onto the hood of the car and confronted him, hands on hips. "Cal, you're making a fool of yourself."

"I don't care!" he shouted. "That's better than letting everybody make an old man of me!"

"If you have another heart attack in this parking lot, I'll kill you, Cal. I swear I will!"

From below, Casey's voice wailed up at them. "Daddy! Mom! I don't believe this! Get off that car right now!"

"I'm not coming down without him."

"And I'm not going anywhere until you admit I don't need a stretcher."

"Cal..."

Another voice boomed up at them. "Hey, buddy, that's my car! Get your butts off it!"

"You didn't think I needed a stretcher at the lake last week," Cal taunted.

"You're going to need one when I get through with you, buddy!"

"You thought I performed pretty well for a decrepit old—"

"That's enough, Cal. You don't need to broadcast your performance for the whole neighborhood."

"Daddy, I can't believe you're doing this! What if somebody sees you? I don't believe you two. You're acting like children!"

The embarrassed hysteria in Casey's voice captured Patrice's attention. She looked around to watch her daughter cover her eyes and stalk away. She turned to Cal; he was watching their daughter walk away, too.

"How about that?" she said. "Did you ever think we'd get too outrageous for her?"

He chuckled, sheepishly at first. Then she joined him. They laughed so hard they had to throw their arms around each other to keep from sliding off the hood of the car.

When they finally stopped laughing long enough to get down from their precarious perch, Cal apologized to the owner of the car that had been in the wrong place at the wrong time. The man merely shrugged as he examined the unmarred hood.

"Forget it, buddy. I've got an ex-wife, too. They all make you crazy. No question."

CASEY LEANED AGAINST the door frame as she and Will watched her parents scamper onto the stage, waving jauntily at the festive audience looking forward to roasting one of Charlotte's favorite personalities.

It was the first time she'd seen them smile at each other for three days—since the day they'd made such spectacles of themselves in the middle of Providence Road.

Parents!

"Are you sure this is going the way you thought it would?" Will asked, leaning close to be heard above the enthusiastic applause.

"Of course it is."

"They didn't look very buddy-buddy to me before this shindig started."

She gave him a look she hoped was withering. In fact, all that felt withered at the moment were her spirits. But she wasn't about to admit that to Will.

Her parents were not cooperating at all. Sure, they had presumably been making mad, passionate love in her mother's condo, if her understanding of these things was not totally whacked out. And unless her dad had merely been ribbing her mom big-time that humiliating day on Providence Road, some kind of hanky-panky had gone on once she'd left them at the lake, too.

So far, so good.

Except that the higher things got cranked up between them, the worse they seemed to get along.

She had thought that once her mom found out about his heart attack and her dad stopped playing those silly games about Tory, they would open up to each other. Her mom would realize how much she cared about Dad; knowing she'd almost lost him had certainly made Casey feel that way.

But it didn't appear to make any difference. In fact, his heart attack seemed to have become just one more thing for them to bicker about.

"If she looks at me that way one more time, I'm going to skydive off the NationsBank tower," her dad had grumbled after last night's rehearsal of the roast.

"And what will that prove?" Casey had retorted, irritable because he might be crazy enough to do just that. After all, any man who would jump onto the hood of a stranger's car in a restaurant parking lot might do anything.

"That I don't need constant supervision."

"You couldn't prove it by me."

As annoyed as she was with her dad—and he had, after all, started the whole thing—Casey didn't hold her mom blameless, either. After all, she had sent out the Worry Patrol in full force. A good sign, maybe, but Casey knew all too well how suffocating it could be to know that Patrice was sitting somewhere worrying herself into a state over you.

Still, the two had managed to avoid being alone together for the past two days. That was, in fact, why she and Will were looking on from backstage as her parents emceed the roast. They had all driven over together.

That, too, Casey took as a good sign. If they couldn't trust themselves alone...

She wondered if her mom could still get pregnant. It had worked once; it might work again, she supposed.

"Hey, they're pretty good," Will whispered.

Casey dragged herself away from her thoughts long enough to listen to her parents. She had been young when they ended their on-camera partnership, but she remembered that they'd always seemed so magical together. Laughing into each other's eyes, shutting out the rest of the world, except for Casey. And because they were her parents, that private world had somehow included her even as it excluded her.

Then they weren't partners any longer.

She had wondered for years how they could have acted so well, fooled so many people into believing the looks they shared were real. Then, one Christmas when she was thirteen, she had seen the look on her mom's face while she talked to her dad by phone from Atlanta.

Casey recognized the look because it reflected the longing in her own heart when she talked to her dad.

She had searched for that longing in her father's face the next time they were together. Sure enough, it was there. And Casey understood. It hadn't been the closeness they had manufactured. It was the alienation.

Again, tonight, she saw the magic between them.

She had mere weeks to get them to admit they knew about the magic, too.

"Come on, Will." She backed away from the stage door. "Let's blow this joint."

"It'll be over soon. We're supposed to ride back with them."

"They're grown-ups. They'll figure it out."

As HE LEFT THE STAGE with the applause ringing in his ears, Cal felt something he hadn't felt in years. He felt the charge of having Trish at his side while the world looked on.

The sensation had always been a tremendous aphrodisiac; he'd never felt like that with any of the other women the station had paired him with after Trish left.

He didn't let her get far away as they looked up and down the narrow backstage corridors for Casey and Will. He kept close enough to inhale the musky fragrance of her perfume and to absorb the warmth emanating from the body encased in silver lamé.

"How was it for you?" he asked, using the voice of naughty suggestion that always drew a rise out of her.

She turned a reproachful look on him, but he couldn't mistake the high color in her cheeks or the glitter in her eye. His groin tightened. He'd always thought it would be exciting to make love backstage. He'd never found out.

"The earth moved, Cal."

He chuckled softly and followed her into the tiny dressing room. "I thought so."

Trish found the note tucked into the corner of the mirror. Checking to make sure the dressing room door actually locked securely, Cal didn't notice her grimace until she thrust the note at him. Casey's sprawling scrawl informed them that she and Will had left already. Cal's keys were on the dressing table.

There might be a fairy godmother after all.

"I guess she got tired of baby-sitting us," he said, tossing the note beside his keys.

"I'll call a cab."

She was fussing with her wrap and her purse, nervously, he thought. He draped the silk wrap around her bare shoulders, holding it in place by resting his hands between her breasts. He felt her heartbeat.

"You've been avoiding me."

"It's best that way."

Her voice was breathy. His body responded.

"No, it isn't."

She tried to back away but there was nowhere to go. She raised her chin and tossed her hair—a trifle haughty. She played that role so well. He loved her confidence, her pride, the surefootedness with which she walked into every situation.

"We never made love in the dressing room, Trish."

"And we're not going to, Cal."

"We're not?" He let go of her silk wrap. It slithered off her shoulders. She shivered. He saw her nipples pucker. He was lost. "You can't mean that."

"Yes, I do. I told you, Cal, it's not a good idea."

She had said that before. The revelation about his heart attack had overshadowed her own confession, but it had haunted him in the days since. He was jealous and possessive and in love.

And the last thing he could do was let her see that.

"Why, Trish? Because there's someone else?"

He saw her hesitate. He didn't believe her; or was it only that he didn't want to believe her? Either way, he had to know.

"Did you ever make love to this someone else in your dressing room, Trish?" He feigned casualness.

"That's none of your business."

"Yes, it is. I want to know. I want to know who he is. And I want to know before I make love to you."

CHAPTER SIXTEEN

"I AM GOING TO MAKE LOVE with you, Trish."

She held her breath to keep from gasping as Cal slipped one French hook out of her left ear and pocketed the glittering dangle of rhinestones.

"Right now. Right here."

"Don't be ridiculous."

Her voice held not one iota of conviction.

He slipped the earring from her right ear, his fingers warm, powered with just enough voltage to draw a shiver.

"Would you like to wear the diamonds?" He laid a hand at her throat, where a diamond choker encircled her neck. "That would be nice, I think. Nothing but diamonds and bare skin."

Her hand fluttered toward her throat but couldn't complete the journey. She felt weak all over.

He picked up her wrist and slipped her watch over her hand. It, too, disappeared into his pocket. "Now, why don't you tell me about this fellow while I undress you?"

"No. I... there's nothing to tell."

His hands slid down her shoulders, dragging the spaghetti straps of her dress with them. "Nothing? Does that mean you made him up? Or isn't he much to talk about?"

He turned her, pausing to caress the hollow of each shoulder blade with his lips. She heard the zipper slowly unthreading down her back.

"Cal..."

"Which is it, Trish?"

"I did not—" the dress puddled at her feet and her voice dropped to the barest whisper "—make him up."

His fingertips danced along the curves of her back and hips, following the lines of the satin and lace bustier. "Then he isn't much to talk about. Good. I like that. That bothered me more than I would admit to you if I weren't under duress. What's his name?"

"Tr—" She closed her eyes and swayed as he drew an index finger along the inside of the champagne-colored garter that ran from the hipline of the bustier to the top of her shimmering silver stocking. She tried to think about what Cal had just said about being jealous and what that might mean. But very little was computing right now. "N-never mind his name."

"Travis? Trenton?" He left the garter attached, then took her by the shoulder and turned her to face him once again. He was smiling; she was melting. She barely registered the instant of recollection when his eyes grew wider. "No, I know. Truman. Is that it, Trish? Truman Matthews, the ICN reporter?"

She put her hands out to push him away. But his chest beneath the crisp white of his tuxedo shirt was so firm, so deliciously molded. Cal was no boy. He was all man. She longed to feel all woman, as she always felt in his arms. She longed for the inner closeness that always came after.

"Doesn't matter," she murmured, pretending to herself that she would remove her hands from his chest soon. Any moment.

"But he's so young." His soft voice took on a teasing note as he slipped his hand inside her satin panties and cupped it against her. She tried not to gasp, but it was hopeless. "Good for you."

"Cal..."

His fingers explored. She felt herself become slippery and hot against his touch. Then his touch disappeared. He pulled her panties down. She wasn't sure her knees would hold out much longer.

"But I can tell, you're aching for a mature man. Aren't you?"

She reached for him, but he captured her wrists in his hands. She struggled against him briefly, hoping he would resist. He did. Sensation spiraled through her. She could almost climax without a touch when he played these games.

But *with* his touch was much better.

"What's the matter, Cal?" Her voice was husky. "Afraid you can't stand up to the competition?"

He chuckled. The sound whisked through her. "Lie back, Trish."

And he lowered her to the floor, then stood above her as he unzipped his tuxedo pants. He dropped slowly to his knees. She tried to smother the small cry that rose in her throat as he knelt, poised between her thighs.

"I can make you forget him."

And he thrust into her, pinning her hands to the floor above her head.

On a jagged sigh that shuddered through every hidden crevice of her body, she whispered, "Forget who?"

PAYING HIM BACK, torment for torment, must have been Trish's motivation for insisting that they mingle with the crowd that had gathered at the Radisson Hotel for Ralph Walters's retirement bash.

All Cal wanted to do was hurry back to her condo, take her in his arms and talk about all the ways they could reweave the threads of their lives. He wanted to coax some small admission of an emotional connection from her. He wanted to tell her how different it could be this time. He wanted to talk about forever and ever.

But Trish, it appeared, wanted to play games.

"Grayson, so good to see you again. How long has it been?" She greeted the head of the hospital authority, all the while discreetly running her fingers up and down the arm of Cal's dinner jacket to make sure he didn't forget the throbbing in his body.

And as a group of Junior Leaguers for whom she had written a guide to Southern gardens at the height of her local career clamored and fussed over her, she turned to Cal, a hand at her earlobe, and said, "Why, Cal, you haven't seen my earrings, have you? I seem to have misplaced them."

Cal felt close to bursting with the longing he had barely tamped during their moments of explosive coupling in the dressing room. As he watched her coy flirtations, catching her occasional glance at him from beneath her half-closed lids, the heat in him built.

He excused himself long enough to find them a second glass of champagne punch. When he turned back, she was no longer surrounded by admirers. She was standing to one side of the crowd, her body rigid, her eyes focused across the ballroom. He followed her gaze.

Jeanine Dawkins.

Ralph Walters's petite brunette assistant, still attractive in that glittering, brittle way, was raising her glass in a toast. Cal's first impulse was to hurry to Trish's side to forestall any chance of a confrontation. He had never forgotten how manipulative and self-centered Jeanine could be; he had learned it the hard way, the way foolish men sometimes discover such things.

He had always counted himself lucky nothing had ever happened between the two of them. Nothing physical, at least. Looks had been exchanged, most of them halfhearted on his part, the result of his bruised ego and Jeanine's carefully plotted stroking.

When it had come time to go beyond flirtation, Cal's heart hadn't been in it.

But he'd still felt guilty for the last eight years, because he couldn't claim to be completely innocent. After all, he had responded to Jeanine in the first place because he wanted a little help. And Jeanine hadn't been above a bit of scheming—especially if it meant putting a hitch in Trish Sullivan's soaring career.

No, the last thing Cal wanted tonight was for Trish to learn the truth he had hidden for so long. He watched the emotions play almost imperceptibly over her face as she struggled with the sight of the woman she had always at least half blamed for the breakup of their marriage. His mouth was dry.

When she took a step in Jeanine's direction, Cal moved into action. Grabbing two fresh glasses of champagne from a passing waiter, he double-timed through the crowd and reached Trish's side just as she came within three feet of the one person he didn't want her mingling with.

He touched the cool glass to her bare upper arm and leaned close to her ear, praying he could keep his voice in control when he spoke.

"You look like a woman who needs her nose tickled."

She stared down at the bubbles in the fluted glass, then up at him. Her eyes were skeptical. His heart was thudding, and he reassured himself that Doc Tipton had said it was in perfect working order these days.

"I'm not sure that's what I need at all, Cal." But she took the glass, being painstakingly careful to avoid brushing fingers. Her gaze moved from their hands to the direction she'd been headed.

He pretended not to notice. "I have an idea."

"So have I."

He swallowed half a glass of the champagne, but it didn't ease the nervous dryness of his mouth. Trish never had been one to make things easy.

"I think you should stay in Charlotte." He watched for her reaction. She was too good. Her eyelids, lowered to sultry slits as she gazed in the direction he refused to follow, barely flickered in response.

"And join your harem?"

Her voice was wryly casual, but he heard the edge to it.

"I thought we'd resolved that issue."

"So we did."

"Tell me the truth, Trish."

She turned her eyes sharply back in his direction. "I always do."

"Always?"

"Mostly always."

"This Truman fellow. Is he important?"

"This Tory person. Is she important?"

But he could tell it was no longer Tory who concerned her. He took her by the elbow and started leading her to the edge of the room, toward the door that opened out on a balcony. "No games, Trish. I'm serious."

"So am I."

"She is important, but not the way you think."

She followed him into the darkness. Her smile disappeared. "Then how?"

"She helped me regain my confidence. Helped me figure out I wasn't a doddering old man teetering on the brink of my grave." He drew a deep breath and told her how Tory had helped him regain control of the body he felt had betrayed him. He told her about sweating and straining to the tune of Tory's encouragement; he told her about learning to work through his fears.

For the first time since she'd laid eyes on Jeanine Dawkins, the edge in her voice softened. "She sounds remarkable. Especially for one so young."

"She is."

He took her empty glass and set it, with his, on a small wrought-iron table. When he finished, Trish was studying him. "Did you really feel so vulnerable after your heart attack?"

"I really did."

"Why didn't you call me?"

He thought back to hospital smells and the breathless, helpless feeling of being on a stretcher and the sound of tense, pressured voices. He remembered the fear. "I wanted to—more than anything."

"But?"

"I didn't want you to see me like that."

She nodded.

"It changed me, Trish. A lot of things have changed me." He saw the skepticism mixed with hope on her face. "What about Truman Matthews?"

She hesitated, then shook her head. "He's sweet. It flatters me. But it's nothing... real."

"Has there been anyone real?"

She looked out into the night. "I've had other things to worry about. My career."

"And now? Is the career still that important?"

She hesitated. "Sometimes I hate it. The competition. Worrying about your looks, as if that's all we have to offer. You know, when I was in Chicago, I can't tell you how many times a day I studied myself in the mirror and worried..."

"Your looks should be the least of your worries, Trish."

She smiled. "You know, now that I'm away from Chicago, I can believe that. I'm older. I'll get older every year. But it doesn't matter. Unless I go back. Then it matters again. Cal, I've accomplished so much and now I wonder if it all wasn't wasted effort."

"Not wasted. We all change directions, Trish. It's part of life. Maybe it's time you took a few detours."

"And you have a few suggestions?"

"I do. Like figuring out what kind of future our relationship has."

"Cal, don't you think it's obvious? Our relationship is in the past, not the future."

"No, Trish. I don't think that's obvious at all. Our problems are in the past. I believe we're finally adult enough to make the relationship work."

He knew from the look on her face that she wasn't convinced. Yet. But several weeks remained until Casey's wedding. And he planned to put every moment he was in town to good use convincing Trish they never should have given up on their marriage.

A half hour later, after they had said their goodbyes and were walking to the car, Cal heard the rapid click of a woman's high heels behind them. As he unlocked the passenger door for Trish, the clicking came to a halt just behind them.

"Well, well, and here I thought I was coming to a farewell. I didn't know it was going to be a reunion, as well."

The sickness in the pit of his stomach returned as Cal recognized the voice of Jeanine Dawkins. He felt Trish tense and straighten herself.

They both spoke at once; the coolness of Trish's voice hid the anxiety in Cal's. At least he hoped so.

"Isn't reliving old times fun?" Jeanine said, then turned and walked away.

The ride home was silent. Cold, brittle silence. Cal didn't know what to say. Damn the woman, anyway. Wasn't it enough to screw up his life once?

When they pulled into Trish's parking lot, she didn't wait for Cal to come around to her side. She jumped out of the car and stalked toward the door. She was impatiently punching the elevator button when he caught up with her.

"No need to follow me up, Cal. I'll be perfectly safe alone."

"Trish, don't."

She whirled to face him. "Have you really changed, Cal?"

He looked her squarely in the eye. "I have."

She pulled her wrap more tightly around her shoulders. Neither of them moved when the elevator rang and its doors whooshed open.

"Why wouldn't you come with me to Atlanta?"

She spoke so softly he could barely hear the question, but it might have been run through an amplifier for the force with which it hit him. All that had come before her move had been insignificant, stuff they could have overcome.

Refusing to move had been his fatal mistake. After he'd made that decision, professional mediators would have been required to get them into peace talks.

Now, he knew, his only real choice was to come clean.

"I wasn't brave enough to give up my career so you could work on yours."

Well, almost clean. He still couldn't bring himself to mention Jeanine. He almost hoped she would. At the time, she'd thought Jeanine was half the reason. And maybe she had been, but not in the way Trish thought. At the time, he'd felt so guilty he'd believed he didn't deserve to hold on to their marriage.

If she asked, he vowed, he would tell the truth. The whole truth. No matter what the repercussions, he would tell her what a louse he'd been. At least then she wouldn't think he'd been fooling around behind her back. It would be a relief to finally come clean after all these years.

And if she doesn't believe you?

And if she believes you but won't forgive you?

She didn't ask, although he knew it was on her mind. And he couldn't bring himself to tell her unless he was backed against the wall.

She went upstairs alone. He went home alone.

To Patrice, the next week felt suspiciously like a courtship.

When Cal was out of town, he called late at night to talk over the day and lure her into deeper conversations than she wanted to indulge in.

When he was in town, the days ended in a tangle of arms and legs and lips and shared emotions and started with cheese Danish and fresh-squeezed orange juice. She needed the emotional indulgence almost as little as she needed the cheese Danish, she told herself. Although to hear Cal tell it, a few extra pounds wouldn't bother him at all.

"When did you get so thin?" he asked, studying her backside one night while she drifted on a float in his pool, a piña colada within reach.

"When I found out TV adds ten pounds."

He ran one hand along each thigh, disrupting the serenity of the night air and the moonlight. "I like you better the way you used to be. Ten more pounds and you'd be perfect."

It was hard not to love a man who wanted you to gain weight. She smiled lazily and downed the rest of her piña colada. "Bless you."

She tried reminding herself that this man who suddenly knew the fine art of saying all the right things was the same ex-husband who had irritated and needled her for the past eight years. She tried to remember the gulf that had opened up between them with the appearance of Jeanine Dawkins, but keeping that in mind grew tougher as the days wound down.

"I'm jealous," he announced one day as they walked around the lake at Freedom Park, tossing the leftovers from their picnic basket to a family of ducks.

"Of what?"

"You make love better now than you did when we were married."

"Why should that make you jealous?"

He swept her into his arms. "I don't like wondering where you got all that vast experience."

She foolishly allowed herself to be caught up in the moment—and fell into the trap she hadn't permitted herself around Cal in almost a decade. Honesty and openness.

"There hasn't been a lot of vast experience, Cal."

He brushed the hair back from her forehead. "There hasn't?"

She shook her head.

He pulled her to his chest and whispered, "I love you, Trish. I never stopped loving you."

He'd caught her at a weak moment. Eyes closed, nose nuzzled into the warmth of his neck, she whispered, "I never stopped, either, Cal. It was always you."

TORY DIDN'T REALIZE anyone else had pulled into the circular driveway when she leaned across to the passenger seat of her ancient VW bug to grab the bag of groceries.

Apple juice, sugarcoated kiddie cereal and hot dogs peeped from the top of the bag. Everything she needed for a day with Whitney. She tried not to let her jitters overtake her. It would all work out. Soon. In six days, to be precise. Cal's attorney had called with the news this morning. In six days, a judge would decide.

Tory's hand trembled as she hoisted the bag onto her hip and closed the car door.

Then she heard the squeak of another car door behind her.

She turned. A woman stared at her from beside a fading and rusted wagon with fake wood grain painted on the side. Her brown hair flyaway in the brisk breeze,

she fixed pale eyes on Tory and remained unmoving.
Her face was pinched and sallow, her thin nose casting
a shadow on her tightly pursed lips. A yellow print dress
hung on her frail frame.

Something eerie in the woman's pointed face made
Tory shiver. "Yes? Can I help you?"

The woman didn't move or speak for a long time, and
it was some moments before Tory realized that she, too,
had frozen in place. Only when another car, an impos-
ing gray Mercedes, pulled into the driveway beside the
station wagon did the woman speak.

"You won't get her, you know."

Fear flooded Tory's body.

"She's mine now, and you won't get her back.
Whatever I have to do, I will."

Tory's voice came out barely louder than a whisper.
"Who are you?"

The woman didn't answer right away, but it didn't
matter. Tory knew the answer. This woman with the
obsessive expression on her face was the foster mother
in whose care Whitney had been entrusted.

The door of the forgotten Mercedes closed. The
woman turned toward the sound. Then she spun around
to face Tory again.

When she spoke, her voice trembled. "You're not fit
to be her mother." Like a windup toy suddenly set in
frenetic motion, she scrambled into the car and started
the engine. "I'm not going to let you hurt her again,"
she shouted, then sped away, tires spinning in the gravel.

Tory was aware of nothing but the woman's threat
until Trish walked up and took the bag of groceries that
had begun to slip out of her grip.

"Who in the world was that?" Trish stared after the
car.

"I..."

Tory couldn't speak. She couldn't move. She had worried for so long about what kind of harm her own careless actions had inflicted on her daughter. Now, it seemed, there was another danger.

Through her fog, she felt Trish's hand on her arm, heard Trish's commanding voice. "Tory? Tory, what's wrong? Who was that woman?"

"She's..." Tory forced herself to pull her thoughts together. She had to think. She had to figure out what to do. "I don't really know her."

Trish frowned. "You don't?"

Tory shook her head.

"Good. She sounded a little off center to me."

Tory's face crumpled and she fell back against her car. "Don't say that. Please, don't say that."

"What's wrong, Tory? Tell me. Right now."

Tory responded automatically to the command in Trish's voice. "She has my baby. She has my baby and she said she won't give her back."

With a small gasp, Trish propelled Tory toward the house. "Come on. You're going to tell me exactly what's going on here."

PATRICE PINCHED OFF just enough of the fresh mint from her window herb garden to flavor a pot of tea. She held it to her nose as the water burbled in the copper kettle. Fresh. Cool. Grown by her own hands. She felt the familiar peacefulness despite the upheaval surrounding her.

She wondered where Cal was tonight. In Portland, perhaps. Or was he already in Walla Walla?

He'd barely been gone two days and already she felt as if she couldn't get through another day without him.

Already? She'd felt that way since the morning before, after she drove to his house to pick him up and give him a ride to the airport. Right after she'd stumbled onto that strange encounter in his driveway.

At least now she knew the whole story about Tory McIntyre. She shook her head as she poured water over the tea infuser she had latched onto the side of her teapot. As soon as they'd dashed Cal to the airport, she and Tory had been on the phone to Cal's attorney.

Imagine that. Her helping Tory.

"I can't believe you're doing this for me," Tory had said as they sat in a musty-smelling coffee shop in the courthouse, waiting for Cal's attorney to come down. She looked vulnerable and young and frightened and absolutely nothing like the femme fatale Patrice had assumed her to be for the past two months.

Patrice shrugged, then smiled as reassuringly as she could. "You need help. Cal's not here, so..."

Tory looked down into her barely touched cup of vending machine coffee. "I know, but... you know, I was a little... jealous of you when you first showed up."

"You were?" Patrice tried not to sound stunned.

"Before you came, Cal had a lot more time for me."

Patrice wondered uneasily if she was about to hear something she didn't want to hear.

"He was a good friend. Almost like a father. Not that he's that old, I mean. But..."

"He took care of you."

Tory nodded. "When I needed it most. And I didn't have anybody else. I guess I... depended on him too much. And when you came along..."

"I made you feel insecure?"

Tory looked her squarely in the eye. "Yes."

"If it's any consolation, you made me feel pretty insecure, too."

"Oh." Tory toyed with her plastic stir stick. "I thought for a while if I just . . . if Cal would just . . . that all this could be fixed somehow if Cal would . . ."

Patrice waited.

"I decided to seduce him, you know."

The words settled somewhere in the region of Patrice's stomach with a heavy thud.

Tory grinned wryly. "He didn't even notice."

"What do you mean?"

"All he could talk about was you. And I was so glad. What if it had worked?"

What, indeed?

Patrice jerked the tea infuser out of the teapot and put it in the sink.

Cal's attorney hadn't been able to accomplish much. The woman with the eerie voice had a long, stable history as a foster mother. She pushed all the right buttons when the authorities spoke with her. And after all, Tory was the one everyone viewed skeptically.

Everyone except Patrice, who now saw Tory as just another sweet young girl who needed—and deserved—friends she could depend on.

Nevertheless, she wished Cal was here to help. To bolster Tory's sagging spirits. Tory's only option now was to wait out the next few days until the date of the custody hearing rolled around. If Cal were here, his influence in town might accomplish more than Patrice had been able to do.

She sighed.

She had told herself she should be relieved he was gone. A few more days and she would've been agreeing to give up her career and move back to Charlotte and marry him again.

At least the wedding would be over soon—five more days remained before Casey made the mistake of her life—and Patrice could escape before she joined her daughter in doing something truly foolish.

As she poured a cup of tea over a sprig of the fresh mint, the doorbell rang. Frowning, she walked into the entrance hall and peered through the peephole. Casey stood waving and mugging in the direction of the tiny hole in the door. When Patrice opened the door, she swept in carrying a take-out pizza box, which she plopped down on the side of the dining room table that wasn't occupied by the debris of Patrice's work.

"Dad made me promise to try to curve you up while he's gone," Casey announced, flipping open the box to reveal a pizza topped with black bean sauce, Caribbean chicken and andouille sausage. "So here I am, always the obedient daughter."

Patrice tried not to smile as she brought plates and napkins from the kitchen. Cal had a big mouth.

"I do not need curving up."

Casey shrugged, dragging a wedge of pizza onto each plate. "Hey, who's to argue with an excuse to pig out?"

Inhaling the spicy aroma, Patrice decided once again there was no reason to object to Cal's preference for women who were more filled out. She could worry about the extra pounds when—if?—she went back to Chicago.

They pulled out chairs and sat down to enjoy the pizza.

"So, I guess this means you two are ... um ... getting ... um ... friendly again."

Patrice tried not to squirm. How to explain this to her nineteen-year-old daughter when she didn't even understand it herself? "I guess you could say that. At least, we've decided to call a temporary truce."

"Wow. A full-scale amnesty would really be something to see." Casey swallowed half a can of soft drink and grabbed another slice of pizza. "Listen, I didn't come here to lecture you about Dad."

"Well, thank goodness for that."

"Or to fatten you up, either."

"Oh? Does that mean you had some other reason for showing up at my door with a bribe?"

Casey grinned. "Yeah. I came here...well, I came here to talk about money."

"Money?"

"Yeah." Casey put her pizza on her plate and wiped her hands. "Well, I've been thinking. This wedding isn't costing very much, is it?"

"I'd have to say this is the most economical wedding I've ever been to. Mine excluded."

"Yeah, that's what I thought. Anyway, I wondered if...well, you haven't said anything about a wedding gift, and I don't mean to sound like a greedy little brat..."

A wedding gift. Patrice realized she had been wishing so hard for this wedding to get off track that she hadn't even thought about a wedding gift. She put her hand out to cover Casey's. "Don't be silly. Is there something you and Will want?"

Casey drew a deep breath. "Money."

"Oh. Money. Well, of course. That makes sense." Well, she would hardly have expected china and silver patterns.

"I thought so."

"You have discussed this with Will?"

Casey immediately glanced down. "Don't worry about Will, Mom."

Something felt fishy, but Patrice didn't know how to find out what. "Is it . . . that is, would you mind letting me in on what you plan to do with this money?"

"It's a surprise."

This didn't sound good. Another of Casey's schemes. "I see. Did you have a particular amount of money in mind?"

Casey hesitated, then quoted a sum that almost made Patrice choke on her pizza. "Actually, Mom, I have a business investment in mind."

"You aren't going to buy that tattoo parlor, are you?"

Casey laughed. "Don't be silly. You don't think I want to spend the rest of my life hanging around bikers and exotic dancers, do you?"

"Exotic dancers?"

"You should see what I did for Dee-Light. She's got more silicone than a Hollywood plastic surgeon and . . ."

"What kind of business, Casey?" Patrice really didn't have the stomach for hearing how—or where—her teenage daughter had adorned an exotic dancer.

"It's a surprise. Okay?"

"Have you talked to your father about this?" If she'd talked to Cal and wouldn't tell her own mother, that was the last straw.

"Not yet. Say—"

The bleat of the doorbell interrupted her. Irritated, Patrice wiped her fingers. "We'll finish this later."

Casey looked perturbed. "Sure, Mom."

Patrice peered through the peephole. Truman Matthews peered back.

CHAPTER SEVENTEEN

HE WAS BLOND and blue eyed, with a sculpted chin and nose just strong enough to save him from looking like a surfer. But when Truman Matthews walked into the room she had shared so often with Cal, Patrice wondered what on God's green earth had ever possessed her to think he was in any way appealing.

Truman had the same sort of wicked smile as Cal—or at least time and distance had convinced Patrice it was the same. Now, with her impressions of Cal so vividly recent, Truman's dimples merely seemed boyish.

Truman had made her laugh, which she also realized now was simply another way of harking back to her relationship with Cal.

Truman made her feel attractive, something she had desperately needed when they met, a few weeks before her thirty-ninth birthday. But knowing that she set Truman's young hormones raging now seemed far less enthralling than seeing Cal's dark eyes spark with a desire that was underscored by long years of familiarity and—yes, she had to admit it—understanding.

Truman hadn't minded her success, and that had been different from Cal. But in retrospect she wondered if Truman's enthusiasm might have been fired by the hope that her success would somehow rub off on his neophyte career.

Good Lord, how did middle-aged men manage to stomach fawning younger women?

Whatever the motivation for her temporary madness, she had to do something. Fast. Cal was due back tomorrow, and Truman was dropping his expensive leather suit bag—expanded to accommodate a full week or more on the road, she noted with a tightness in her chest—onto the floor and sweeping her into his arms.

Think, Sullivan. Fast.

She wasn't fast enough to avoid the enthusiastic kiss he planted on her lips.

Behind her, Casey cleared her throat insistently.

Patrice extricated herself from Truman's embrace. "What are you doing here?"

His smile dripped anticipation. "I'm here for the wedding. You invited me. Remember?"

She remembered. She wondered if a migraine would be any help at all at this point.

"Mo-om."

Truman looked over her shoulder. His Pacific-blue eyes lit up politely; he smiled. The smile was warm and disarming and totally devoid of any allure.

Didn't he used to be sexy?

"Casey, right?" He walked around Patrice and took Casey's hand, holding it between his palms. "You know, you really have your mother's looks."

Casey seemed torn between glaring at him or succumbing to the spellbinding effect Truman had on most things female. She chose her route quickly.

"I have my *father's* smile," she snapped, failing to demonstrate the resemblance as she turned her eyes on Patrice. "Who is this?"

"Truman Matthews. He's a reporter for ICN." Casey's suspicious look told Patrice her answer was not sufficient. "He's a friend of mine."

"And you invited him to the wedding? Without even telling me?"

Patrice wasn't certain of the reason for the shrill note creeping into Casey's voice, but she was certain that now was not the time to indulge her daughter's outspokenness.

"Casey, why don't you open a bottle of wine and pour us all a glass?" She gave her daughter a pointedly commanding gaze. "I'm sure Truman had a tiring flight. Let's give him a few minutes to relax, okay?"

Casey looked at Patrice with mistrust before disappearing into the kitchen. The moment Patrice was alone with Truman, he reached for her, an unmistakable look in his eyes. She slipped beyond his grasp, gesturing to the couch. "Please, sit."

She wondered how difficult it would be to manipulate him into a room at the Omni before Casey left. She dropped into the chair that was farthest from the couch.

Instead of sitting, Truman walked around behind her and leaned close. He brushed annoying kisses along the side of her neck while he murmured, "How soon is she leaving? You have no idea how much I've missed you. If she doesn't leave soon, I may..."

"Not now, Truman." She squirmed away from his touch. "This is not a good time."

He hesitated, then backed away. Looking at her as if she were on mind-altering narcotics, he perched on the edge of the couch. "What's wrong?"

"Truman, I..."

"Wine is served," Casey's strident voice broke in. She had that Mother-how-could-you look on her face as she deposited the tray on the coffee table. "So..."

"What's going on at ICN, Truman?" Patrice knew her voice was too bright and too brittle the moment the words were out.

Truman looked at her oddly. Casey looked at them both impatiently, then sprawled on the floor beside the coffee table. Patrice barely listened while Truman filled her in on the latest gossip, none of which registered.

"But the big news is Cmienski and Cinda."

The names of her boss and her trainee instantly drew Patrice out of her distraction. She'd meant to return Cinda's call, but she hadn't been prepared to embroil herself in whatever was going on at ICN. "Oh?"

"For a while, it looked as if they were going to be the hottest ticket since..." He halted his automatic glance in Casey's direction almost in time, but Patrice knew better than to suppose Casey had missed it. "A hot ticket," he finished lamely. "Anyway, turns out Cinda has scruples."

"She was going to sleep with him?" Casey's voice was incredulous. "Totally heinous."

Truman grinned. "She must know Cmienski."

"So what happened?" Patrice leaned forward. *And what about Lettie?*

"My sources close to the top say he's prepared to up his offer to you." He settled back on the couch, his satisfied smile telling her he was confident he was bringing welcome news. "Doubling it, I believe."

"Ridiculous."

Casey sat up straight. "Doubling what offer?"

Truman shook his head. "Patrice, you know better than to doubt my sources. Come back next week and the money's yours."

Knowing that her decision was now tougher—and that she could not stall much longer—heightened Patrice's discomfort.

"Mo-om!" Casey's voice was now distinctly shrill. "What is he talking about?"

Reluctantly, hoping her lack of enthusiasm didn't show, Patrice explained the situation she had been running from at ICN. Without, of course, explaining the running part. Casey's face grew dismal as the story unfolded.

"You've been offered a full-time anchor job? You didn't tell me that."

"Well, I...nothing is certain. I haven't accepted it...yet." She was surprised at the gloom on her daughter's face.

"But you will. It's what you've always wanted."

"Yes. Well, I suppose it is."

Casey stood. "Mom, we need to talk. In the kitchen."

"Casey, we have a guest."

Casey's eyes narrowed in a challenging expression that felt uncomfortably familiar to Patrice; she was fairly certain she used that look herself. "I know that, Mother. But I have to leave. And I have to talk to you first."

She followed her daughter into the kitchen, but before Casey could speak, Patrice whispered, "Don't go."

"Don't go?"

Casey's glassy glare threatened to turn into a knowing smirk.

"Please."

Yep. There it was. That got-your-number smirk.

"But, Mom, I thought you'd want to be alone with your boy toy."

"He is not my boy toy."

"He thinks he is."

"Well, he isn't," Patrice hissed. "And I don't want to be alone with him. Just yet. Until I figure out . . ."

"What to do with him?"

Patrice nodded.

"I don't know, Mom. I think you need to handle this yourself. You know, you have to learn to take responsibility for your own actions, and . . ."

"Casey, right now I do not need your smart mouth. Is that clear?"

Casey dimpled sweetly, her eyes gleaming with mischief. "Mom, don't get testy." She glanced at her watch. "Besides, you don't need *me* as a buffer."

"Yes, I do. I do need—what do you mean? Why are you looking at your watch?"

"Well, it's just that Dad should be here anytime."

"What? He's not due until tomorrow. He told me so. He very distinctly said tomorrow."

"Are you going to hyperventilate?" Casey folded her arms across her chest, a calm, satisfied smile on her face. "He called me earlier. He couldn't stand to be away a minute longer. As soon as he finished his last talk, he caught the next plane out. He wanted to surprise you. Isn't that sweet?" She glanced at her watch again. "Yeah, he should be here anytime now."

Patrice knew she was on the verge of doing something uncharacteristically frantic. She had to get a grip. Had to stay calm. "Casey, tell me you're lying."

"You are losing it. Totally. I like this side of you, Mom." Casey put her arm around Patrice's shoulder and spoke soothingly. "Now, listen, I just came over to make sure you didn't take off before Dad got home. So now that Truman is here, I think I'll run. You won't be going anywhere now, will you?"

"Don't do this, Casey. You can't leave. If your father comes and finds Truman here..."

"You're worried about what he'll think?"

"I don't want to cause a scene."

Casey nodded sagely. "I understand. But don't sweat it, Mom. Exes *never* get along. Although I do appreciate the effort you and Dad have been making—for my sake."

Patrice narrowed her eyes and leaned close, her voice as menacing as possible. "Cassandra Hilton Sullivan, if you want that check for your wedding gift, you'll help me get rid of Truman. No more games."

"Really? You'll give me the money?"

Patrice reached for the purse she had dropped onto the kitchen counter when she came in earlier in the day. "I have my checkbook right now."

Casey instantly snapped into a serious, cooperative mode. "Okay. What do you want me to do?"

Patrice tried to disguise her sigh of relief. "Just stay. And help me figure out how to get Truman and his suitcase out of this condo and into a suite at the Omni."

"Do you want me to seduce him?" She peered over the bar into the living room. "I'll bet I could. That would get him out of your hair."

Patrice almost forgot how many zeros to add. "Casey! You're engaged! And he's a perfect stranger."

She looked up in time to see Casey's dimples twitching. "But he's really a hunk. And you wouldn't be fooling around with him if he had anything contagious. Would you?"

"The wedding, Casey. The wedding is Saturday."

"Okay, okay. Just write the check. I'll stay. You can count on me, Mom."

Patrice tore out the check, folded it and tucked it into the patch pocket on the front of her daughter's shirt. "And, Casey?"

"Yeah, Mom?"

She put her hand under Casey's chin and looked her straight in the eye. "All kidding aside. The check? It's because I love you. If you're going to...get married...I want you to be happy. And I want you to know I'll always be there for you. No matter what."

Casey looked down, a sheepish smile on her face. "No foolin'?"

"No fooling."

"Don't worry, Mom. I really do know exactly what I'm doing."

We all think that, Patrice wanted to say. She merely gave her daughter a hug. "Then stay away from Truman. He's not your type."

When they returned to the living room, Patrice realized quickly that Casey's loyalty went only so far. Although her daughter had agreed to stay, she hadn't agreed to be docile.

"So, Truman, you must like weddings, huh?"

Ever polite, Truman nodded. "Love 'em."

"Yeah, me, too. I think you'll *really* enjoy Saturday, then."

"I'm sure I will."

"It won't be exactly what you're expecting, though." She delivered the devilish smile that always made Patrice uncomfortable. "Of course, I couldn't have done it without Mom and Dad. They were such a help. I mean, they've been together, like, day and night for the past month."

"They have?"

Casey nodded. "Day and night. It's been...well, it's been like we were family again. Hasn't it, Mom?"

"I wouldn't exactly put it that way, Casey."

"Of course, they're used to working as a team. But I guess you knew that."

"I did?"

"You didn't tell him, Mom?"

"Casey..."

"They were the morning team on local TV for years. That's how Mom got her start."

Truman turned his searching blue eyes on her. "I didn't know that."

"Mom, I can't believe you didn't tell Truman all about you and Dad." She dimpled at Truman, and the look she gave him was far too provocative to suit Patrice. "I could tell you all about that when I drop you off at your hotel. Where did you say you were staying?"

Truman turned to Patrice, confusion replacing his momentary fascination with Casey's beguiling eyes. "Where am I staying?"

Casey leaned forward to refill his wineglass. "You did make reservations, didn't you?"

"Patrice..."

"Don't worry. Dad will be here any minute and I'm sure he can make a call for you, even though it *is* late. He knows simply everybody, doesn't he, Mom? I know he'll be glad to help you, since you and Mom are such pals. Right, Mom?"

"Casey, I'm sure Truman won't need your father's help."

"No prob. Dad can handle it."

"Your father is coming here?"

"That's right. Listen, if you don't want to meet him right now, that's perfectly understandable. We could leave now, if you like."

Truman settled back and crossed his arms. "I wouldn't dream of leaving yet."

By the time the doorbell rang for the third time, Patrice was grateful that, one way or another, the evening would soon be over. She sent Casey to open the door for Cal, solely to avoid receiving another unwelcome welcoming kiss.

"Dad, look who's here," Casey said as Cal walked in. "Mom's boyfriend."

Patrice would have bet the raise Truman had hinted at that Casey had stressed "boy".

"Well, isn't that nice." For one fleeting instant, Cal gave her a look that was almost dangerous before he turned a practiced smile on Truman, who stood and extended a hand. "Truman, I presume?"

"Daddy, you knew? How come nobody told me? I thought the husband was supposed to be the last to know."

"*Ex*-husband, Casey." Patrice bit out the words through her tightly clamped jaw as Truman and Cal shook hands. Neither of them sat. They simply held each other's gaze. Cal was taller. Truman was thinner. Too thin, it seemed to Patrice, after weeks of getting accustomed to Cal's broader shoulders and deeper chest.

"I guess Trish invited you for the wedding?"

"*Trish?*" Truman turned a questioning gaze on Patrice. She smiled thinly. "Yes, she did."

Cal turned to her with a reproving look. "Now, Trish, did you remember to add him to the caterer's list? And what about the rehearsal dinner? Don't forget, someone will need to know if there's an extra man at the rehearsal dinner."

"Rehearsal dinner?"

In the back of her mind, Patrice registered the note of alarm in Casey's voice.

"Daddy, nobody mentioned a rehearsal dinner."

"Trish, did you fail to spearhead efforts for a rehearsal dinner?" Cal asked with exaggerated astonishment.

Patrice glared at him; she couldn't believe how glad she was to lay eyes on him.

"Daddy, maybe we don't need a rehearsal dinner. Okay?"

From the corner of her eye, Patrice noted that Truman was looking from unconcerned Cal to agitated Casey to resigned Patrice as if they had gone collectively bonkers.

He was probably right.

"Well, whatever. I just want to make sure your mom's fellow doesn't get left out." Cal loosened his tie. "When did you arrive, Truman?"

Truman glanced at his watch. "About an hour ago."

"It was a surprise," Casey added.

Cal glanced at Patrice; his mustache twitched. "I'm sure it was."

Patrice was astonished how disappointed she was that Cal's welcome home had turned into Grand Central Station.

"Daddy, he doesn't have anywhere to stay."

"You don't have reservations?" Cal asked with innocent disbelief.

Truman's irritation began to show. "Actually, I assumed Patrice would have room for me here." He looked at her for support.

"Here?" Cal frowned. "Trish, I've only been in—uh, seen—the one bedroom. You aren't hiding another one, are you?"

"No, Cal."

He shook his head. "Well, obviously, that will never do."

"Listen, Sullivan..." Truman's patience gave way.

Cal glanced at Casey. "Casey, dear, could you excuse us for a minute. Maybe run in and clear out the dishwasher or something?"

"Da-ad."

"Now, Casey."

To Patrice's astonishment, Casey complied. And when she was out of the room, Cal put his hand on Truman's shoulder in a man-to-man gesture that could almost pass for genuine. "Listen, I understand that you and my wife—sorry, my ex-wife—may have a close relationship up in Chicago..."

"Cal—"

He completely ignored Patrice's threatening tone, and she would have sworn his Southern drawl was slowing to a crawl the longer he strung Truman along. "Now believe me, I know that's none of my affair. But I know you'll understand if I am concerned about the kind of example she sets for our daughter."

Daughtah. May lightning strike if he didn't say daughtah.

The two men looked toward the kitchen.

"Casey is sensitive. Impressionable. I don't want her getting the wrong idea about her mother having some young man who doesn't happen to be her husband sleeping over." He shook his head. "I know you can understand my position on this."

If she hadn't been so eager to get Truman out of her condo for the night, Patrice would have clobbered Cal. But right now, anything seemed better than having to deal with Truman and his great expectations.

"Well, I certainly wouldn't want to be responsible for any kind of rift."

"Good man. Listen, I have the perfect solution. Stay at my place. I have plenty of room and—"

"No!" The two men turned toward Patrice. Truman looked distinctly uncomfortable. Cal looked supremely pleased with himself. "Cal, I don't think that's a very good idea."

"Nonsense. It's no bother at all. How about it, Truman?"

"Well, I don't think . . ."

"I have a workout room. And a pool. It'll be like being on holiday."

Truman looked at Patrice and she discovered she was irritated with him for more than his inopportune arrival. She was irritated with him for looking to her for permission. "It's up to you, Truman."

Truman was apparently struck dumb. Cal was not.

"Great! That's settled then." Cal rubbed his hands together. "Listen, let's get going. I've had a long day and I'm sure everyone else is tired, too. Besides, Truman, I bet you and I will find a lot to talk about over a nightcap."

Cal tossed a wicked wink at Patrice as he left with Truman.

CHAPTER EIGHTEEN

CASEY ALMOST COMMITTED mayhem when Mr. Bartlett Crookshank told her the bank would have to freeze her account for five working days to allow the out-of-state check her mom had written to clear.

"I'm most apologetic." The officious branch manager pushed his bifocals up the knotty bridge of his nose, disturbing the lie of the reddish brown fringe encircling the rim of his shiny, freckled pate. "But a check this size requires certain precautions. I'm sure you understand."

She did, indeed, understand. She understood that if she couldn't convince this little chipmunk in the cheap suit to forget his stupid regulations, her whole plan was flushed. And in three days, her mom would be on a plane back to Chicago. With Truman holding her hand, no doubt.

Serious measures were required. Failure was not an option.

So she lied.

Clutching the little man's doughy hand in a death grip, she wished for once that she owned at least one reasonably sane outfit like the ones that filled her mother's closet. Credibility was an issue here, and she knew tie-dyed leggings did not project such trust. Nevertheless, she exhaled dramatically and launched an explanation of the bone marrow transplant, impressing upon him the necessity for prompt action. Life and death, she insisted in a low, choked voice.

Mr. Crookshank waived the regulations. She was a genius, no question. The Goddess of Small White Lies was perched on her shoulder today.

Two hours later, Casey had written the check that was bound to be the coup de grace of her entire brilliant scheme. She had signed papers. And she was terrified. What if this didn't work? Would she end up in jail?

Perhaps she should ask her boss at Body Designs what to expect from a life behind bars.

At least a protracted court battle would force her parents to hang around together for the next few months, she told herself. But she had to make sure Will didn't get wind of this final bit of strategy. He was already in a red-hot panic. Another little nudge and he would be over the edge.

"I want out," he had announced the afternoon before, when she had broached the topic of falsifying a marriage license in her parents' names. Just in case, she had explained.

"Okay, okay. We won't get the license. They can do that later."

"You have lost what little bit of gray matter you ever had," Will had announced, sounding disconcertingly like all the adults who had ever fussed at her over the years.

Casey sincerely hoped she never turned into an adult.

"You're stirring up something you're not going to be able to control. You know that, don't you? They're both likely to disown you when they find out what you've done."

"Don't be silly." But his words did give her a moment of apprehension. She let it pass. "You haven't seen them together. They're crazy about each other."

"Sure they are. That's why your mother invited this Truman bimbo down from Chicago."

"For your information, she hasn't seen him for the past two days. She's working on her book and can't be disturbed."

"Your whole family is crazy. You know that?"

"It's okay. Truman is occupied."

With telephone calls to Chicago, she wanted to say but didn't. She didn't even want to think about that. When she had dropped by her dad's earlier in the day to see what was going on, Truman was into some kind of heavy negotiations with somebody—this Cmienski stiff, she supposed.

"Just authorize me to make the offer official," he was saying. "That's all you have to do. I can nail her down if you give me the authority."

Standing out of sight in the entrance hall, Casey held her breath while Truman listened to the response on the other end. She wondered if she had time to make her way to the extension in the kitchen.

"If you don't? I predict we lose her."

Despite feeling sympathy at the hint of sadness in Truman's voice, Casey couldn't help but smile into the mirror over the library table. The smile faded with Truman's next words.

"Good. You're doing the right thing. Now leave it to me. You know I can handle her."

Great. Now she had two things to worry about. One, would she end up in jail for signing a contract she couldn't hope to honor without her mom's cooperation? And two, would Beach Boy here seduce her mom back to Chicago with the promise of lots of money and the job she'd wanted for years?

TORY STOOD. Her knees were shaking. She couldn't concentrate on the words being spoken by the woman in the robe with the piercing eyes and the stern voice. The Honorable Judge Gullane. Tory tried to listen, but she needed every bit of concentration she had just to stay on her feet.

Trish was right behind her, the way she'd been more than once during the past six days. Cal was standing by, the way he had for months. He'd said nice things about her on the witness stand. She had listened with a dry mouth, the four-hour hearing roaring in her ears.

Her need for them was so great right now, maybe they were just another crutch, a replacement for the one that had caused this whole nightmare. But even if they were, that was okay. At least one thing was certain. She would never again be weak enough to lean on drugs. She had survived the past six days without even considering drugs. She would never need that particular crutch again.

Even if the judge took away Whitney for good.

Whitney. She hadn't seen her today. She tried not to picture her, plump faced and smiling, playing with toys in a nearby waiting room while a social worker watched over her.

She had seen the foster mother. She was in the back of the courtroom. She had testified. Tory thought she had sounded too frantic, on the verge of losing control. Tory understood that feeling. She hoped she hadn't sounded that way herself.

She tried to listen to the judge, but it was no use. When the noisy reaction broke out behind her, Tory knew the judge had announced her decision. She turned to Trish and Cal. Tears had gathered in his dark eyes, but his dimples showed. Trish waved her fist in victory.

"Yes?" she breathed, unwilling to celebrate until she was certain.

Cal reached across the railing that separated them and hugged her. "She's yours, Tory. It's all over."

Tory cried in the arms of the man who had given her this chance to start over.

Once everyone had finished sniffling, Cal went to get the car. Tory clutched Trish's arm during the long walk down the corridor to the room where Whitney waited. Trish squeezed her hand, as if sensing Tory's sudden uncertainty.

"It's all over now, Tory. Nothing else to worry about."

Tory gave her a shaky smile. "Thanks to you. If you hadn't been there last week, I don't know..."

"Then we're even."

"Even? What do you mean?"

"I mean if you hadn't been there when Cal needed you, where would all of us be now?"

Tory didn't get a chance to respond. At that moment, a plump little face peered around the door to the waiting room. Whitney looked uncertain, a little shy. Tory wondered if she was learning her alphabet yet. If she could sing "Itsy Bitsy Spider." What her favorite bedtime story was.

So impatient to know all those things that she ached, Tory dropped to her knees and held out her hands. "Whitney, baby? Are you ready to come home?"

Whitney looked up at the social worker, who nodded and smiled. Then the little girl smiled shyly. "Mommy? Go home now, Mommy?"

PATRICE CLOSED OUT chapter thirty-one and slowly stretched to get the kinks out of her neck and back. She glanced at the clock. Two-nineteen in the afternoon. She'd been at it since four in the morning this time. But she was almost done. Three more chapters—chapters that were already well formulated in her mind—and she would be finished.

And by the time she finished, it would be time for the wedding.

Then you can go back to Chicago.

She groaned and stood.

With Truman. To back stabbing and deadlines and double your salary.

She was too tired to think about the unpleasant decisions that awaited her. Could she really bring herself to take her own best friend's job? Could she stand not to, after all the years she had worked so hard in pursuit of such an opportunity?

But you don't want it anymore.

Then what do I want?

She had asked herself that more than once during the past three days. It would be nice if, just once, she could ask it without Cal's image dancing into her head.

She had managed to avoid him—and Truman—by using her book as an excuse. Cal hadn't pushed. Truman had. Guilt had almost prompted her to promise him a lunch and an afternoon of sight-seeing.

Until he said, "You have to see me. We have something very important to discuss."

He was right. He just didn't know what it was.

"I've talked to Cmienski, Trish, and . . ."

That was it. When he started calling her Trish and speaking on behalf of Cmienski, she decided she owed him nothing more.

She cut him short and went back to her manuscript. For the first time, she actually welcomed the time spent on the book. It was the only time she wasn't thinking about Cal and Cmienski and Truman and Lettie and Casey. All the things she no longer seemed to have any control over.

She shut down the laptop computer. Ten hours was enough for one day. She took a walk, then a long soak in a hot tub with the scented mixture Casey had brought her from the New Age shop down the street from the tattoo parlor. Then she pulled out the dress she and Casey had picked for the wedding. With all the pizza and other indulgences Cal had coaxed her into in recent weeks, she hoped she could still wear it.

The doorbell rang. She prayed it wouldn't be Cal—or Truman—although she doubted she could avoid either for much longer. She would likely see Cal at the family dinner tomorrow night, the eve of the wedding. And she supposed she owed it to Truman to spend some time with him tomorrow. After all, she had invited him.

The doorbell rang again. It was Casey, looking spindly in lime-colored bike shorts and an orange stretch camisole.

"So, how's the hermit?"

"Tired."

Casey walked over to the table and looked at Patrice's notes and resource material. "Have you really been working?"

"One hundred and one pages in the last three days."

"Wow! I can't *read* that much in three days. Are you going to be a famous author now, too?"

The thought of traipsing from major city to major city on the book tour her editor had suggested had little appeal now. At the time it had sounded almost exciting.

What was happening to her? She seemed to have lost her enthusiasm for everything. She thought of Cal. Almost everything.

"Let's hope not," she replied.

"Mom?"

"Hmm?"

"It's been great having you here."

"It's been great being here."

"Really? I mean, I haven't, like, totally aggravated you the whole time?"

"Not totally." She grinned at her daughter; her daughter grinned back. "I think I'm getting used to it."

"Used to what?"

"The idea that you're a real person."

"Of course I'm a real person."

"And not just my little girl. Sometimes mothers feel that way, you know. We can't help remembering when you were a part of us. When you needed us to survive. When you don't need us anymore, when you insist on being your own person—that's tough."

Casey shrugged. "Yeah, well, I guess things change. I mean, I realize more and more that you're right about stuff. You think it's a bummer watching your kid grow up? It really weirds you out when you start thinking like your parents."

Patrice laughed. "I know. I remember."

"Yeah? Cool." Casey pulled out the chair Patrice had been sitting in most of the day and flopped down. "So, is Truman going to be, like, your date for the family shindig tomorrow night?"

"I suppose I don't have much choice."

"You kinda screwed up there, didn't you? I mean, I could tell you weren't exactly thrilled to see him."

"Let's just say I've realized Truman's limitations."

"Are you going away with him? Back to Chicago, I mean?"

Through the fog of her own uncertainty, Patrice spotted the dread in her daughter's eyes. "Casey, if I go back to Chicago, that doesn't mean I'm going back with Truman."

"If?"

"When."

Casey looked so forlorn it worried Patrice. The ever-effervescent Casey never looked forlorn. The fact that she did so two days before her wedding worried Patrice.

"You know, don't you, that if you're worried about anything, anything about the wedding…well, it isn't too late. To have second thoughts."

Casey smiled unconvincingly. "Worried? What in the world is there to worry about?"

THE MOMENT PATRICE SAW the infamous Jeanine Dawkins, she told herself to turn and walk away.

SouthPark Mall, apparently, was still the one place in Charlotte you couldn't go without seeing someone you knew. As she shopped for something to wear to the family dinner the following night, Patrice had already run into two fans and the woman who had owned the apartment where she and Cal had lived before Casey was born.

Then, as she stopped to sniff the scent of fresh-baked chocolate chip cookies in the food court and wish once again that Casey had opened up more that afternoon, she saw Jeanine. The woman who had caused Cal to stray.

It doesn't matter now, she reminded herself. *It's yesterday's news.*

But she made the mistake of staring at the woman's petite form and short, sophisticated hairstyle a moment too long. Jeanine dropped her soft drink cup into a trash receptacle, turned and saw Patrice. As Patrice had done, she seemed to pause to collect her thoughts. Then she walked, unsmiling, directly toward her.

Patrice felt as sick and afraid as she had eight years ago, when this woman had cornered her at work with the words, "I think you and I have something to discuss."

Eight years ago, a younger and less courageous Trish had fled. She had no choice this time, it seemed, but to stand her ground.

"I tried to catch up with you alone at the roast," Jeanine said with no preamble. "But you still make a fast getaway."

But are you still a troublemaker? Patrice thought, not at all ashamed of feeling catty. She made her face placid and pleasant. "So nice to see you, Jeanine."

The woman's smile was knowing. "If it helps, I did my damnedest and it didn't do one whit of good."

"What are you talking about?"

"To get you out of the way. So I could get Cal."

A surge of futile rage filled Patrice; she had never before believed in those scratching, screaming, hairpulling fights that women got into in old westerns. Right now, though, she felt capable of one herself.

"Your disappointment must have been intense," she answered coolly, not even caring that her words revealed an old bitterness.

Jeanine had the grace to look away. "I thought it was a disgrace, the way you were upstaging Cal. A man shouldn't have to put up with a woman who's more successful than he is. That's what I thought at the time, anyway."

Cal had expressed his own insecurities in much the same way. Now Patrice wondered how much those insecurities had been fueled by this manipulative woman. She shoved her hands deeper into the pockets of the knit skirt she wore to quell the temptation to throttle her onetime rival.

"I knew I had a chance to come between you when Cal first talked to me. He wondered if a word to Ralph Walters could take you out of the running for the Atlanta job, you know."

Cal had done that? Tried to ruin her chances in Atlanta? The words stunned her, stealing her breath with the sting of his deceit. The revelation hurt more, she realized, than hearing that this woman had purposely set out to seduce her husband. Cal had betrayed her; he had planned to sabotage her career.

She wanted to walk away; she wanted to hear the rest.

"So I made it my campaign to keep filling Cal's head with ideas about how you were moving too fast for him, leaving him behind. I told him if he was really first with you, you'd never consider the job in Atlanta."

And Cal had fallen for it.

"The clincher was when I told him how well you and the general manager in Atlanta had hit it off. *Really* hit it off. And about his reputation with women, you know?"

Patrice knew. And she knew now why Cal hadn't fought her when she packed and left. Thanks to this woman, he had believed the same about her as she had believed about him. And none of it was true.

What *was* true hurt even more. He had tried to ruin her career.

"Anyway, the whole sorry truth is, it was pointless. Cal never wanted me. He never thought of me as anything but Ralph Walters's assistant. And I just wanted to... apologize, I guess."

The woman waited, expecting absolution, Patrice supposed. But she had no forgiveness in her heart. For Jeanine or Cal.

"Apology noted," Patrice said, chin high, eyes cold. She turned and walked away.

Her breath came in short, labored gasps as she walked blindly to the mall exit, and she wished she were a big enough woman to offer forgiveness. Jeanine Dawkins had set out to destroy her marriage at a time when it was most vulnerable, and now, when it had seemed almost possible to erase the past, to recapture what had been lost to them for eight years, this woman had unwittingly revealed a poison Patrice had never known existed.

She might have been able to forgive infidelity, a one-time indiscretion now regretted. But the kind of deceit it must have taken for Cal to throw up a roadblock to her success, that she could never forgive.

She hurt as deeply and wrenchingly as if she were losing Cal all over again. And this time she could never turn back. Never.

CHAPTER NINETEEN

FOR THE PAST twenty-four hours, Cal had told himself Trish wasn't worth the headache.

He didn't believe it but expected to convince himself at any moment. He was a firm believer in the power of positive thinking, and he was positive he was damned sick and tired of the way she was purposely avoiding him.

Any minute now, he told himself as she edged away from the buffet table in his crowded dining room, his body would get the message from his head and he would no longer feel the urge to follow her with his eyes.

"Daddy, you have to do something."

Casey's nearness startled him; he tore his attention away from Trish, who was mingling with family—whatever family was farthest from Cal at any given moment, although Will's parents didn't seem to be there yet. If he wandered toward his older sister and her son, Trish would no doubt slip away and ease up to her mother. And if Cal decided to wish his former mother-in-law, well, Trish would simply—

"Daddy! You're not even listening to me!"

Cal shook his head and looked into Casey's reproachful eyes. "Sorry, Case. What's the problem?"

She sighed the sigh of the oppressed. "You are. You and Mom."

"What did we do now?"

"You're fighting."

"We're not fighting. We're not even speaking."

"Exactly. You're going to ruin everything."

Cal put his arm around Casey's narrow shoulders and hugged her to his side. "Don't worry. We won't take out our machetes and go after each other tomorrow."

"But you can't…I mean, if there's something wrong between you…everything's going to be spoiled."

She was right, of course. And even without that excuse, Cal knew he had to do something. He was not willing to let Trish ship herself back to Chicago without a battle. Maybe they should bring out the machetes after all.

"Casey, the last thing in the world I want to do is ruin tomorrow for you." He faced her and pressed a kiss to her forehead. "I want it to be perfect. Because I love you and all I've ever wanted is for you to be happy."

She wrapped her arms around him in an enthusiastic hug. "Oh, Daddy, I know. And I will be, if…"

She looked up at him beseechingly.

"Okay. I'll fix it."

He stalked Patrice, giving her just enough distance to set her at ease. And when she let her guard down and ducked out the French doors, he knew he could pick her off easily.

The pool, deep and dark in the fading dusk, reflected the rosy glow of the setting sun. Her face picked up the color.

"You might as well surrender."

She started at his voice but didn't turn around. "I'm not in the mood for banter."

He was surprised how cold her voice was. She hadn't withdrawn on a whim; something had happened.

"What's wrong, Trish?"

"Leave it alone, Cal."

"I want to know."

She whirled on him. "Take my word for it, Cal. You don't want to talk to me right now."

"I don't want anything between us tomorrow. I was thinking . . . tomorrow could be like a fresh start for us, too. If we let it."

"It's too late for that."

"What's happened, Trish? Just a few days ago you were . . ."

"I'm warning you, Cal. Drop it."

"I'm as stubborn as you are."

"You're going to be sorry."

"Then make me sorry."

"I saw an old friend of yours at the mall today."

Her eyes were like brittle, blue-green ice. Uneasiness rumbled in his chest. He couldn't bring himself to ask. He knew he wouldn't have to. He had pushed her. This battle would proceed in earnest now, with or without his participation.

"Jeanine."

She was right. He was going to be sorry. "Yes?"

"She told me."

His throat went dry and his heart raced. He figured if he didn't have a second heart attack within the next few minutes, he never would.

"Trish, I don't know what she told you, but there was never anything between us. Never."

Patrice smiled, but it was a smile that did nothing to ease his mind. "I know. She told me."

"Well . . . good."

"That's not all she told me."

Ah, Lord. She knew it all. He was surprised at the relief he felt. At least now he would know just how bad it could get.

"She told me you weren't happy with how my career was progressing. I think her sense of it was that you felt threatened."

"I told you that."

"Why didn't you tell me the whole thing, Cal? Why didn't you tell me you asked Jeanine's help in stopping me?"

The only answer he had was the truth. "Because I was afraid you'd react just the way you're reacting. And I didn't—"

"What did you say to Ralph, Cal? Did you tell him I couldn't carry my own weight on the show? That I was nothing without you? Or maybe you said a woman simply wasn't right for the job. Is that it, Cal?"

He didn't know whether to let her spew it all out or to try to step in now and stem the tide of her anger. Obviously, Jeanine hadn't exactly told the *whole* story. She had stopped short of the part where Cal realized his mistake and absolutely refused to interfere. But how could he get Trish to believe that now. Lord, would he ever quit screwing up with this woman? "You don't know the whole story, Trish. After I—"

"Are you telling me you didn't want to dead-end my career right here in Charlotte?"

"Well, no. But there's more to it than that, Trish. I—"

"Thank you, Cal. It's taken eight years, but I do appreciate finally hearing the truth. It's very…liberating."

She whirled and faced the sky, which had darkened while they argued. He knew he had been dismissed, but he was determined this would not be the end of it. He knew how he felt about Trish and, dammit, he knew how she felt about him, whether she did or not. He was going to stay right here and hash this out. And once—

Truman's voice filled the muggy night. "I think she's said all she has to say to you, Sullivan."

Cal bristled. And he suspected from the sudden tension of her shoulders and the more pronounced jut of her chin that Trish was bristling, too.

"So why don't you leave us alone. *We* have things to talk about."

"Trish and I aren't finished, Truman."

Under her breath, Trish muttered, "Oh, yes we are."

"See, Sullivan? Oh, yes you are." Truman shrugged, his apologetic grin unconvincing.

Cal figured he had twenty pounds on the young reporter. He thought he could take him. Easily. And that, he knew, would really tick off Trish.

But, hell, it couldn't get much worse.

"I'm not going anywhere, Truman. If you've got anything to say to my wife, say it."

"Ex-wife!" Trish's mutter was more vehement this time.

Truman studied him. Cal smiled pleasantly but implacably.

"Okay. You might as well listen. You'll know soon enough anyway." Truman walked around and faced Trish. "Trish—"

"If you call me that one more time, I'll push you in the pool and hold you under until you stop struggling."

Truman looked marginally less confident, but he didn't back down. "Sorry. Listen, I've talked to Cmienski. He's authorized me to offer you the anchor."

Now Cal felt considerably less confident. An important job offer at a time when she was already furious at him was not good. Maybe he should pop Truman after all.

"He *what?*"

Another wave of relief. Trish sounded peeved at this development, too.

"He asked me to—"

"I heard you," she snapped.

"It's a good offer."

Then, with a quick glance at Cal, Truman announced the offer. He was right; it was a good offer. A damn good one. Cal felt himself squirming again. That much money *and* the visibility of an anchor position. Who could turn that down?

He wondered how much trouble it would be to pick up and move to Chicago.

Truman didn't give Trish time to respond. "So I think you should go in right now and call him. He's expecting to hear from you anytime." He pulled a memo sheet from his breast pocket. "This is his home number. I told him you'd call and we could make all the—"

"You told him I would call?"

"That's right. Now listen, let's go in and—"

In a flash, Trish grabbed the note from Truman's hand, balled it up and pitched it over his shoulder.

"Not another word!"

Truman looked confused. Cal took a step backward. Truman turned to see the paper floating on the surface of the lighted pool.

"Now, why did you do that?"

Trish stared at him.

"I think she's a little upset with you," Cal confided with a sympathetic smile.

"But..."

"I am not a *little* anything." Trish's voice was a throaty roar now. "I am a *lot* furious. At you." She thrust a finger at Truman's chest. Then she turned and jabbed the same finger into Cal's chest. "And at you."

"Me?"

"I've had it with both of you."

"Patrice, I don't get it. I..."

"I've had it with men who think they can run my life. Men who think they know what's best for me. Men who try to make my decisions for me."

"Now, Patrice..."

"You call Cmienski. Better yet, get on the next plane to Chicago and see him in person. You tell him if and when I want his job, I'll let him know how much it'll cost him to get me."

"But..."

"And *you*..." She turned her wrath on Cal. "You...you can..."

When it was clear she could think of no justice gruesome enough to cover his eight-year-old indiscretion, she turned and stalked away, leaving him alone with Truman. She wouldn't be angry for long, he consoled himself. And at least she wasn't headed for Chicago.

He forced himself to smile at the bewildered young man. "Truman, you need to work on your timing, pal."

THE LAST TWO CHAPTERS WERE the hardest, and not just because Patrice found it hard to concentrate.

Yes, she was thinking of the wedding, now less than twelve hours away. Yes, she was thinking of her confrontation with Cal—the Final Confrontation, she had already labeled it in her mind—five hours earlier.

The only thing she wasn't thinking about was Chicago and Cmienski and Truman. In her heart, she now knew. They were all ancient history.

But as she stared at her computer screen at 2:15 a.m., struggling with the final chapters of her fearful weeks behind enemy lines in the Persian Gulf, Patrice struggled with something else, as well.

She struggled with memories she had buried almost as quickly as her rescuers had arrived.

She hadn't been tortured by captors. In fact, she had never been captured. She hadn't been wounded. No, the worst that had happened to her was that she had been alone with memories of her life. Alone with her regrets for all the things she had really wanted to do with her life but hadn't because of all the things she had felt she *should* do.

She remembered the night she'd spent lying on the desert under more stars than she had ever seen in her lifetime, terrified that she would never see such stars again. Terrified of dying on the desert without ever seeing her daughter's face again. Without ever holding a grandchild in her arms. Without knowing the peace that comes from rising each morning to the prospect of work that satisfies and soothes. Without ever again feeling her heart burst with the knowledge of love.

Staring into the cloudless sky, listening to the silence of sand and the occasional scuttle of desert creatures she was unwilling to search out in the darkness, she had vowed to turn her life around. She would recapture her joy. If she survived, she would make the rest of her life what she wanted it to be.

And as if she had learned what fate had intended her to learn, she had been rescued the next day.

Her vow was quickly submerged by the return to her frantic life. She realized, as she stirred through her memories, that the feelings she had buried once again had no doubt spawned the dissatisfaction she had felt during the past year.

Her face in her hands, she was swept by the overwhelming need to talk to someone who would understand.

She thought of Cal, who had faced his own epiphany.

She forced herself to remember his betrayal and to ignore the voice protesting that the betrayal had occurred almost a decade earlier. Mistakes should be forgiven.

Especially if you love someone.

She finished the book in time to shower and dress for the wedding. And the second part of her own life.

THERE WAS NOTHING traditional about the purple, washed-silk sheath Casey had helped her select as her mother-of-the-bride dress. When she got back to Chicago, she told herself as she drove to the wooded lake, she would pitch out every single corporate suit she owned.

If she went back to Chicago.

First she had to decide what she wanted to be now that she wasn't so sure she wanted to be grown-up anymore.

Tomorrow would be plenty of time for that. Right now she had a wedding to celebrate.

The clearing was already growing crowded. The barge, painted the same shade of bright red as the accessories Patrice wore, sat at the end of the dock, flowers and balloons tied to its four corners. Tidy white folding chairs ringed the lake. Caterers were setting up a buffet. The air of a medieval festival prevailed.

She saw Tory, carrying a toddler. She saw Cal, casually elegant in a white silk shirt and black raw silk jacket shot through with teal. She tried to catch his eye, but he was seeing that his mother and hers had the best seats in the house. It didn't matter; she knew, somehow, that there would be plenty of time to talk to him later.

She was looking for Casey when Ralph Walters's familiar voice captured her attention. She turned and smiled, returning his greeting.

"I never got a chance to thank you for the roast," he said. "It was a great send-off."

"You don't have to thank me." She gave him a hug; for some reason, she felt like hugging everyone today. "I should be thanking you."

"Thanking me?"

"If not for you, I wouldn't be where I am today." Never mind that she might not be where she was today by tomorrow; the knowledge only added to her serenity. "You gave me my break."

Ralph pursed his lips and shook his head. "You know..." He seemed to hesitate. "I'd love to take the credit. I really would. An old man can't have enough beautiful young women grateful to him, you know."

They laughed.

"But I really can't take the credit. If it weren't for Cal..." He shook his head again. "You know, I was so damned mule headed. I told him no at first. Told him TV was no place for a husband-wife team. But you know Cal. He was stubborn."

Patrice stared at Ralph's face for signs of duplicity, for some hint that he had been bribed or blackmailed.

"Anyway, I was always glad I gave in. But you knew that. Hell, I wasn't ready to let you go when the Atlanta offer came. But Cal insisted. Said if I didn't call the station manager there and tell him what a fine job you'd do, you'd both quit anyway." Ralph gave her shoulders a fatherly squeeze. "Never could understand how he could let you go like that. But he said it was what you wanted. So I called 'im. Recommended you. Always wished I hadn't. But you deserved it. Cal was right."

When Ralph at last drifted away to speak to some of the other guests, Patrice discovered her legs were feeling too wobbly to hold her.

Cal pushed Ralph into recommending her? If she didn't know better, she might have wondered if Ralph Walters had grown suddenly, irrevocably senile.

Cal hadn't betrayed her. Even if he had initially asked Jeanine Dawkins for her help, he'd apparently had second thoughts. He hadn't been able to go through with it. He had supported her. Silently and without credit for all these years.

No, the only betrayal had belonged to Jeanine Dawkins. And Patrice had almost allowed her to betray them both again.

Excited, she stood, her eyes darting around the clearing, searching for Cal. She had to find him. Had to tell him. Had to—

Before she could spot Cal, someone tapped her shoulder. Will. He looked green around the gills, as befitted a nervous bridegroom. Swept up in a feeling of well-being she wasn't sure was justified, Patrice put her arms around him and hugged him.

"Don't worry, Will. Everybody feels this way right about now." In a flash that was almost physical in its intensity, she remembered her own wedding day. "You're going to be family soon, so we're all on your side."

"Oh, Lord," he groaned.

"By the way, where is your family?" She looked around.

"Oh, Lord."

"Is anything wrong, Will?"

"Uh, listen, uh, Casey, uh..." He swallowed hard and gestured. "Uh, could you come talk to Casey?"

She followed the direction of his gesture. Casey stood away from the crowd, wearing the strapless pink bubble dress she'd had her heart set on, a worried expression on her face. Looking from Will to Casey, Patrice set out for her daughter's side.

"What's wrong, Casey?"

"Grandma said you and Dad had a big fight last night. Oh, Mom, you and Dad aren't mad at each other today, are you?"

She sounded on the verge of tears. Nerves, Patrice supposed. She smiled and patted her daughter on the shoulder.

"Now, Casey, don't you worry about your father and me. This is your day, and we're not going to do anything to spoil it."

Casey looked at Will. "I think I'm gonna hurl."

"Case, I told you. I told you all along this was not going to work."

"Put a lid on it, Will. Okay?" Casey drew a deep, ragged breath, then looked Patrice straight in the eye. "Mom, did you ever think about staying in Charlotte? I mean, like, for good?"

"Casey, I swear, everything is going to be fine." Feeling so benevolent that she was determined to spread her inner peace around, Patrice gave her daughter a warm hug. "No matter where I am, I'll be there for you. I'm on your side and..."

"Mo-om." Casey's wail was low but frantic. "I just need a straight answer."

It was somehow reassuring to see Casey so over-wrought; perhaps she was taking all of this more seriously than Patrice had realized. So seriously that nothing she said seemed to have much relevance here. "Well, no. I don't think so. Although, actually, maybe. I'm not sure."

"Terrific. This is just terrific."

Will looked at his watch. "Case, you've got ten minutes till blast-off."

"Mom, the money you gave me? The wedding gift?"

"What is it, Casey? Is something wrong?"

"I bought something with it."

"Casey, if you don't quit beating around the bush and tell me what's wrong, I'm going to shove the buffet table in the lake."

"Okay. Okay. I put a down payment on the florist shop and I'm going to buy it and run it, but the only problem is I don't know anything about florists or business and I really don't have any other money to keep it going at first and I was counting on you to be my partner and run it with me." Her breath ran out. She almost looked relieved. "There. I did it. Now you can kill me."

"You bought the Garden of Temptation?"

Casey nodded. "Well, actually, not completely bought it. I made an offer. I, like, signed a contract." She groaned. "I used the money you gave me for the earnest money. I thought if you didn't want to stay, we could just kind of tell them it was a mistake, but Will said they'll keep the money anyway. I think I'm gonna be sick, okay?''

"You gave them money?''

"I'm supposed to fill out all the loan papers tomorrow. But I don't think they'll go for it unless you're part of the deal.''

"So you signed a contract making an offer on the Garden of Temptation and you expect me to stay here and go into business with you?''

Casey nodded. Patrice frightened herself with the flood of satisfaction that washed through her.

"Casey, I have a job. In Chicago.'' Even as she said it, she was calculating how quickly she could get rid of everything she owned in Chicago. Her car. Her condo. Her rooms full of practical modern furnishings. Hadn't she decided last night that ICN was behind her now? And what else did Chicago hold?

"I know. But... well, I just thought... I mean, you looked so happy when we went through the florist's and...''

"Okay. I'll do it.''

"I know it was maybe, like, the dumbest thing I've ever done and I suppose I could get in deep rabbit pellets for this, but...''

"Casey, I said I'll do it.''

Casey stopped babbling. Her mouth, however, remained wide open. Patrice smiled and patted her on the arm.

"There. Does that make you feel better?''

"You'll do it? No foolin'?''

"No fooling. Now, can you relax and enjoy yourself today?''

The pleased astonishment on Casey's face vanished. "Oh. Right." She looked at Will. At least they were matching shades of green. "That's not all, Mom."

"There's more?"

"What's going on over here with my two favorite ladies?" Cal walked up. "We've got to take this show on the road in about ten minutes. Is everybody ready?"

Will groaned again. Patrice began to have serious doubts that he had the constitution for living with her daughter.

Then the most surprising thing of all happened. Casey burst into tears.

Both Patrice and Cal instantly wrapped their arms around her and exchanged worried looks over their daughter's head.

"Casey, what's wrong, baby?"

"Whatever it is, Casey, we'll work it out. We're on your side."

"Promise?" she whimpered through her tears.

"Of course."

"Absolutely."

"No matter what?"

Patrice lifted her daughter's narrow chin and stared sternly into her damp eyes. "Unless you make me wait another single minute to find out what in the devil is going on here. Then we may have problems."

Casey managed a weak smile. "I'm not getting married."

"What?"

"I didn't plan this wedding for me at all."

With another of his weak groans, Will sank to the ground. Patrice wasn't certain she might not have to join him.

"What are you talking about?"

"It's for you and Dad."

"Me?"

"Me?"

Casey nodded, her expression a combination of hope and misery.

"You see, I know you still love each other. I've known that for years. And I've tried and tried to do something about it, but nothing ever worked. Not the appendicitis. Not the religious cult."

"*What?*"

"Do you mean to tell me—"

Casey swallowed a sob. "Please, don't be mad. Don't hate me forever and never speak to me and disown all your future grandchildren. Okay?"

Patrice looked at Cal. His dimples were twitching. She felt seriously close to laughing out loud herself.

"It was just such a great idea. That if you had to spend all this time together, you'd both realize you loved each other, too. Only now the whole thing's ruined."

Cal looked at Patrice. "Should we disown her?"

"I'm afraid I can't."

"Can't? Why not?"

Casey dropped to the ground, bunching her poufed dress between her bony knees, where she propped her elbows. "And now you're mad at each other again. I mean, you've been running around panting after each other for months and I *know* you've spent the night with each other, for criminy's sake, and you still don't have the sense to know what anybody else could see with one eye closed, even Grandma, 'cause I told her all about this and—"

"No, I can't disown her. She's my business partner now."

"Are you sure you know what you're getting into?"

Casey looked up. "Still? You'll still stay?"

Suddenly Patrice was laughing. Laughing so hard she felt tears welling up in her eyes. She dropped to her knees beside her daughter. "Do me a favor, Casey."

Casey sniffled. "Sure, Mom."

"Never change."

"Huh?"

"Stay just like you are. Silly and impulsive and true to whatever your heart tells you to do."

Casey looked confused as she rubbed tears out of her eyes.

"And never, never do anything just because you think it's something you *should* do. Promise?"

"Um, sure. Does that mean you're not mad at me?"

"That means I think you're probably the only one in the family who's had the right idea for the past eight years."

She looked at Cal and saw the emotion in his warm brown eyes. How foolish, how unyielding she'd been for far too long. He smiled, a soft smile of hope.

"Does that mean you'll do it, Mom?"

"Do what?"

"Get married."

Giving Casey a final pat, Patrice then walked over to Cal. She took the lapels of his jacket between her fingers. "Marry this man again? Never."

She knew from the quirk of his dimples and the mischief that suddenly rose in his eyes that, no matter how Cal might have changed, he hadn't changed in all the ways that mattered. Thank goodness she'd learned to appreciate them before it was too late.

"But I'm going to stay right here in Charlotte."

Cal slipped his hands around her waist. "Now there's an excellent idea."

"And embark on a long, sordid affair with my ex-husband."

"Mo-om, you can't do that. You have to marry him. After all I've gone through, I deserve to get my family back. You should—"

Cal's eyes didn't stray from Patrice's. She saw the apology and the forgiveness and the understanding and, yes, the maturity she had never been able to acknowledge before. "Don't push your luck, Casey. Your mother is finished doing what she should just because somebody else expects her to."

Patrice nodded. "Now it's your turn, Cal."

"For what?"

"To be the grown-up. I'm going to take a few years off and play."

"Why can't we both play?"

She pretended to consider the suggestion. "I'll get back to you on that."

Then she kissed him. She savored the softness of his mustache tickling her upper lip and the hardness of his chest and the bayberry scent of him. She savored the mastery that was born of years of understanding and familiarity. She savored the excitement that was born of renewal.

"Come on, Cal."

"Where to?"

"I'm going to promise to love you and be faithful to you and to be crazy with you as long as we both shall live."

"Right here? In front of all these people?"

"They might as well start getting used to the new me right now."

"Am I going to like the new you?"

"You're going to love the new me. She's a lot like the old me. Only better."

She led him to the barge, and the two ponytailed attendants from Casey's favorite natural foods store paddled it to the middle of the lake. Holding Cal's hands in hers, Patrice looked up at the man who had shared so much of her life.

She made her promises, her voice faltering only when she got to the part about forever.

Then Cal made his. "Trish Sullivan, I promise to love you and be faithful to you and try to get you to make an honest man of me again."

She laughed. Everyone around the lake cheered. And although no minister blessed the vows and no rings were exchanged, everyone who witnessed the ceremony knew that this time their vows would never be broken.

S HARLEQUIN SUPERROMANCE ®

COMING NEXT MONTH

#582 MOONCALLER • Patricia Chandler
Logic told Whitney Baldridge-Barrows to hate Gabriel Blade. He
was planning to turn the Havasupai village at the bottom of the
Grand Canyon, where she worked as a doctor, into a posh tourist
resort. But logic had nothing to do with Whitney's response to the
man....

#583 IF I MUST CHOOSE • Lynda Trent
After her divorce, Lacy Kilpatrick wanted nothing to do with
romance—but she hadn't counted on sexy Austin Fraser showing
up. Nor had she counted on her family calling him "the enemy" and
forbidding her to see him.

#584 McGILLUS V. WRIGHT • Tara Taylor Quinn
Never mind that sparks flew between them—Tatum McGillus and
Jonathan Wright should never have said hello to each other. The
timing was wrong, and they couldn't agree on anything. As if that
weren't enough, they stood on opposite sides of the law. This was
one relationship that would need a miracle to survive.

#585 DIAL D FOR DESTINY • Anne Logan
The last thing Lisa LeBlanc's sister Dixie said before she disappeared was that she was going to meet a man named Gabriel
Jordan. Lisa managed to track Gabriel down, but the man denied
ever speaking with Dixie. Somehow, Lisa was sure he knew more
than he was telling. To uncover the truth, she had to stay close to
Gabe. An idea that was not altogether without appeal.

AVAILABLE NOW

#578 THE LAST BUCCANEER
Lynn Erickson

**#579 THE DOG FROM RODEO
DRIVE**
Risa Kirk

#580 SIMPLY IRRESISTIBLE
Peg Sutherland

#581 THE PARENT PLAN
Judith Arnold

Where do you find hot Texas nights, smooth Texas charm and dangerously sexy cowboys?

$ $ $  $ $ $
$ $ $ $ $

EVERYBODY'S TALKIN'
by Barbara Kaye

To catch a thief—Texas style!

Somebody's been taking money from Carolyn Trent's savings account, and bank manager Cody Hendricks is determined to find the culprit. Carolyn's bookkeeper, Lori Porter, is just as anxious to find the thief, but when she and Cody team up, she finds his motives are more than strictly business.

CRYSTAL CREEK reverberates with the exciting rhythm of Texas. Each story features the rugged individuals who live and love in the Lone Star state. And each one ends with the same invitation...

Y'ALL COME BACK...REAL SOON!

Don't miss *EVERYBODY'S TALKIN'* by Barbara Kaye.
Available in February, wherever Harlequin books are sold.

My
Valentine
1994

Celebrate the most romantic day of the year with
MY VALENTINE 1994
a collection *of* original stories, written by
four of Harlequin's most popular authors...

MARGOT DALTON
MURIEL JENSEN
MARISA CARROLL
KAREN YOUNG

Available in February, wherever
Harlequin Books are sold.

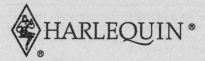

HARLEQUIN ®

VAL94

**Fifty red-blooded, white-hot, true-blue hunks
from every State in the Union!**

Look for MEN MADE IN AMERICA! Written by some
of our most poplar authors, these stories feature fifty of
the strongest, sexiest men, each from a different state in
the union!

Two titles available every other month at your favorite
retail outlet.

In January, look for:

DREAM COME TRUE by Ann Major (Florida)
WAY OF THE WILLOW by Linda Shaw (Georgia)

In March, look for:

TANGLED LIES by Anne Stuart (Hawaii)
ROGUE'S VALLEY by Kathleen Creighton (Idaho)

You won't be able to resist MEN MADE IN AMERICA!

HARLEQUIN SUPERROMANCE ®

Women Who Dare will continue with more exciting stories, beginning in May 1994 with

THE PRINCESS AND THE PAUPER by Tracy Hughes.

And if you missed any titles in 1993 here's your chance to order them:

Harlequin Superromance®—Women Who Dare

#70533	DANIEL AND THE LION by Margot Dalton	$3.39	☐
#70537	WINGS OF TIME by Carol Duncan Perry	$3.39	☐
#70549	PARADOX by Lynn Erickson	$3.39	☐
#70553	LATE BLOOMER by Peg Sutherland	$3.50	☐
#70554	THE MARRIAGE TICKET by Sharon Brondos	$3.50	☐
#70558	ANOTHER WOMAN by Margot Dalton	$3.50	☐
#70562	WINDSTORM by Connie Bennett	$3.50	☐
#70566	COURAGE, MY LOVE by Lynn Leslie	$3.50	☐
#70570	REUNITED by Evelyn A. Crowe	$3.50	☐
#70574	DOC WYOMING by Sharon Brondos	$3.50	☐

(limited quantities available on certain titles)

TOTAL AMOUNT	$
POSTAGE & HANDLING	$
($1.00 for one book, 50¢ for each additional)	
APPLICABLE TAXES*	$ _____
TOTAL PAYABLE	$ _____
(check or money order—please do not send cash)	

To order, complete this form and send it, along with a check or money order for the total above, payable to Harlequin Books, to: *In the U.S.*: 3010 Walden Avenue, P.O. Box 9047, Buffalo, NY 14269-9047; *In Canada*: P.O. Box 613, Fort Erie, Ontario, L2A 5X3.

Name: _____

Address: _____ City: _____

State/Prov.: _____ Zip/Postal Code: _____

*New York residents remit applicable sales taxes.
  Canadian residents remit applicable GST and provincial taxes.

WWD-FINR

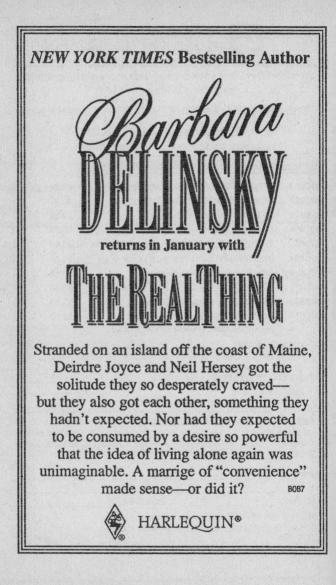

NEW YORK TIMES Bestselling Author

Barbara DELINSKY

returns in January with

THE REAL THING

Stranded on an island off the coast of Maine,
Deirdre Joyce and Neil Hersey got the
solitude they so desperately craved—
but they also got each other, something they
hadn't expected. Nor had they expected
to be consumed by a desire so powerful
that the idea of living alone again was
unimaginable. A marrige of "convenience"
made sense—or did it? B0B7

HARLEQUIN®

Relive the romance...
**Harlequin and Silhouette
are proud to present**

by Request ™

A program of collections of three complete novels by the most requested authors with the most requested themes. Be sure to look for one volume each month with three complete novels by top name authors.

In January: **WESTERN LOVING**   Susan Fox
JoAnn Ross
Barbara Kaye

Loving a cowboy is easy—taming him isn't!

In February: **LOVER, COME BACK!**   Diana Palmer
Lisa Jackson
Patricia Gardner Evans

It was over so long ago—yet now they're calling, "Lover, Come Back!"

In March: **TEMPERATURE RISING**   JoAnn Ross
Tess Gerritsen
Jacqueline Diamond

Falling in love—just what the doctor ordered!

Available at your favorite retail outlet.

REQ-G3

HARLEQUIN®

Don't miss these Harlequin favorites by some of our most distinguished authors!

And now, you can receive a discount by ordering two or more titles!

HT#25409	THE NIGHT IN SHINING ARMOR by JoAnn Ross	$2.99	☐
HT#25471	LOVESTORM by JoAnn Ross	$2.99	☐
HP#11463	THE WEDDING by Emma Darcy	$2.89	☐
HP#11592	THE LAST GRAND PASSION by Emma Darcy	$2.99	☐
HR#03188	DOUBLY DELICIOUS by Emma Goldrick	$2.89	☐
HR#03248	SAFE IN MY HEART by Leigh Michaels	$2.89	☐
HS#70464	CHILDREN OF THE HEART by Sally Garrett	$3.25	☐
HS#70524	STRING OF MIRACLES by Sally Garrett	$3.39	☐
HS#70500	THE SILENCE OF MIDNIGHT by Karen Young	$3.39	☐
HI#22178	SCHOOL FOR SPIES by Vickie York	$2.79	☐
HI#22212	DANGEROUS VINTAGE by Laura Pender	$2.89	☐
HI#22219	TORCH JOB by Patricia Rosemoor	$2.89	☐
HAR#16459	MACKENZIE'S BABY by Anne McAllister	$3.39	☐
HAR#16466	A COWBOY FOR CHRISTMAS by Anne McAllister	$3.39	☐
HAR#16462	THE PIRATE AND HIS LADY by Margaret St. George	$3.39	☐
HAR#16477	THE LAST REAL MAN by Rebecca Flanders	$3.39	☐
HH#28704	A CORNER OF HEAVEN by Theresa Michaels	$3.99	☐
HH#28707	LIGHT ON THE MOUNTAIN by Maura Seger	$3.99	☐

Harlequin Promotional Titles

#83247	YESTERDAY COMES TOMORROW by Rebecca Flanders	$4.99	☐
#83257	MY VALENTINE 1993	$4.99	☐
	(short-story collection featuring Anne Stuart, Judith Arnold, Anne McAllister, Linda Randall Wisdom)		

(limited quantities available on certain titles)

	AMOUNT	$
DEDUCT:	**10% DISCOUNT FOR 2+ BOOKS**	$
ADD:	**POSTAGE & HANDLING**	$
	($1.00 for one book, 50¢ for each additional)	
	APPLICABLE TAXES*	$ _____
	TOTAL PAYABLE	$ _____
	(check or money order—please do not send cash)	

To order, complete this form and send it, along with a check or money order for the total above, payable to Harlequin Books, to: **In the U.S.:** 3010 Walden Avenue, P.O. Box 9047, Buffalo, NY 14269-9047; **In Canada:** P.O. Box 613, Fort Erie, Ontario, L2A 5X3.

Name: _____

Address: _____ City: _____

State/Prov.: _____ Zip/Postal Code: _____

*New York residents remit applicable sales taxes.
Canadian residents remit applicable GST and provincial taxes.

HBACK-JM